DEAD HEAD

A DIRTY BUSINESS MYSTERY

Dead Head

Rosemary Harris

THORNDIKE
CHIVERS

This Large Print edition is published by Thorndike Press, Waterville, Maine, USA and by AudioGO Ltd, Bath, England.
Thorndike Press, a part of Gale, Cengage Learning.

The text of this Large Print edition is unabridged.
Other aspects of the book may vary from the original edition.
Set in 16 pt. Plantin.

LIBRARY OF CONGRESS CATALOGING-IN-PUBLICATION DATA

Harris, Rosemary.
    Dead head : a dirty business mystery / by Rosemary Harris.
        p. cm. — (Thorndike Press large print mystery)
    ISBN-13: 978-1-4104-2776-2
    ISBN-10: 1-4104-2776-5
    1. Holliday, Paula (Fictitious character)—Fiction. 2. Women gardeners—Fiction. 3. Fugitives from justice—Fiction. 4. Connecticut—Fiction. 5. Large type books. I. Title.
PS3608.A78328D43 2010b
813'.6—dc22   2010015365

BRITISH LIBRARY CATALOGUING-IN-PUBLICATION DATA AVAILABLE
Published in 2010 in the U.S. by arrangement with St. Martin's Press, LLC.
Published in 2010 in the U.K. by arrangement with the agent.

U.K. Hardcover: 978 1 408 49203 1 (Chivers Large Print)
U.K. Softcover: 978 1 408 49204 8 (Camden Large Print)

Printed and bound in Great Britain by the MPG Books Group
1 2 3 4 5 6 7 14 13 12 11 10

To Bruce, for everything

ACKNOWLEDGMENTS

Since my first book, *Pushing Up Daisies,* was published, I've had occasion to meet many wonderful and generous people in the mystery community. That community is made up of writers, retailers, librarians, conference organizers, readers, publishers, bloggers — people who just love the genre. They are a tremendous source of inspiration for any new writer, and I am grateful for the support that they've shown me.

In particular I would like to thank Carolyn Hart, Molly Weston, Jane Murphy, Bernadette Baldino, and my indefatigable friend and blog sister (at www.jungleredwriters.com) Hank Phillippi Ryan.

I'd also like to thank copy editor extraordinaire Martha Schwartz for her exhaustive research and incredible attention to detail. Any errors or omissions are mine and not hers.

dead head (also deadhead) vt **1:** to decapitate or cut off fading flower heads to promote a second bloom **2:** trucker's slang for driving an empty vehicle n **1:** someone who travels without paying, a freeloader **2:** a loyal fan of the band the Grateful Dead

PROLOGUE

So many lies. The day you start telling them, you expect a hand on your shoulder at any moment. Every time you open your mouth and the fake history comes out — the fake family, the fake anecdotes. If not the hand, then the stony gaze, as if to say "I know that's not true" or "like hell you are." The challenge is anticipated. It may be delivered casually with a slightly puzzled look and a muttered "really?" Or more forcefully by a relentless questioner pressing you for names and dates, distances between the cities where you say you've lived, and the names of the schools you say you've attended, because miraculously the speaker has a relative in each of them.

When the challenge doesn't come — or the hand or the handcuffs that would eventually follow — there's a whoosh, like a plane slipping through a layer of clouds or a diver breaking the surface, coming up for air. You're free. And after years of that happening and *feeling* free, maybe you are. When every trace of who you were has disappeared or been buried and all that's left is the new person.

Everyone remembers the crooked financier who turned himself in to the authorities — the one who stole billions with a decades-old Ponzi scheme. Springfield was abuzz with gossip. The names of those who'd been hit and were quietly deaccessioning boats and pied-à-terres were spoken in hushed tones as if the victims should somehow be ashamed for having been bilked out of their fortunes. People were astonished at the greed and the lavish lifestyle the man's crimes had supported. At how otherwise smart people had handed over millions of their hard-earned dollars apparently without checking the man out.

I marveled at how the man had kept the lies straight for so many years — the nonexistent meetings and transactions, the phantom companies, the fictional world he'd created a thousand times more complex and intricate than the one I'd devised — and how it had all come crashing down around his ears and whether the same thing might happen to me.

But then, I had no intention of confessing.

ONE

"It's a false lamium," I said.

Babe Chinnery folded her muscular arms, appraised the plant, and said simply, "If it's not a lamium, why in hell do you keep calling it one?"

"Things aren't always what they seem to be."

"Thank you, Yoda."

The woman had a good point. She usually did. Despite the rock 'n' roll outfits, the hair color that changed with the New England seasons, and the boyfriend twenty years her junior, Babe had more common sense than most of the people I knew. It was a perfectly legitimate question and I couldn't answer her.

"Don't give me a hard time. I'm just a gardener, not Linnaeus."

"Who's Lin-ay-us?"

"Some Swedish guy who named plants," I said. "Don't worry — there won't be a quiz.

I was just trying to dazzle you with my smarts."

"Consider me dazzled."

In fact, Linnaeus hadn't named this plant. There was a lot of deception in the garden. Beautiful plants that were poisonous to the touch. Things that look like one thing but were something else — false spirea, false hellebore, false Solomon's seal. I suppose it's accurate to label them false, but why not just call them what they are? When I'm queen, I'll change that and give them all their own lyrical, poetic names, like *Kalmia latifolia* or *Platycodon grandiflorus* or a new favorite, nicotiana 'Only the Lonely'. Roy Orbison would be so pleased.

"Trust me, you don't want real lamium in these planters. You said you want more yellow. This may not look like much now, but when this baby flowers, believe me, it'll be yellow."

Babe squinted and walked around the parking lot. She held a nursery catalog near each planter to visualize what it would look like next year when it was in full bloom. I resisted the urge to tell her the images in the booklet were almost as unrealistic and unattainable as the ones in the Victoria's Secret catalog. Why burst her bubble?

14

Optimism was a critical ingredient in any garden.

Babe had specifically requested yellow because that color would work with the diner's new hot-pink shutters. Not exactly ye olde New England color scheme found in regional magazines, which always wanted to call red, Betsy Ross red, and blue, Heritage blue, as if the building's occupants all wore knee breeches and white hose and were called Lemuel or Goody. But Babe was not your garden-variety New Englander and the colors worked for her — a little punk rocker, a little Caribbean beachcomber — to go with the lakeside setting and the tiki-bar feel of the place.

"Damn," she said.

What now? She stood at the far side of her outdoor café, looking perturbed. Behind the lattice and the flaking hand-painted HOMEMADE DONUTS sign stood the small utility shed where Babe stored her trash cans and where a Dumpster was temporarily parked. The top and side doors of the shed were open, and the industrial-sized cans beside it had been knocked over.

"They can't be bargained with. They can't be reasoned with. They don't feel pity or remorse or fear. And they absolutely will not stop."

Where had I heard that?

"Raccoons." She smacked the side of the shed in frustration. "How can they have lifted those rocks off the top?"

"Beats me. The rock trick works at my place. You want me to help clean up?"

"Nah. I shouldn't do it now, either. I'm needed back in the kitchen. I'll take care of it tonight. Just chaps my butt, though. Look at this — papers and food scraps strewn all over." She hauled off and kicked one of the rocks that had held down the top of the shed, and it bounced off one of six metal cans lined up in formation behind the shed.

"What are you saving the empties for?" I asked. "Deposit?"

"They're not empty. It's WVO — waste vegetable oil. I leave it out for the people with the fat wagons."

I'd read about the fat wagons, or French frymobiles. Serious environmentalists or loonies, depending on which side of the gas pump you stood, reconfigured engines to run on waste vegetable oil; and, apart from making their cars smell like a death wish-sized tub of onion rings, it sounded like a good idea. Maybe it was a diet strategy, too. Perhaps if you smelled fried food all day long, you were less likely to eat it.

"You think it was one of those guys?"

"Looking for what? I leave all the good stuff out. There's no need to go through the trash. And most of them aren't poor. One guy has a Mercedes fat wagon. He just hates paying for gas. For some it's the carbon footprint; for others it's the dependency-on-foreign-oil issue. I think the Mercedes guy just wants to relive his radical youth. It kills him that he's turned into his dad. I'm happy. They recycle my garbage. And it makes me feel less guilty for not having traded in my SUV for a Prius, like I told my sons I would.

"No," she said, rubbing the hand that was still smarting from the ill-advised smack. "These were four-legged culprits with glow-in-the-dark eyes and pointy little noses. I'd think they were cute if I saw them on the Nature Channel, but not in my parking lot!"

I empathized; I felt the same way about deer. In a national park, Bambi. In my garden, Godzilla.

In the years since we'd become friends Babe and I had transformed the glass- and rubbish-strewn parking lot outside the Paradise Diner into a tropical oasis. Never mind that this part of Connecticut frequently saw ten to fifteen snowstorms a season. Babe chose to live on island time. She had made her own rules and blissfully

17

ignored convention for so long that people in Springfield rarely commented on it anymore, unless it was to acknowledge her latest makeover — her current look featured spiky blond hair and fingernails the color of Granny Smith apples.

We walked back to the planters. She circled one anemic lamium, moved it slightly to the right, and gave it careful consideration before giving it a thumbs-up. The plant had made the cut. We reenacted the same pas de deux with each perennial and shrub every planting season, and she'd never yet turned down one of my suggestions.

"Why do you do this," I asked, "when you always say yes?" I made a note to order six more false lamiums from the nursery.

"I just don't want you to think I'm a pushover."

As if that were likely.

I'm Paula Holliday, sole proprietor of Dirty Business, formerly known as PH Factor, but the longer I did it the more dirt I dug up, so I changed the name and it caught on. It was also my intentionally vague way of saying that I'm not a licensed landscape architect and I'll do pretty much anything garden related from long-range design plans to houseplant care.

The traditional property maintenance business had all but disappeared these days. People were cutting back, and I'd had two clients stiff me for an entire summer's work last year by moving out and neglecting to leave a forwarding address so that I could send them a final bill. Anna Jurado, my part-time bookkeeper, felt responsible, but it was my own fault. I should have read the telltale signs — the tag sale, the rented Dumpster, the "Oh, no, we're just doing some fall cleaning." Right, and I'm just doing this because I'm a madcap heiress waiting for my inheritance to come through.

The good news was that those two miscreants inspired my latest professional brainstorm — the quickie curb-appeal face-lift. Makeup for your home. With all the *for sale* signs dotting the area, these instant-gratification jobs had turned into the most lucrative and least-labor-intensive part of my business. I suppose I had cable television to thank.

For three to five hundred bucks, depending on the size and selling price of the house, I'd sweep in with a horticultural Band-Aid for a plain house — containers, annuals, and a few small trees. Pumpkins and ornamental kale in the fall. Just about the only thing I couldn't orchestrate was a thin wisp of smoke emanating from the chimney to give it that final Norman Rockwell touch. *If you lived here you'd be happy, warm. Your house would be filled with the smell of homemade bread or apple pie. Your kids wouldn't smoke pot or give you a hard time. And all your in-laws would be people you'd actually hang out with if you had a choice.* All courtesy of a few plants, a vivid imagination, and a fondness for Norman Rockwell.

At the Paradise, on the other hand, that wasn't required. Not that Babe had anything against Norman Rockwell, but she saw my work at the diner as a calling card — not unlike the display gardens at a flower show. Babe had insisted I put Designed by Dirty Business signs on the planters as a way to drum up business. It had worked for the past three seasons, and I had my fingers crossed for next year.

I allowed myself to think about a vacation. I hadn't had one since leaving my old job, but once my assets and debits were on speaking terms I was heading to Jost Van Dyke. I'd lie in a hammock and read the water-swollen paperbacks — thoughtfully left by previous travelers — that smelled of the sea and suntan lotion. And the biggest decision I'd have to make was which high-calorie local drink to order, the painkiller or the bushwhacker.

In the meantime the Paradise Diner would serve as my Caribbean surrogate. Earlier in the season, Hugo Jurado and I had turned one corner of Babe's parking lot into an outdoor café, something sorely missing in suburban Springfield. Hugo was Anna's husband and my part-time helper; sometimes it seemed as if they were the brains of the business and I worked for them instead of the other way around.

Springfield's downtown had evolved, even in just the few years since I'd arrived. We had an art house movie theater and an all-night deli, but further out of town Babe's and the Dunkin' Donuts were the only two gastronomic and social destinations. Double D had the edge on the coffee, but no one could touch the donuts at the Paradise.

Hugo and I had constructed wooden flower boxes two feet high and four feet deep creating a modular enclosure for a twenty-by-twenty-foot area in the front of the diner. In the spring and summer the boxes dripped with colorful annuals and perennials, and Babe wanted to extend the season with a fall display that included shrubs and ornamental grasses. All of them were a charming counterpoint to Babe's deliciously trashy message marquee and neon sign, where one of the bulbs was always burned out or smashed. I half suspected that kids came by at night when the diner was closed and tossed rocks at the lightbulbs, to help Babe maintain the diner's slightly seedy look, or maybe it was Babe herself, who knew?

She had added picnic tables and unmatched tag-sale umbrellas, so now in addition to being a must stop for every trucker in this part of the state, the shabby chic café was attracting the Main Street Moms who had previously been too timid or too snobby to venture in, preferring the overpriced gourmet bakery three towns away.

One or two curmudgeonly regulars had grumbled that Babe was tarting up the place, but just as many appreciated the new and better-looking faces. The early shift of day laborers and long haulers who camped out at Babe's — whether they were hungry or not — was now followed by clusters of suburban matrons, sometimes with their kids, fresh from soccer or ballet or dressage. Sometimes they overlapped.

"When you pay my bills," she told the complainers, "you can tell me how to decorate and who to serve."

I didn't pay her bills either, and she rarely paid mine, except for materials. For the most part, Babe and I had an in-kind arrangement. I worked on her outside space and she let me use a corner booth at the Paradise as an informal office where the coffee kept flowing and Pete number two (so named to distinguish him from Babe's late husband) used me as a guinea pig for new recipes. It was an arrangement that suited me fine despite the three or four pounds I'd put on since I had relocated to Springfield from New York City and our unspoken agreement had started. And Babe's bulletin board was my private ad space, touting my services to residents and small businesses up and down the Merritt Parkway, which brought Babe many of her non-truck-driving customers.

This was a far cry from Babe's previous life twenty or so years earlier when she was a backup singer traveling with a band and the dear departed Pete number one. Late in the day when there were no kids around, she would let slip one of her more outrageous anecdotes, and she never failed to gather a crowd at the diner's counter, leaving most of her listeners feeling Walter Mittyish for living vicariously through her adventures instead of getting off their butts and having some of their own. Once in a while a story sounded suspiciously like something I'd seen in a movie or read in a novel, but if she was embellishing, who cared? Who didn't relive the past and burnish some stories to make herself seem smarter, hipper, and funnier? And she told the stories well, with enough brio and detail to make you feel as if you'd been there with her, partying with rock stars and dancing on yachts.

"I miss it sometimes," she'd said, "traveling with the Jimmy Collins Band. A different city every week. Hell, sometimes every night. That was a lifetime ago. I have no complaints. Somebody once told me there are only two stories: a man goes on a journey, and a stranger comes to town. The first half of my life, I went on the journey. Now I'm here and the people who come to the diner are the ones who come to town." A bittersweet smile had crossed her face when she said it, and I wondered if she was thinking about Pete number one and how they had come to this town so many years ago.

Babe brushed her hands on her tight black jeans, held the diner's screen door open, and shooed me inside. "C'mon, Linnaeus," she said. Babe was a quick study.

"Town" was Springfield, Connecticut, somewhere between Boston and New York and light-years from both. I had come to Springfield from New York City years earlier as a summer renter, thinking everything was so much smaller and simpler than my life in New York. People said hello. After only two trips to the diner I was asked if I was having "the usual."

Arrogantly, I found everything *quaint.* Then a few years back I lost my job and my boyfriend in one sixty-day period. I came here to lick my wounds and I never left. Small and simple was just what I needed.

"Speaking of a man going on a journey, have you heard from Neil?" I asked casually, sliding onto a counter stool and positioning my backpack on the one next to it. I peeled off my garden gloves, shoved them into a back pocket, and checked out the day's specials on the blackboard. I made an extra effort to appear to be studying the menu in case the subject of her relationship with Neil was off-limits.

Babe's face softened. Neil was her sweet young thing. He had gone home to Scotland because his mother was ill and wound up staying longer than any of them had expected. "He's supposed to be back in two weeks, according to the last round of elec-

25

tronic missives."

Neil had been e-mailing and Twittering lists of movies, foods, and recreational activities he expected to indulge in once he got home. They were sweet, like two teenagers separated during summer vacation. Babe smacked her lips as if Neil were one of Pete number two's architectural, Food Network desserts. "His mom is out of the woods medically, but it sounds like she didn't change a lightbulb or hang a picture in the seven years he's been in this country. You'd think no one else in Scotland knew how to use a spanner. That's a wrench . . . or a hammer. I forget which."

"C'mon, isn't it just the mom thing? Don't you have it have with your kids?"

"My kids? They've been independent from a very early age."

That's right. I recalled one of Babe's late-night storytelling sessions. She told us how one night her sons, Dylan and Daltry, had borrowed a friend's car to catch Hootie & the Blowfish at a club called Emerald City, more than a hundred miles away. They almost made it, when a couple of bored staties pulled them over on the Jersey Turnpike for driving with a broken taillight. Her sons were eleven and thirteen at the time and the only thing that bothered Babe was that they'd done it all to see Hootie and not some edgier, hipper band. *Independent* was an understatement. So independent that I'd never met them and neither had anyone at the diner. They hadn't been back east since their father had died. That was a subject I didn't touch. People were funny when it came to their kids.

I placed my order — red, white, and blueberry waffles, probably the reason for my extra four pounds — and went to wash my hands. When I got back, Babe was peering out the window through the miniblinds.

"What have we here?" she said under her breath. "If it's Tuesday it must be . . . what, horseback riding or lacrosse? Convoy of Main Street Moms arriving, Pete. Crank up the cappuccino machine." Which was a joke, since she didn't own a cappuccino machine, although Pete was lobbying hard for one, as well as a copper milk steamer he'd seen on QVC.

I half stood in my seat to see what was holding her attention for so long. A flotilla of sleek cars had arrived and pulled into the angled parking spots adjacent to the entrance as if they were a team of synchronized swimmers or trained seals. Just as gracefully, out the drivers came, first one smooth fair head, then the next.

27

All the moms wore slightly different permutations of the same early fall outfit — turtlenecks, leather vests, quilted jackets, quilted vests, leather jackets, with well-coordinated gloves, scarves, and bags that were like the colors on creamy decorator paint chips. Pricey paint.

Four or five kids who could have belonged to any of the women piled out of the back of the largest SUV. Towheaded angels, a cross between the psycho kids from *Village of the Damned* and those from the latest Ralph Lauren ad campaign whose little duds probably cost more than my first car, although that wasn't saying much. Something about the mothers suggested they had just parked Thoroughbred horses, like their cars, on similar angles, and left them in the nearby Mossdale Stables.

Caroline Sturgis was the last to dismount from a silver, or maybe it was a Paul Revere pewter Land Rover. Caroline was one of my first customers in Springfield. We'd met at a local thrift shop — I was buying, she was donating. Despite the differences in our ages and socioeconomic groups, she seemed to gravitate toward me. As a newcomer with a business, I needed all the contacts I could get, so I responded.

This would be the third year I'd looked

after Caroline's property, weaning her from the pedestrian triumvirate of impatiens, marigold, and red salvia and steering her toward more adventurous plantings, or at least my notion of them. But I'd kept my distance for the last month or so because making a house call inevitably involved a pitcher of something alcoholic. I'd succumbed in the past and it resulted in my losing a day's work and once, a dozen flats of pansies that had sat wilting in the sun for hours while Caroline and I got very happy on a bottle of Mouton Rothschild. Getting loaded early in the day was something a rich suburban matron might be able to do, but it was a no-no for a woman of modest means who was struggling to keep her small business afloat.

It was just cool enough to turn up your collar without looking too affected, so Caroline and the Moms settled in at a table outside — one farthest from the road, mostly out of the sun, and at an appropriate distance from another table of women whom they acknowledged but didn't join. Their kids commandeered a picnic table nearby.

These were the well-heeled ladies of Springfield and its neighboring towns. They traveled in packs to book groups and charity events, prep school fund-raisers and the occasional local art show or dramatic performance. They were attractive, polite, and just standoffish enough to make you feel justified in not feeling all warm and fuzzy toward them. If there was a Junior League in Connecticut I wasn't aware of it, but I imagined that the Main Street Moms — as Babe had christened them — were the unofficial New England equivalent. I had a love-hate relationship with them. Two or three more on my client list and I could stop worrying about the rising cost of mulch and start packing for the Virgin Islands, but with a last shred of independence, self-respect, or city slicker stupidity — I didn't know which — I couldn't bring myself to suck up to them the way any other small businesswoman would have.

Babe motioned for one of her young waitresses to go outside and take their orders.

"Why me?" the girl said, her expression changing from sullen to stricken. "They always look at me as if I have two heads." She didn't. She had one head, but she did have more than the requisite seven holes in it. Thank goodness my generation was satisfied with a few extra holes in our earlobes.

"Hey, Terry, you don't wanna be looked

at, lose the nose ring and the eyebrow bolts. Otherwise wear your freak flag proudly," Babe said, sympathetic but firm. She swished a handful of menus under the girl's pierced nose.

"Great. Now I'm going to have to google *freak flag*. I don't know what that means, but I'm going," the girl said, shaking her head. She snatched the menus and let the screen door slam as she went out, but her chin was the tiniest bit higher than it been earlier, getting the spirit of the advice if not the actual reference.

"Good girl!" Babe said.

"What *does* that mean?" I asked quietly.

"Et tu, Paula? You girls are sadly lacking in a basic cultural education," Babe said. "I told them to write down everything they heard in the diner that they didn't understand and then look it up. Freak flag? Woodstock? The Dead? Frank Zappa? Crosby, Stills and Nash? What are you girls going to listen to when you get old, sitting in that rocking chair on the nursing home porch? The Spice Girls? Salt-N-Pepa?"

Outside, shielding her eyes, Caroline Sturgis twisted in her seat and peered through the miniblinds until she located me at the counter. She wiggled her fingers in my direction, said something to her friends,

31

then excused herself and headed for the front door. I knew I should have parked the Jeep farther in the rear, she might not have known I was there.

"Hello, partner," she sang, accompanied by the screen door's bells. She walked in my direction with just the hint of a cowboy swagger.

"That's premature," I said. "I haven't agreed to anything."

For months Caroline had been pursuing me. She wanted us to start a business together, but I wasn't sold on the idea. I worried there would be lots of celebrating and not a lot of working. *She* might be able to write off a failed business as this year's uncompleted pet project, like a quilt or an exercise program, but I couldn't. Besides, I didn't like partners and hadn't had one for a while. Professional or otherwise. Having been thrown recently, I was finding it hard to get back on the horse.

"You've been avoiding me," Caroline said, wagging a finger at me. "I know it."

Of course she knew it. I was the worst liar on the planet. That's how my mother always knew when I stayed out too late or sneaked beers and cigarettes with my girlfriends and then tried to mask the smell with Altoids. That's why I'd had a string of two-date relationships. What's the point? If it's not happening, it's not happening. And that was why it was a good thing I was no longer in the television business, where lying was practically a job requirement.

"This is not just a bored housewife's fantasy," Caroline said. She'd read my mind.

"I've written a business plan. I have spreadsheets and everything, and I'm going to sit here until you agree to meet with me to discuss it."

That last line was delivered with all the certainty of a three-year-old who announces that he's going to hold his breath until you do something, knowing full well that you're not going to let him turn himself blue, even if he could.

Caroline had unwittingly just listed everything I hated. I came to Springfield to get away from spreadsheets and business plans. I was hardly going to be lured back into harness by a pie chart. And I'd gotten used to being the boss. Okay, my full-time staff was sitting on this counter stool, but at least I didn't think my boss was an idiot, as most people do.

Still, I liked Caroline. What started as a business relationship had developed into something more — a friendship not based on history and "remember when." And it wasn't as if I had any burning plans for the next few months other than keeping this counter seat warm and keeping Babe company. I'd briefly considered an off-season job but didn't really see myself plowing people's driveways, which was what most of the other gardeners did during winter.

Maybe it wouldn't be so bad getting toasted before noon during those long, cold months between November and February when business was slow or, let's face it, non-existent. Caroline drank the good stuff, too, no screw-top bottles for her. I could resurrect my fondness for Veuve Clicquot and premium vodka on her dime, instead of indulging in the Two Buck Chuck I'd been sipping and pretending to like on those chilly evenings alone by the fire.

I was driving into the city the next day, picking up my pal Lucy, and heading to Bucks County for an old colleague's wedding. Now that nuptials lasted five days and required interstate, if not intercontinental, travel I wasn't likely to be back in Connecticut for almost a week, especially if I tacked on a few days visit with Lucy.

"When were you thinking of getting together?" I asked, taking out my phone and scrolling through the calendar.

"I knew it! I knew you'd say yes!" Caroline said. "We're going to buy Chiaramonte's!"

"I *haven't* said yes. I agree to talk about it when I get back and perhaps advise you, that's all."

Caroline nodded, not hearing me. Why are blond women always so sure we're going to do what they want? And why do we do it? I was sure it had something to do with the vestigial scars from high school. We're still hoping the cool kids will want to have lunch with us. How pathetic is that?

She pulled out an old-style planner, blood-red leather, with her initials stamped in gold on the front. All the pages still had hard edges, and there were no stray papers or business cards sticking out. Brand-new for her brand-new venture. It was endearing. She flipped through a few pages with a fat ceramic pen.

"I can't do next week, either — college visits. Jason's only fourteen, but that's when you have to start looking. He's had a wish list since he was nine. How about the following week? I told Sarah I'd go with her to the doctor's, but I don't know which day yet. She'll need my support," she said, almost to herself. "She's getting Brandon's DNA results back to see which sports he'll be good at."

I wracked my brain trying to think which of the little blond urchins was Brandon. "Isn't he just a toddler?"

"That's when you're supposed to do it, or else Sarah might waste a lot of time taking him to the wrong classes."

That's right, heaven forbid Brandon spends time at an activity for which he is not genetically predisposed.

"How about meeting on the twelfth, nine A.M. at my place unless I let you know otherwise? Does that work for you?" Caroline asked. "I'll come straight home from my morning ride."

It did indeed. In the fall, almost everything worked for me, especially when someone asked that far in advance. It was the time of year when I remembered the concept of weekends, too. And exercise that involved colorful weights instead of forty-pound bags of topsoil or manure.

In any event, our scheduled appointment gave me enough time to figure out how to let Caroline down gently when I eventually said no. It was a hundred to one I'd actually want to go in to business with her, but why blow her off completely; no point in totally burning bridges or alienating my biggest customer.

Mission accomplished, Caroline left to

rejoin her pals outside, chirping to Babe on her way out to think of a good name for our new gardening venture.

Babe and I answered at the same time, "What's wrong with Dirty Business?"

Caroline laughed like a teenager. "*Dirty Business* — that *is* a good name, better than Chiaramonte's. Done!" She snaked through a knot of recent arrivals and tried unsuccessfully to ignore the comments of a handful of truckers waiting to be seated. She smiled but sidestepped them, backing up against the Snapple fridge, as if coming too close would somehow contaminate her or rough up the nap of her tan suede jacket. It was all very faux friendly.

In the group was one long-haired, bearded guy, not bad looking if you liked that slightly grungy Johnny-Damon-when-he-was-a-Red-Sox look. He wore Oakley sunglasses, a dark green windbreaker, and a baseball cap with an ornate letter D on the crown.

He took off the glasses to get a better look at Caroline or perhaps to give her a better look at him — I couldn't tell which. Neither Babe nor I heard the exchange, but from Caroline's reaction something he said shook her up. She rushed out the door, and Babe shrugged as if to say, "what the hell?" Caroline must have made some excuse to her friends because without even touching her coffee she left a few dollars on the table and hurried to her car. "Johnny Damon" walked to the door and put his hand on the handle as if he was going to go after her.

"What did I tell you boys about scaring the locals?" Babe said it loudly enough to stop him in his tracks. He turned around and smiled. "Do you know what the markup is on coffee and a fat-free muffin versus the lumberjack specials and endless cups of coffee you animals are gonna suck down?" Babe might not have looked like much of a businesswoman, but she knew where every penny went and where it had come from. Anna and I could take a page from her book.

"I didn't mean nothing, honest," he said, walking back to the counter. "I just said she looked familiar. You look familiar, too, pretty lady," he said. "Can I buy you a coffee?"

"That's highly original. Are you, by any chance recently divorced? Because I don't think I've heard that one since leg warmers were in style. Next time, you could try asking what her sign is. I hear that one's making a comeback, too."

She was busting his chops but in a gentle, flirty way, smiling and leaning over the counter. Few people left Babe's without wanting to be either her friend or her lover. This one was a toss-up.

One of his pals chimed in. "Give him a break, Babe. It's his first time here. JW don't know the rules."

What were the rules, anyway? Were they posted somewhere? Did I know them? The man looked sheepish and said nothing, rejoining his friends. His buddies laughed; then they all piled into a booth closest to the front door before the table was even bussed. One of Babe's singing waitresses went to clean it up and take their orders.

"Not bad," Babe whispered, advance scouting for me as usual.

I ignored her. One of *my* rules is not to think of someone as a potential mate or date until I've at least said a complete sentence to him and gotten a semi-intelligent answer.

"I've thrown back better. How's the new help working out?" I asked, changing the subject. The help was three girls who had stumbled in, in tears, after a singing gig that hadn't gone well. Of course Babe had hired them on the spot and promised to help them with their act. Now they worshipped her and copied her every move.

"That's a very slick segue. They're not so new anymore. But they're doing okay, thanks for asking. They've got more physi-

39

cal presence on-stage," she said, holding the ketchup bottle like a mike and pretending to sing into it. "They'll be at Ringwald's in a coupla weeks. Alba's singing lead."

They all looked the same to me. Alba must have been the one inside — more confidence than the one with the multiple piercings. She was holding her own, sparring with a table full of burly guys; no mean feat for a ninety-pound teenager in heavy makeup and black Frankenstein shoes that looked like cinder blocks, spray painted and strapped to her heronlike legs. Her life flashed before my eyes. I saw her strutting her stuff, sucking on a ball microphone and posturing like Madonna or Mick or Avril or Amy, getting deliriously famous and then crashing and burning before she was twenty-one, rehab by twenty-two — video at eleven. Perhaps I took too dim a view of the music business.

The girl outside, with the eyebrow bolt, was more introspective. Probably the songwriter, writing a lot of angry chick, why-did-you-dump-me songs. Jeez, I was turning into a cranky broad. Was I really jealous of a couple of young girls?

"You should go," Babe said, as if she were clairvoyant.

"Lots of guys at Ringwald's."

"Twenty-year-olds."

"Nothing wrong with young stuff for whatever ails you."

That was as aggressive as Babe got in her matchmaking efforts. A few times a week she remembered that I hadn't had a date in a while and gave it a shot, but she never pressed.

Sometimes it seemed as if she and Lucy Cavanaugh, my friend the bridesmaid, were having a private contest to see who could hook me up first. Despite Lucy's vehement denials, I knew there'd be a fix-up sometime over the course of the upcoming five-day wedding. That was the real reason she'd asked me to drive her. And while I wasn't actively dreading it, I wasn't looking forward to it either.

"I'm going to a wedding. There will be ample opportunity for me to listen to some boring guy's whole life story before telling him I'm not interested. Besides, as you say, plenty of cute guys right here. No need for me to pay a cover charge for some watered-down drinks at some shabby joint downtown. I can just stay in this shabby joint and watch the passing parade."

"Shabby? I'm cutting you off. Pete, no more taste testing for Paula," she yelled.

Moments later, Eyebrow Girl pushed

through the door, butt first, muttering, with two trays of cups and small plates, one of them precariously balanced on her forearm. Something on her sleeve, or maybe her studded leather cuff, snagged on the door handle and one of the trays flew out of her hands like an oversized Frisbee. The other one fell with a clatter, splashing beverages up in the air like minigeysers.

"Holy shit!" she said, laughing and only half covering her mouth, in deference to the father sitting at the counter, who gave her a disapproving look and covered his toddler's ears as if the kid could recognize a naughty word at that tender age.

No one was hurt and just a few were splattered by the mug puddles; someone applauded. I've never quite understood that. Is that supposed to make the person feel better? *Yes, I am a klutz and a loser, thank you for acknowledging. I feel so much better.*

The bearded trucker who'd spoken to Caroline was closest to the door, and he got up to help the girl who was crab walking in a circle collecting the items she'd dropped. He said something to her, and it was the first time I'd ever seen the kid crack a smile, although she went to some pains to hide it.

Babe came around from behind the counter and picked up the cups and plates that had traveled farthest. "All right, Mr. Nice Guy, you've redeemed yourself for your formerly boorish behavior. Go eat your food before it gets cold. I'll get this."

"Don't worry, Terry, it's no big deal," she whispered, bending down to help the girl. "Doesn't really count unless you send one of them to the emergency room." She handed the girl a soggy five-dollar bill. "Take your tip and go wash your hands." Babe brought the mess back to the counter near where I was sitting with my coffee and waiting for my order.

"Look at this. Pete makes these phenomenal, food orgasm muffins and the Moms barely touch them. They don't need utensils, they need scalpels."

The cranberries had been picked off and a thin layer of crust was almost surgically shaved off the tops. I remembered that calorie reduction tip well.

"*You* used to be like that," she said. "A damn picky eater. Before you got some sense."

Sense. To Babe that meant ordering the waffles. Or the cake or the sundae or whatever it was you really wanted. Whether it was food, men, or adventures, Babe did not believe in living a life of denial.

"These women," she said, motioning to

43

the group outside. "I still don't get some of them." She cleared off the tray and put the cups and dishes in a rubber basin underneath the counter.

"So what is it the queen of the cul-de-sacs wants you to do now? Plant marigolds in the shape of clinking martini glasses?" Babe was referring to my first fall in Springfield when Caroline had asked for tulips planted in the shape of giant crossed tennis rackets. Which worked out well until, inevitably, they flopped over and resembled nothing more than an enormous handlebar mustache.

"That's very creative," I said. "I may offer that next year. I could do martini glasses. Champagne flutes should go over well during bridal season." I was semiserious.

"You remember last spring when Caroline was calling me three times a day," I said, "and practically stalking me here at the diner?" Babe nodded.

"She's got some notion to buy Guido Chiaramonte's old nursery. And she's written a business plan, which I have foolishly agreed to take a look at. She'd have a garden gift shop and I'd offer design services. We'd collaborate on special projects."

"Sounds good. What's wrong with that?"

"They want two million dollars for the

property, and it probably needs another five hundred thousand just to open the doors. She wants to front the money and put it all in my name."

That raised an eyebrow. She looked around as if to appraise her own lot with its charming waterfront view. What was her lakeside property worth? One million? More? "Okay. Unusual but, I repeat, what's wrong with that?"

I couldn't put my finger on it, but in my gut there was something about Caroline's plan that didn't sit right with me. It was too good to be true, like those Nigerian e-mail scams — *just send me the postage, my friend, and we will split a fortune.* My knee-jerk reaction was to say no. But that was generally my knee-jerk reaction to things — not unlike the overcautious lawyer who says, "We could have a problem there. . . ." There is no problem, but there could be one.

That was also the reason I owned a ten-year-old car, a fifteen-year-old television, and a four-year-old cell phone that the company's Web site refers to as a "legendary" model. It took me awhile to say yes to new things.

"C'mon, what's the downside?" Babe said. "I mean, not to put too fine a point on it, but she's loaded and you've got two, maybe three nickels to rub together."

And where does *that* expression come from? Why would anyone want to rub two nickels together? Are they supposed to make babies if you rub them together? From anyone else, I would have been offended, but Babe was close to the truth. I was fantasizing about an island trip, but I was treading water financially. It happened every year at this time. I sucked it up, ate big breakfasts — the least expensive and most filling meal of the day and frequently free, if Pete had gotten a new cookbook or watched a new cooking program. I had soup for dinner and generally lost my three or four donut pounds by the time garden season rolled around. Not the end of the world, lots of mammals put on a layer of fat and hibernated for the winter.

I nursed my third cup of coffee and picked at Pete's all-American waffle — strawberries, blueberries, and heaps of powdered sugar — when the truckers finished and came to the counter to settle up. The bearded guy was last to pay. He lingered at the register to talk to Babe after his pals left. He motioned outside to where Caroline had been sitting.

"I don't suppose you'd like to tell me that pretty lady's name?"

"Who's that?" Babe said.

"He means Caroline," Eyebrow Girl said, trying to be helpful.

"Caroline? That was the woman I was talking to?"

The young girl nodded. She didn't understand Babe's hesitation. Who else could he have meant?

"Sure," Babe said. "She's Mrs. Caroline I've-got-a-big-dog-an-even-bigger-husband-and-a-security-system-the-Pentagon-would-be-proud-of. Who wants to know?"

The trucker held up his hands in mock supplication. "Wow. What are you, her bodyguard? Forget it. No biggie. I'll catch up with *Car-o-line* next time."

He held up two fingers in a peace sign and backed out of the diner with a smile. Once outside, he zipped his jacket, took a last look around, and then strolled past the last of the Main Saint Moms now reloading their kids into their cars. He tipped his hat theatrically and made his way over to his truck, where his buddy was waiting for him.

"I must be slipping," Babe said, inspecting her reflection in the small fridge behind the counter. "Not to be conceited, but usually they want *my* number. Maybe it was a mistake sucking up to the velvet headband crowd. Too much competition."

"Like you've ever been worried about competition. You think he was hitting on Caroline?"

"Who knows? If the Paradise can bring two people together, my work is done. I'm not one to stand in the way of either true love or unbridled lust. No judgments here. I was just looking out for her. He could have been a serial killer."

I'd heard Babe say that a hundred times. As friendly as she was, the first time she met anyone, he was a potential mass murderer until she had evidence to the contrary. Coming from a large city, I tended to agree with her.

"I don't know," she said, "baseball hat, long hair, even the peace sign. Sometimes there's a thin line between cool and creepy. And who wants to be responsible for giving a friend's name and address to the next Hannibal Lecter? Am I right?"

"You're getting dangerously close to profiling. What would the Maharishi say?"

"He was before my time, wise guy. I'm just saying the guy looked like he should be on his way to a Grateful Dead reunion, not sniffing around a white-gloved suburban lady, who, by the way, is still happily married as far as I know. If I'm wrong and either of them is interested, it's their business to pursue, not mine to facilitate. He may be back anyway. I think he was driving for the same company as Retro Joe."

Retro Joe was hard to miss. Despite the fact that he was over sixty years old and 100 percent gray, he sported an oiled pompadour with a big curl on his forehead that swirled like the inside of a nautilus shell or the top of a soft ice cream cone. In the summer he wore his sleeves rolled up tight on his biceps. Mercifully, it was fall and we were spared the peculiar sight of his ashen skin stretched over surprisingly cut muscles.

"Joe's here a few times a month. Works for two or three different companies depending on where he feels like driving and where the next Elvis tribute concert was being held. I'll ask him about his new colleague the next time he's in."

I teased her again about betraying her Woodstockian peace, love, and music roots, but Babe was right to be cautious. One town over, an elderly woman brought in her luxury car for a tune-up and wound up dead at the hands of the mechanic's greedy girlfriend, who bludgeoned her with a tire iron after the older woman thoughtlessly failed to have any jewelry or money to steal.

So much for things being quieter in the suburbs.

Two

The next day, I was home packing for the marathon wedding trip when Gretchen Kennedy called. Gretchen was one of the real estate agents I was counting on to keep me in big breakfasts and soup throughout the long Connecticut winter.

"I didn't even know they were thinking of selling the company," she said. I could hear the long, deep exhale of her cigarette smoke. "Two offices are merging, that's the official story. I'll still have my properties, but you know how it is. There's a glut in the market right now. Sellers aren't selling and buyers aren't buying. People keep waiting for things to bottom out."

Hadn't they bottomed out yet? I tried hard to share her pain but wanted her to get to the point. How would it affect our arrangement? Would there be more work? Finally she blurted it out. "The curb appeal trick won't work for the new listings I've inherited. These are distress sales — condos and townhouses without a Chia Pet, much less a garden. They're less expensive and I've a better chance of moving them before the junior exec minimansions you've been helping me with. In this economy . . ." She took a long drag on her cigarette and babbled on, but I'd stopped listening. I was getting tired of hearing sentences starting with that phrase. And I was tired of delivering them, too. *In this economy,* landscaping was one of the first things cut when people economized. A lot of people thought they could handle it themselves — and they *could* do it themselves — if they lived in an apartment with two hanging plants and an air fern. Otherwise it was as lunatic as trying to cut your own hair. Suburban homeowners needed me or someone like me, but it wasn't always easy to make the case. The women got it, but the men were harder to convince. They thought ten minutes with a flashy power mower was all any home needed until they tried it and gave up halfway through to watch the big game, even if the big game that day was a Norwegian curling competition.

"You've had two or three jobs a week for me for the last two months. Are you saying that's dried up?" She didn't have to say any more. It was as if a lover had told me he needed his space. I got the message: she'd call me if and when business picked up.

I stopped packing and went online to check my bank account. In the spring and summer, Anna Jurado looked after me. She kept the books, made sure I got paid, made sure I ate, and generally took over the role of older sister and *mami* from March until October, when she and Hugo went back to Mexico for the winter. It would be four months, maybe five with next to no money coming in, just a few upcoming jobs and outstanding invoices — and they wouldn't cover one large heating oil delivery. Maybe I should have gone to Mexico and worked for them.

I wasn't anyone's idea of a spendthrift but I could economize. I'd turn down the thermostat and wear a sweater in the house, like Mr. Rogers. I'd get a dog to keep me warm at night, one that didn't eat much. Or three, like the Eskimos. Wasn't that how the band Three Dog Night got its name? Three dogs would keep you warm on a really cold night. (I'd have to ask Babe.) I'd run my car on waste vegetable oil from the diner . . . once I learned how to do that.

No I wouldn't. And I wouldn't get three dogs either. One, tops.

Grimly, I tallied up what the wedding trip was going to cost. Perhaps I could take home a very large doggie bag for my not yet acquired dog. Why didn't people elope anymore? It was so colorful and romantic. And so much cheaper for one's friends. I barely remembered this woman. How had I allowed myself to be roped into going to her wedding?

Caroline Sturgis's business proposition was starting to sound better. I dialed her home number but the phone rang off the wall.

The next morning before I left I tried again. "At the request of the customer, this number has been temporarily disconnected."

THREE

The wedding was a gaudy, over-the-top affair that was desperate to be featured in the Vows section of the Sunday *New York Times*. It wasn't. I was happy to escape early on Sunday before the last round of ostentatious celebrating, which over the course of the weekend had me alternating between feeling pathetically single, righteously indignant about all the waste, and shockingly poor. I hadn't shared my financial concerns with Lucy, but that five-year-old black sleeveless sheath I wore told the tale.

I dropped Lucy at her apartment, not intending to stay, but she dragged me upstairs and forced three glossy shopping bags into my hands. Recent acquisitions or retail therapy gone awry, many of the items still had tags on them.

"It's too late to return these, but they'll look better on you than they do on me anyway." I peeked in one of the bags — a sequined jumpsuit, a velvet miniskirt, and a huge red patent-leather handbag with so many grommets on it I'd be surprised if they'd let me through airport security with it. Not that I was going anywhere. What did she think my life was like these days? Could I weed in a sequined jumpsuit? The next bag was more promising — a few sweaters and a huge white fur hat, which would come in handy if I happened to get the lead in the local theater group's production of *Dr. Zhivago,* but would otherwise just collect dust in my closet. I thanked her.

"Call me. I don't want you trapped in the hinterlands all winter. You've got new clothes. You need places to wear them!" I tried to think of that quote about avoiding activities that required new clothes, but it escaped me. Lucy hugged me, then I hit the road.

If I was no longer the downtown, all-in-black girl or the uptown I-have-so-many-names-on-my-clothes-I-look-like-a-Nascar-driver gal, I wasn't the Junior-League-let-me-take-my-kids-to-a-playdate woman. I was a hybrid. A false something, like the false lamiums I'd be planting in Babe's garden. A city girl in the suburbs and a suburbanite in the city. That observation gave me a lot to think about. And I did, all the way back to Connecticut.

The sun was setting over the river, and the orange glow was reflected on the limestone buildings on Riverside Drive. Farther north, I passed the Cloisters, a four-acre shrine to the Middle Ages that the Rockefellers shipped from Europe piece by piece, and that small Pantheon-like structure where I always imagined it would be fun to dance or drink or just sit and watch the river.

What did I care if some woman I used to know just got married? Good for her. And her husband seemed like a nice guy, once you got over the fact all his relatives were named Weena or Bitsy — nicknames that after a few drinks sounded vaguely like dwarves or euphemisms for genitals. For goodness sake, they'd named their dog Patrick. Couldn't they find human-sounding names for their children?

Once I crossed the bridge I felt the big city trappings slip away. And the snarkiness. The clothing from Lucy would probably make their way to Goodwill, except the hat — she'd ask about that and expect to see me in it. And one of the sweaters she'd most likely bought after seeing Michele Obama wear one just like it, even though I'm of the opinion that argyle is for socks or golfers or

Japanese schoolgirls carrying Hello Kitty backpacks. And I was none of those. I thought about my new fall wardrobe until I hit the Merritt Parkway.

At that time of day and that time of year the odds of seeing wild turkeys or deer on the highway were pretty good. I had the gardener's natural antipathy toward deer, but I got a huge kick out of seeing a rafter of turkeys. I had planned to stop at Babe's for coffee and one of Pete's desserts — what the hell, I'd passed on the wedding cake — but when I got there the diner was closed. Babe rarely kept regular hours, so I thought perhaps Neil had surprised her and come home sooner than expected. That made four people I knew who were getting lucky that night, including the newlyweds. Alas, I wasn't one of them.

I made a wide U-turn in the empty parking lot and out of the corner of my eye noticed it wasn't entirely empty. Something had moved behind the lattice enclosure and donut sign.

Probably the Terminator raccoons again, who feel no remorse and won't be bargained with, or maybe wild turkeys living it up in the last few heady weeks before Thanksgiving. I'd make sure to tell Babe next time

I saw her so that she could put out the Hav-ahart traps.

FOUR

It took days of fall cleanups to pay for my long weekend away. They were standing gigs from some of my regular customers and I'd enlisted three of Hugo's compatriots who'd stayed in the States for leaf season, recruiting them at the bodega near the downtown car dealerships where men gathered every morning, rain or shine, hoping for a day's work.

After the leaf blowers were turned off and the day laborers piled into their trucks, I'd sweep in to cut back perennials and fling annuals onto the compost pile or into the back of the used pickup that I went halfsies on with Hugo. Now that he was back in Mexico for the winter, I sometimes used it for the messy jobs to lengthen the life span of my Jeep, which was nearing 100,000 miles. The truth was, apart from the lousy gas mileage, I liked the idea of driving a pickup. I was still getting used to the stick and the strange center of gravity, but it made me feel tough, adventurous. *American,* even.

I didn't pay much attention to the time, preferring to stop whenever the truck got full or when I got hungry, whichever came first. Then I'd head to Babe's for sustenance. In the past, I'd brought my lunch like the men did, to save money, but without the social life the diner provided I could conceivably go for days without uttering a complete sentence, and that probably wasn't healthy.

When I got to Babe's, I found my usual seat at the counter occupied by a lanky guy in a gray sweatshirt and grimy down vest that looked like all the feathers had been sucked out of it. Just seeing him reminded me to wash up, so I did and came back and sat catercorner to him at the diner's long L-shaped counter, as far away as I could sit without its being obvious that he grossed me out.

I scanned the blackboard for the day's specials, but nothing appealed to me. Either I was feeling virtuous for having worked off the weekend's calories or my grubby dining companion had put me off my feed.

"Just coffee, for now."

"You sick?" Babe asked, mildly interested.

"No, I just need a few minutes."

She brought my coffee and topped up my neighbor's. He moved his keys and phone to one side with a veiny, calloused hand. We dutifully nodded like two people without the slightest interest in each other who were required to be cordial.

In a gravelly voice the guy said his name was Chase and he was in town for a couple of weeks to help a buddy of his who was in the countertop business. During the last week or so he'd become something of a regular at the Paradise while I'd been away and then working my tail off at my fall cleanup jobs.

"Is that right?" I said, hoping I sounded polite. Countertops held about as much interest for me as backsplashes, but every ten or fifteen years homeowners were forced to think about them and my number was coming up soon — the tiles on my kitchen island were popping up like cardboard shutters on an Advent calendar. So far my method of dealing with them was to put a heavy pot or vase on the ones that had erupted, but I was losing valuable counter space and would soon have to adopt another strategy.

"What kind of countertops?" I asked.

"Oh, the usual. The black stuff, the speckled stuff. Stuff like this." He tapped a fork on Babe's counter.

"Let me guess," Babe said. "You're not in the sales side of the business, am I right?"

He smiled, revealing a set of alarmingly bad teeth. "Yeah. I do the heavy lifting."

You didn't need to be a detective to see that underneath the down vest, the sweatshirt, the flannel shirt, the thermal, and who knew what other layers of insulation, this guy had all the brawn of an anemic coyote. Heavy lifting would not seem to be his forte. He saw what we were thinking.

"My pal is helping me out. We met in the service."

Having had a brief flirtation with countertops the previous spring when the tiles in my kitchen started popping up, I happened to know that most of the stone and granite companies in Springfield were owned by Eastern Europeans. Babe knew it, too, since most of them were her customers. Was this guy trying to convince us that he'd been in the Bosnian army? Another dubious look must have crossed our faces.

"Okay, it wasn't the service. We got in a little trouble when we were kids. Nothing serious — kids' stuff."

Something about the Paradise Diner acted like truth serum on certain people. Maybe there was something in the water. They came in and spilled their guts as if Babe were a therapist, a priest, and a parole officer all rolled into one. They shared things they'd never told their husbands, wives, or analysts. And then they left a tip commensurate with how much they'd unburdened themselves.

"Hey, pal, stop right there," Babe said. "We really don't need to know where you met The New Granite King of Springfield or what you did to get there. Today is the first day of the rest of your life and all that jazz. Besides, whatever *you* did, we can probably top it."

"You don't say." Chase leaned in to hear more.

"I once served coffee to a double murderer right where you're sitting — not that I knew it at the time. Right, Paula?" I nodded, not eager to talk about it. I had worked for the murderer and it had not been my favorite job.

The man gave us a strange, almost admiring look, and there was an awkward silence when that particular line of conversation evaporated.

"Look, I didn't mean to cut you off," Babe said, refilling his cup and giving him a donut on the house. "It isn't that we don't care about you, but we're a *don't ask, don't tell* kind of diner. At least until we know you better. One of Babe's rules."

"Fair enough," he said. "Babe. That's not what your mama called you, is it?"

"As a matter of fact she did, but it's not what's on my birth certificate, if that's what you're driving at."

I knew Babe's given name was Wanda and so did anyone else who cared enough to take a magnifying glass to the health department inspection certificate hanging on the wall near the cash register, but this guy was either stupid or flirting. Quite possibly both. He startled both of us by taking a picture of her with his phone and staring at the image although the original was standing right there.

"Let me guess. Your name's Darlene."

"No."

"Brittany?"

"Please, do I look like a Brittany? Listen, pal, there are about a million women's names, not including the New Agey ones and the ridiculous meant-to-be-creative spellings of old names, and the odds of your guessing mine in the next two minutes, which is all the time I have before the party at booth five wants their checks, are about a trillion to one. So, give it your best shot because now you're down to thirty seconds."

"You're Monica." The triumphant look on his face suggested that he thought he'd hit the jackpot. He waited for a reaction.

"Game over." Babe patted her apron pockets for her receipt pad, found booth five's tab, and excused herself to bring them their checks.

He looked shell-shocked, as if he didn't believe her, and looked to me for confirmation.

I'd never realized it before, but Babe really was trapped at the diner. As much as she held court and had a steady stream of admirers and friendly faces every day, she also had to deal with loonies like this. What was next? Guessing her weight? It made me appreciate my business, where I rarely saw my clients from March through October, unless they had an infestation of slugs or leaf miners.

"So what is her name?" the guy said, sliding over one seat closer to me. He slurped down the dregs of his coffee and wiped his mouth and his nose on his cuff. If I'd regained my appetite, I'd lost it again.

"Like she said. Her mother called her Babe." I got up to leave.

"Where you going?" Babe yelled. "Pete's got a new Nigella cookbook. He's making converts with it. Two women already left him their phone numbers and asked if he did private parties. Can you beat that? Let's just hope they were looking for baked goods."

"I'm going to the nursery. Gotta pick up some orders, including yours. And I may drop in on Caroline. I've been trying to reach her. I may catch you on the way back. Otherwise I'll see you tomorrow when I work on your planters." I nodded briefly to the man at the counter, who was now staring at me in a way that made me glad I was leaving.

For some reason, I dragged my feet in the parking lot. I didn't want to simply hop in my car and take off alone, so I sat there, fidgeting with my mirror, my seat belt, and anything else I could think of, waiting to see if Mr.-I-can-guess-your-name would come out soon. He didn't disappoint. Two minutes after I left he emerged, holding his phone at arm's length and shuffling towards a dirty white pickup that had streaks of rust on the side I could see and probably more on the side I couldn't. He was trying to look casual but failing miserably. Neither of us was fooling anybody. I pantomimed searching for something on the passenger seat, in case he was looking in my direction, wondering why I hadn't driven away. Then I turned off the engine and went back inside the diner, ostensibly to retrieve whatever it was I'd forgotten. I could feel his eyes on my back as the screen door slammed behind me.

Babe was surprised to see me back so soon. "It was the Nigella reference, right?" she said. "You're having second thoughts? Dang, Pete could turn out to be a domestic god. I may send him to culinary school. It could be a very good business investment." I shushed her and dragged her to the farthest booth in the back of the diner.

"Is he still there?" I asked.

"Who?" she asked, looking over her shoulder.

"Countertop Man, who wouldn't know black honed granite from Black Oak Arkansas. Is he still out there in the white pickup?"

She looked again. "If I had my periscope, I'd be able to answer more intelligently, but from where I'm sitting, no Countertop Man." She gave me a look that bordered on maternal. "Have you eaten anything today or just guzzled coffee and diet Red Bull? You're acting kinda jumpy. Five dollars says you're overcaffeinated."

"Something is not right with that guy."

"Tell me what you think over food, okay?"

She ordered for me, a Paradise Special —
eggs, pancakes, French toast, bacon — well
done. And a large decaf.

"Make double sure it's from the orange
pot. No more high test for this girl."

FIVE

I did feel better once I'd eaten. After the lunchtime crowd had thinned out, Babe came back to sit with me and brought over a plate of warm chocolate chip scones. She gave me one. Periodically I checked the door, waiting for Countertop Man to re-appear.

"You know, everyone didn't go to prep school," Babe said, "and maybe he doesn't have a meaningful relationship with his dentist."

I'd had a crush on my dentist when I was little — until he hired that big blond dental hygienist. Barbara, I think her name was. I was only eight, but I was no fool. I knew what was going on and I hated her.

"And so what if he's a con?" she said, breaking off a hunk of scone. "If he's out, he's paid his debt. What are those guys supposed to do — put themselves on ice floes? You gotta be open-minded."

Between the deliriously rich scones and my memories of my first crush, I'd lost the thread of the conversation. Prep schools? Ice floes?

I was surprised to hear Babe talking this way. I'd never given ex-cons and prison recidivism much thought, even less than countertops, but it seemed that Babe had.

"You see those tables and chairs outside?" she said. "Look pretty good, don't they? They're con jobs — refinished by convict labor."

"Are you kidding me?"

She wasn't. She'd heard about the program from Ms. Baldino, one of the town librarians. Apparently all the benches at the library had been refinished by convicts, too. Who knew?

"They learn a craft, make a few bucks, and maybe find a different line of work when they get out instead of whatever got them locked up. Everybody wins." I hadn't realized convict labor still existed in this century. It seemed so Dickensian. But I suppose I was being naive. There were a lot of things I hadn't experienced either chained to my desk in New York or buried in my gardens in Springfield.

After mopping up every last crumb on my plate, I got up to leave. Again I did recon-

70

naissance in the parking lot. Countertop Man was gone, and I felt foolish for ever having been suspicious. Since it was later I went straight to the nursery and bagged the idea of going to Caroline's. I would see her tomorrow.

I love nurseries, no matter what time of year it is. My new favorite was D'Angelo's, forty minutes west of Springfield, on the other side of the Paradise. The owners did their best to make the place a destination even though gardening season was winding down. They geared up for Halloween with hayrides, a haunted house, mountains of pumpkins and ornamental kale, and a fall sale on perennials that would save me dough and time next season. As long as everything was well watered, fall was an even better time to plant than spring because it gave plants the chance to establish themselves before the growing season kicked in.

I pulled out my shopping list and dragged around a flatbed dolly with uncooperative wheels, piling on threes and fives of my favorites. I stalked the false lamiums.

No matter how hard I tried not to, I invariably fell in love with some plant or shrub that wasn't on my list and would put me over budget or, worse, that I didn't have an appropriate place or client for. Early in my gardening career I'd killed a few spectacular plants by making rash purchases. I still had their sap on my hands and mourned them every time I went to the nursery and saw a magnolia 'Edith Bogue' or a hibiscus 'Lord Baltimore' like the ones I'd killed — as if these shrubs knew what I'd done to their brethren, and would somehow punish me for it if I took one of them home.

I was struggling to lift a lovely but totally unnecessary Japanese cutleaf maple onto my cart when a white pickup pulled into the garden center. Was it the creepy guy from the diner? I hunkered down and hid behind the tree, kicking myself for not having chosen a wider shrub that would have made a more effective screen. I left my cart where it was and crawled on all fours behind a lush, and thicker, miscanthus. I peered around the plant and saw first, work shoes, then a pair of denimed knees, and a beaded belt that claimed the wearer loved, or more precisely "hearted," Guatemala.

"May I assist you with something?" The man's T-shirt identified him as a nursery employee. What could I say? "No, thank you, I'm hiding because I think I see an ex-con who doesn't know a countertop from a kayak?" Nah.

"I think I lost something," I lied and patted the gravel, which had by then had stuck to my hands and made little pockmarks in my palms. The nursery employee bent down to help me look.

"What was it?"

Yeah. What was it? Wallet? Keys? Nope, too big and too noisy.

"An earring . . . No! They're both here! Boy, that's lucky." I grabbed both of my ears.

He stood and was polite enough not to ask the obvious question: Why are you still crouched on the ground if you didn't lose your earring?

I mumbled something about my back, my age, my sciatica, and my inability to stand up fast without the blood rushing to my head and making me dizzy. I rattled off so many fictitious ailments it's a wonder the man didn't ask where my caregiver was.

I made a show of getting up slowly, eyeballing the garden center and looking for the white pickup that I thought belonged to Countertop Man. I saw one idling, all the way to the right in the back lot where pros were shoveling mulch and compost into their trucks.

"Are you taking the maple, senorita?" the man asked when he was sure I was okay.

"No, I've changed my mind. I was looking for the false lamiums. Are they in yet?" Right . . . I mistook a tree for a perennial.

"Maybe our next shipment," he said. "Try again in a few days."

"Just these plants, then." The man pushed my cart to the checkout desk for me, walking at a funereal pace in deference to my wretched physical condition until we reached the outside counter, where yet another employee would tally my purchases and hand me a slip to take inside to the cashier. Everyone's a specialist.

I glanced to the right and saw the white pickup turn around and come barreling toward us. I leaned back slightly so that my face was hidden behind a scarecrow and a towering stack of baled hay.

The Guatemalan nursery employee who had helped me saw me lean backward and must have thought I was fainting. He screamed for someone inside to call 911, and in a clumsy attempt to catch me wound up knocking over the hay bales, the scarecrow, and me on top of them. From my horizontal position in the driveway, I saw the truck pass, with two Hispanic garden workers and what looked like a mixed-breed Lab inside, none of whom I'd ever seen before. All of them, even the dog, appeared to be laughing.

Six

I laughed myself the next morning as I drove to Babe's, thinking about the disturbance I'd created at the nursery, but as I approached the diner, I saw a cluster of Springfield police cars with their lights flashing. All the cops I knew walked across the road to the Paradise. Either someone was having a retirement breakfast or something bad had happened, and I was afraid it was the latter.

I pulled closer and saw a man being handcuffed and led over to one of the cars by Sergeant Mike O'Malley, a Springfield cop I'd gotten to know in the last few years. Not in the biblical sense, but Lucy and Babe still gave it a fifty-fifty chance.

I instantly recognized the vest and sweatshirt on the person now being helped into the patrol car; it was Countertop Man. With all the official vehicles in the lot, the only parking space still available was at the far end near a hair salon that I'd never seen anyone enter or exit. I took it, then jogged to Babe's private office in the back of the diner, where I met Babe and Mike O'Malley.

"What's going on? You okay? Was that Countertop Man?" I asked, pointing to the man in the patrol car. "I knew there was something fishy about that guy."

"I thought you didn't know him," O'Malley said to Babe.

"He said his name but I don't remember it. I know he likes black coffee and fried eggs and he asked me if my name was Brittany. He's been in the last few days, that's all. Said he worked for a countertop company downtown. I just feed them, Mike. I don't ask for references."

Then O'Malley asked what I knew about the man, but I didn't have anything substantial to contribute other than my gut feeling, which didn't seem fair to share with the police given that it was based on the guy's inability to tell Formica from limestone, which was not a crime, although perhaps it should be. I spared Mike the nursery anecdote, since it no longer seemed all that funny.

"So you think he lied about being in the countertop business and he flirted with

Babe and you thought that made him weird? Doesn't everybody flirt with Babe?"

For my benefit Babe repeated what happened. "I closed up around 7 P.M. last night — business was dead, so I came in early today, to make up for it. When I got here, I found that guy, whatever his name is, in my office, curled up on my inflatable bed. He scared the crap out of me, so I backed out of the room as quietly as I could, locked him in, and called the cops after I looked myself inside the diner."

"It's lucky he didn't just wake up and run away," I said.

"He did wake up, and busted my lock in the process, but I'd blocked the door with my SUV. He couldn't get out. Even the windows are painted shut. I've been after Neil all summer to scrape them. Now I'm glad he didn't get around to it."

Countertop Man claimed to have left his ID in his other suit which was kind of funny since he didn't strike any of us as a suit-and-tie kind of guy. All he'd said was that his name was Chase McGinley. He was babbling in the back of the police cruiser, his head rocking back and forth in an animated argument with himself. Against the odds, he appeared to be losing.

McGinley said he'd just been sleeping one

off someplace warm, but apparently he'd gone through Babe's garbage, her files, and a bottle of Bombay gin before passing out on her sofa. When the cops cuffed him, he had bits of receipts, mail, and a picture of Babe and Neil crammed into his pockets.

"Identity theft?" I asked. "That's a pretty low-tech way to do it, isn't it?"

"Could be. Back in the day, people used to steal the carbon copies of credit card transactions. Not all the bad guys are computer savvy," O'Malley said. "Some of them are just thieves."

Identity theft was another thing I rarely thought about that had surfaced lately, along with convict labor, backsplashes, and my old dentist. The list was getting longer. I wasn't even as fastidious as my eighty-seven-year-old aunt, who scrupulously shredded all her documents including sales flyers and newsletters from her congressman. I knew identity theft happened, but there were so many things I worried about before that — like my house payments or world peace or an infestation of bronze borers that would decimate my flowering dogwoods — that identity theft was way down on my list. "Who'd want to be me?" I had said. I had no dough and not much stuff.

"That's not the way it works," Mike had

answered. "They're not stealing stuff. They're stealing your good credit rating. Your good name." Maybe that was what Countertop Man was doing. Babe Chinnery's name was gold in these parts and probably all over.

"You know, I drove by a few nights ago, when the diner was closed. I thought I saw something moving around behind the diner but I didn't get out to investigate."

"That was an uncharacteristically prudent thing to do," Mike said. This was a not-so-veiled reference to the way we first met, on a cold case I'd accidentally unearthed a few years earlier. "Do you think it was him?" he asked after a minute, now more curious. "Is that why you said he was weird?"

"I thought it was turkeys. If it was him, what on earth could he have been looking for for so many days? He was just creepy. Taking Babe's picture and then insisting on guessing her name. And I'm pretty sure he would have followed me if I had left the diner. Call it intuition — just don't say *women's intuition* or I'll have to smack you."

At Mike's suggestion, Babe had checked her office thoroughly to see if anything else was missing. The man had obviously gone through her things, but she couldn't say what, if anything, he'd taken, other than the

80

booze. She didn't keep any jewelry or cash in the office, and since he was still there when the cops arrived, he couldn't have left with anything unless it had been squirreled away on his person and neither of us wanted to stick around for the cavity search.

"It's a good thing I don't keep the Fabergé eggs here anymore, right?" At least she was getting her sense of humor back. Countertop Man saw us laughing and it infuriated him. He stuck his head out the window and yelled at us. "Why are you jerks arresting me? This is just a little criminal trespass. Kid stuff. I'll be out before Oprah goes on."

"Berry, tell that guy to quiet down or we'll tack on disturbing the peace to the charges."

Apparently, the man knew his law. And his daytime television. According to O'Malley, he'd be issued a summons and made to sign a PTA, a promise to appear in court. If he got "belligerent," he might graduate to a $250 bond. But he'd still be let go, probably in just a few hours.

"Define belligerent," I said.

"Broad definition."

"That's it?"

"What would you like me to do with him? We've done away with stocks and pillories in New England. No weapons; no damage, thank goodness; no physical harm to Babe.

81

It's like the man said, trespassing — a misdemeanor in the state of Connecticut. Forget Oprah, he may even be out before Martha goes on."

O'Malley's young partner was exasperated. He had no luck getting McGinley to shut up, and had gotten tired of trying. Finally he rolled up the window of the patrol car and came over to where Babe, Mike, and I had drifted near the side entrance to the diner.

"What's he yapping about now?" O'Malley asked.

The younger cop looked uncomfortable.

"Go ahead," Babe said, smiling. "We've heard four-letter words before."

"That's not it, ma'am. He said, 'She's the damn criminal. She's the one you want.' He thinks we should arrest Mrs. Chinnery."

O'Malley simply closed his eyes for a second or two with a look that suggested this was as novel an excuse for trespassing as he'd ever heard.

"Didn't he like the food?"

SEVEN

False or not, Babe's lamiums had finally arrived. They wouldn't look like much until the following spring, so I filled the bare spots with temporary fixes like annual grasses and mums that could stay in their black plastic pots until the winter came and we composted them. By that time, not too many people would be eating in Babe's outdoor seating area anyway, and no one would notice if the garden was a little bare.

Right then, the diner's business was booming. Indian summer had brought people out in droves and even inspired a few hardy souls to resurrect their long shorts and flip-flops, but not the Main Street Moms, who rarely strayed from their seasonal uniforms. I didn't see Caroline Sturgis in either of the two packs of women at the picnic tables but expected to see her soon for our long-awaited business meeting. I was also mildly curious to learn if little Brandon's DNA tests revealed he could keep up with his swimming lessons.

Outside the diner, not far from the planters, where I was adding topsoil, sat a sandy-haired man, fair skin, around fifty to fifty-five years old — I could never tell anymore. He was extremely fit and attractive despite a nose that had obviously been broken and never fixed properly. If he were a woman, he'd be what the French might call *jolie laide.* I was amused to see a ripple of interest pass through the Main Street Moms' tables, and I made a point of not staring at the man — he was getting enough female attention without my adding to the adoration.

A stack of real estate brochures was fanned out on the table in front of him, and he pored over the booklets with more than the casual interest of diner patrons, who generally leafed through them only after they'd ordered and were waiting for their meals to be served. He even took notes. I could imagine Gretchen Kennedy and her colleagues who filled the Free-Take-One! racks coming to blows over a buyer as motivated as this one.

For some reason I assumed he was single and so did the rest of the women, who consciously or unconsciously sat up a little straighter and spoke with their heads tilted at flattering angles. He wasn't wearing a wedding ring, although that didn't prove anything. But straight or gay, how many guys went house shopping without wife or partner? I had to pass him three or four times carrying large bags of the mulch that I used to camouflage the nursery pots in the planters.

"May I help you?" he asked, getting up from his seat.

"No thanks," I said, breathing heavily. "I've got it covered." And I did mostly. I was out of breath but tried not to show it.

"You're pretty strong."

Was he checking out my muscles the way I'd been checking out his? I kept working and didn't respond.

He dog-eared pages in the brochures and finally got up and approached one of the Moms' tables. Despite the banged-up nose he had an elegant, catlike grace, almost like a dancer.

"Excuse me, ladies. I know this is presumptuous, but I was wondering if I might ask you a few questions about Springfield?" He fanned out the real estate brochures as if to show them he was for real.

The sea of females parted for him, and before long the women from the second table had dragged their chairs over to assist the handsome, well-spoken man. I could almost hear the gears moving as the quickly confirmed single man was being mentally seated next to divorced friends at future dinner parties.

There went my chance — I should have let him help me with the bags of mulch. I could have had first dibs on one of the only eligible men in Springfield. A sudden peal of giggles erupted from the women, who had regressed in age and maturity due to the unexpected novelty of a man in their midst — and during the day. Flirting. It was like riding a bicycle.

I finished up, stored my tools in my Jeep, and went inside. Through the window, Babe had been keeping an eye on the action outside.

"Something tells me if that guy really does buy a place around here, those girls are going to reinstate the welcome wagon, but instead of cookies and kitchen tools there'll be rubber and latex in the goody basket." I cleaned up and joined Babe at the counter, where a cup of coffee was waiting for me.

"He got here an hour before you did," she said. "Had breakfast inside and about five refills on the coffee. If he doesn't come in to pee soon, he's going to make medical history."

When the man first arrived, he'd asked Babe if this was the only diner in the area so many times that she was close to throwing him out, but he apologized and explained that he'd gotten the directions from a friend and just wanted to make sure he was in the right place. That's when he began studying the real estate booklets. When the Moms arrived, he took his research outside. One of them, Becka Reynolds, was being particularly helpful.

"Look at them," I said. "They're fixing him up already and he could be a potential mass murderer. And he hasn't even seen a house yet, much less made an offer. Wait until those real estate harpies get their hooks in him. He'll be toast."

One of the regulars, a guy named Carl, was paying his check and overheard me. "You girls just can't stand to see us single and happy," he said.

"Shut up, Carl, before I tell that sweet young wife of yours what you think about marriage." Babe handed him his change and returned to my end of the counter.

"You never told me about that wedding you and Lucy went to," Babe said. "Did you find your soul mate?"

"That doesn't happen in real life. In real life one bridesmaid looks fabulous because she lobbied for the dress that was most flattering to her, and the rest of them look ludicrous in it, and they'll never wear it again no much how much it's shortened. She may be the one who gets lucky. The other guests are not hooking up. They're wondering which of their friends will marry next and whether they'll be the last lonely member of their group, rolling her walker over to the center of the banquet room to try to catch the bride's bouquet in her gnarled, liver-spotted hands."

"Wow. That's a depressing image," Babe said. "Is that what you were thinking?"

"Only once or twice."

Babe herself had been single for many years since her husband, Pete, had died in a motorcycle accident. They'd moved to Springfield with their twin boys and opened the diner years ago. Not long after, Pete went out for a ride with a buddy and had a smashup on Route 7. She didn't talk much about the years right after that. It must have been hard being a single mom and the sole breadwinner with a young family and a fledgling business to get off the ground. When she did share memories, they were of her happier days with the Jimmy Collins band.

I'd had no idea who they were and had had to look them up. They'd had a few hits back in the days when Babe was a backup singer named Wanda Sugarman — before the band had dubbed her Babe and Pete had given her his own last name.

"Look at that guy," I said, pointing with my cup. "All he had to do was smile and say, *Aw shucks, ma'am, I'm new in town.* If a woman had done that with a group of men, she'd have been handed a scarlet letter and a needle and thread."

"It's a cruel world."

On the day I was to see Caroline, I headed to the Paradise for a hearty meal before our meeting. I was leaning toward Caroline's side of the fence now and wanted a base in my stomach just in case Caroline decided to seal our partnership with a toast or three.

Babe hadn't seen Caroline for days. I tried her again on my cell and I got the same message I'd gotten the previous week — disconnected.

"What's the matter?" Babe asked.

"Her home phone's disconnected. Don't you think that's odd?"

"Plenty of people are dropping their landlines and just going with cells," Babe said. "It's the economy. Don't you have her cell number?"

"I do but her house is in a dead zone. She never uses it at home. Besides, I don't see Caroline and Grant belt-tightening in that way. I'm going to go see what's up." We had a date and Caroline was so anxious to talk to me; it wasn't like her to disappear without leaving me a message. I finished breakfast and headed for the Sturgis house. Halfway to Caroline's I thought perhaps I had screwed up the days. Was this the day she was accompanying one of her friends to the doctor's on a bizarre mission to see whether or not the friend's three-year-old was biologically suited to be the next Roger Federer? What the hell. I'd go anyway. If I had the date wrong, I'd leave a note. When she got home, she'd be thrilled that I was more interested in her proposal than I'd been when we last spoke. And I was. Between losing the real estate gigs and being sent home with hand-me-down clothing, I was a lot more inclined to consider her offer than I thought I'd be. I hadn't seen her business plan yet, but she was a smart woman. And so was I.

When I pulled into the Sturgises' driveway, Caroline's silver Land Rover sat at the entrance of the house. The driver's side door was wide open. I parked behind it. I took my time walking up the front steps and rang the doorbell, expecting to see Caroline, perfectly coiffed, perfectly clad, and given the early hour, holding the perfect Bloody Mary in a lead crystal glass. There was no answer, so I rang again. This time I noticed a sliver of light between the door and the jamb. It wasn't latched. I gave it a gentle push and it creaked open.

"Caroline? Caroline, are you here?" The vestibule was empty. Entering her house uninvited was a breach of suburban etiquette and I wasn't sure I should. Then I heard a sound coming from the family room — a gasping or choking sound.

"It's Paula. Are you okay? Can I come in?" I waited for an answer, then tiptoed into the cathedral-ceilinged room, not knowing what I'd be interrupting.

Caroline wasn't there, but her husband, Grant, was. He was on the sofa, clutching a huge pillow to his chest and mouth and rocking back and forth. Tears were streaming down his face, and his eyeglasses were fogged and slightly askew.

"Where's Caroline?" I asked. I was afraid to know the answer. "Is she all right?" He didn't seem surprised to see me. He took the corner of the pillow out of his mouth.

"Caroline's not here. They've arrested her. They say she's . . . she's not Caroline Beecham Sturgis. I don't know who she is, but she's not Caroline Sturgis. My wife is a stranger."

EIGHT

When you're my age, it's easy to look back and say I should have done this or shouldn't have done that. It's like the aerial view of a garden maze. From above it looks easy. The pathways are clear and it's obvious which way you should go. When you're on the ground, of course, it's much easier to make a wrong turn.

If I'd had that nice clean aerial view when I was nineteen, I wouldn't be walking through O'Hare Airport with two federal marshals, a barn jacket thrown over my handcuffed wrists, rushing to catch a flight to Detroit, back to the city and state I hadn't even wanted to fly over for as long as I could remember.

I'd thought about this moment every day for the last — what is it — twenty years? Twenty-five? Who remembered? Early on, I jumped every time I heard a siren or if the front door open unexpectedly. Gradually, that feeling faded, like an old scar you forget you have until you look for it and see that it's still there, right where it's always been, and you were crazy to think that it had ever disappeared. Now it's over. They know. And I can exhale.

That time and place, B.C., before Caroline, seemed like fiction, a novel I'd read or a movie I'd seen before my real life began. If only.

My friends and family were in shock when I was arrested at cheerleader practice, on the football field with the rest of the squad around me and Coach, who looked stricken. I sleep-walked through the trial and sentencing until I heard the words, twenty years. Only then did it become real for me. Twenty years was longer than I'd been on the planet. I'd be almost forty when I got out, older than my father. Way older than my mother was when she died. People kept saying thank God she wasn't there to see me, but I didn't thank him, I wanted her with me. To tell me what to do. Maybe if she'd been with me, I wouldn't have been in such a mess.

In prison I spent months crying myself to sleep every night — afraid during the day and more afraid to let my defenses down and go to sleep at night. It was like that for eighteen months until one day a dozen of us were chosen for a work release program that was to last two weeks. After a few days I noticed cracks in security, the times when a guard could be distracted and frequently was. I stayed on my best behavior for twelve days. On the morning of the thirteenth day I simply didn't get on the bus that took the others back to prison. Only one other inmate saw me slip away behind a delivery van and all she did was close her eyes, a slight curl to her lips. Maybe she was laughing to herself as the van pulled away with me hunkered down in the back. When the driver stopped for gas and a bathroom break I crept out of my hiding place.

I walked for miles, tearing off my work shirt and tying it around my waist. I turned my prison-issue T-shirt inside out, and in those days the look passed for grunge. Then I hid at a construction site where I knew my brother Luke would be at 6:30 that night. He'd gotten a summer job as a security guard making sure no building materials disappeared overnight. Once I was sure all the workers were gone, I scooted over to the hut where the blue light from a cheap portable television reflected off the window. I tapped on the glass. My brother scrambled out of his chair and opened the window.

"Sweet Jesus! What the — how did you get here?" He pulled me inside, closed the door, and hugged me. We both collapsed and started to cry.

I hid in the booth until 4:30 A.M. By that time, I hoped it would be safe to go to a motel and steer clear of the construction workers who'd start arriving soon. Luke had thirty bucks in his pocket. He gave me twenty-five and I checked into a hot-sheet motel near the interstate highway until my brother returned with a bag of clothing and all the cash he could scrape together without arousing suspicion.

"They're looking everywhere for you," he'd said. "I didn't even drive — I rode my bike because I was afraid of being followed. You can't stay here."

As if I wanted to — waiting for the cops to come banging on my door to drag me back to that place. Early the next morning, after saying good-bye to Luke, I sat fully dressed on the edge of the bed wondering what the hell I was going to do. Then I heard one of the truckers checking out. He was making a noisy exit, he and his vehicle belching and grunting. I ran outside and climbed on his running board before he left the long, narrow parking lot and turned onto the highway.

"Will you wait for me?"

In five minutes I was out the door, grabbing a motel washcloth and a sliver of soap and the bag my brother had brought.

"Not much in the way of amenities here," the trucker said, looking at the pilfered items.

I stuffed the stolen goods into my bag. The

guys who drove me from Ann Arbor to Dayton and from Dayton to Pittsburgh didn't really want to know my name. The first one thought he might make out — teenage runaways were probably less discriminating and undoubtedly found themselves in situations where it was easier to just do the deed than to get beaten up and tossed out of a moving vehicle. But after a few feeble attempts to engage me in sexy chat, he dropped the idea and was just grateful to have a human to talk to on his long drive south, instead of simply singing along to oldies on the radio.

The next driver wanted to replay his own hitchhiking experiences or live vicariously through mine. He looked like an aging hippie, ten or so years past his Woodstock days, and he kept saying things were far-out, which I knew from an old boyfriend meant "good." Up until that point my own travel anecdotes (the Upper Peninsula to visit grandparents and one class trip to Chicago) weren't adventurous enough to keep him interested, so we soon fell into that silence that takes over on long drives when the rocking of the vehicle or the rhythm of the windshield wipers is all the sound you need and keeping quiet is more natural than saying anything. I rolled down my window to feel the nighttime breeze and to stay alert, just in case he tried anything.

In Pittsburgh I was picked up by a woman in a Volkswagen van. She said I looked like an Abigail, and I told her it was remarkable, but she'd guessed my name; so I was Abigail for a few days. I got shorter lifts across the endless state of Pennsylvania, and all the way I tried out various fictional autobiographies and names until I found the handful of story lines I was comfortable delivering. My parents were dead. I grew up with my grandmother, who was back home in Oregon. Oregon was a nice touch. I never met anyone who'd ever been there.

I had a lightweight nylon bag that contained everything my twenty-year-old brother thought I'd need: some clothes, dark glasses, one of the wigs our mother wore during her chemo sessions — I wasn't sure I could wear it — a hat, my passport, and the entire contents of my brother's college fund. Six hundred and forty dollars to start a new life.

NINE

The stranger we'd all known as Caroline Sturgis was named Monica Jane Weithorn. Why do all convicted felons have three names? And she wasn't from Oregon, as we'd thought; she was from Michigan. Caroline/Monica had been convicted on a drug charge when she was eighteen years old and had been sentenced to twenty years in jail — a surprisingly draconian sentence given her age and the fact that it had been her first offense.

By that night, Caroline's story was dribbling out on the local news channels. The following day it was all over the Internet. Springfield, Connecticut, was soon flooded with news media from every major market in the country who wanted to learn all they could about the woman they were calling the Fugitive Mom.

News trucks lined the streets around the Sturgis home. Reporters camped out at the

Paradise Diner. It was impossible to buy a quart of milk without some overzealous helmet-haired reporter sticking a microphone in your face. And my best friend, Lucy Cavanaugh, came dangerously close to being one of them. As soon as she heard the story, she called me.

"Paula, this would make a great feature for sweeps week. If you can get us the story, Danielle might offer you a job."

"You just spent an entire weekend telling me what a jerk your boss is — why would I ever want to work for her? Besides, you know the story," I said. "Everyone knows it by now. She walked away from a work release program, hitchhiked out of town, changed her name, and started a new life."

"You've got to be kidding," she said. "That's like saying *Moby-Dick* is about a guy who goes fishing. This is a huge story and *you know her*. I *met* her. This could be big. I could write that screenplay I've always wanted to write. Meryl Streep — she's from Connecticut, isn't she? Or is it Maine? It's one of those states up there. Maybe she'll be interested. She could play Caroline. No, she's too old. No, she can do anything."

I could almost hear the wheels turning. She'd be planning her Oscar acceptance speech in a minute. "You are officially going off the reservation and I'm hanging up now." And I did. Whatever last shreds of privacy Caroline and her family still had, I wasn't going to be the one to tear them down. Hopefully someone was shielding her kids from the vultures that now circled the family.

Besides, appearances to the contrary, I *didn't* know her. None of us did. Even her husband and her kids hadn't known she wasn't Caroline Sturgis.

I'd told Lucy everything I knew. It was unclear if anyone had helped her escape, but it seemed likely. That was all most of us knew because since her arrest Caroline hadn't given a statement to anyone.

How do you live with something like that hanging over your head for twenty-five years? Constantly covering your steps and worrying about slipping up. Now it made more sense why a smart, creative woman like Caroline didn't work but stayed home, doing her crafts and quietly numbing herself with alcohol. She was hiding, staying under the radar.

The story was like roadkill: it was impossible not to pay attention. People in Springfield who barely knew Caroline were giving interviews, and the residents of her hometown in Michigan dug back decades to find the slimmest reminiscence. One of her second-grade classmates volunteered the significant factoid that Caroline/Monica always liked to make up stories. Which of course meant nothing but gave the talking heads copy to read while nodding gravely. Opinions were everywhere. With each day more snippets of the story leaked out and were rehashed mercilessly all over town, including at the Paradise Diner.

Babe wasn't behind the counter when I arrived, so I grabbed a newspaper, slipped into my favorite booth in the back, and got the attention of one of the singing waitresses with the universal cup-drinking motion that said I needed coffee. Eyebrow Girl brought me a mug and a slice of cake.

"What's this?" I asked.

"Olive oil cake," she said, bored. "Pete wants you to try it." She dropped the plate on the table with a clatter. "Sorry."

Sure she was.

Olive oil and cake are not two things I generally associated together, but for free, I was willing to give it a shot. It was delicious with a slightly nutty flavor, and I was shaving off another sliver of the dense cake with a spoon when Babe slid onto the banquette opposite me. She looked tired, but I was enough of a friend not to say so.

"What have you been up to?" I asked. "Neil back?"

"I wish. Putting in a new lock on the back door. I should be putting in a new door, but I'll wait until Neil comes home. That the olive oil cake?" she said. I nodded, handing her the spoon. "Whodathunkit, right? Giada recipe. Not that that girl looks like she's ever eaten a piece of cake in her life."

Babe's appearance brought the sullen waitress back with an automatic cup for Babe and a refill for me.

"Thanks, Terry. So what do you think?" she said when the girl left.

"I think you're right: she's probably never eaten an entire piece of this cake and I think the boobs are real," I said.

"Not Giada. Caroline . . . Monica . . . whatever the hell her name is. Pretty wild, huh, federal marshals coming to take her away? The Main Street Moms must be having a field day with this one. They'll be dining on this for a year. I guess now we know why Caroline was so hot to put the business in your name. She's been invisible so long it was probably second nature to her not to put anything in her own name."

In all the excitement, that hadn't occurred to me. Had Caroline done something related

103

to the business that had exposed her identity?

"Cripes, I wonder if that's how she got caught, because I resisted letting her be a silent partner."

"Don't start feeling guilty — it wasn't *your* fault. Besides, she hasn't bought anything yet or signed any papers." Babe shook her head at my ignorance. "Where have you been? People are getting e-mail alerts and Twitters on this, details are flying through this diner faster than blackflies in April. Maybe I should just put the latest news on the marquee outside. I almost wish I had a television in here if only so people would stop asking me what I know. No, I take that back."

I knew she didn't mean it; the last thing she'd ever watched on television was *Hill Street Blues,* and that was only because she'd dated one of the actors. Besides, she liked Caroline as much as I did — neither of us would ever exploit her situation. Maybe deep down we'd both seen something else behind the ballet flats and designer clothes. A layer of experience or sadness. We just didn't know it had been caused by a year in the slammer.

Babe blew on her coffee and then took a swig. "It wasn't your fault," she said softly.

"It was an anonymous tip. Somebody intentionally outed her."

"But who? And why?"

"*Quién sabe,* my friend."

Just then Sergeant Mike O'Malley entered the diner. Babe waved him over, and he joined us, sliding onto the seat next to her.

"Brother," he said, "not a very convenient week for this to happen. We've got a new department spokesperson — fresh out of school. He's been hyperventilating ever since this story broke. And we've got a rookie cop who nearly shot himself in the thigh yesterday, like that dopey football player." Mike swung around and called to the girl behind the counter. "Darlin', can I get a decaf here? Skim milk?"

What possible difference could skim milk make when I saw him eyeing the rest of the cake on my plate?

"How awful for you. I'm sure it hasn't been a banner week for the Sturgises either," I said.

"True," he said. "I'm just asking as a neighbor, not a law enforcement official, but you two girls didn't know anything about this, did you?"

"Let me out of here," Babe said. "I will not be interrogated in my own restaurant." It was said in fun, but I had the feeling there was a nugget of truth in it. And, tellingly, she didn't answer. Babe shoved O'Malley out of the booth and then got out herself. "Don't say anything without your attorney present." She gave Mike a playful push and left.

Of course we hadn't known — at least I hadn't. Although I don't know that I would have said anything if I did. It was an ethical dilemma unlike any I'd ever encountered before.

"What was she in jail for, anyway? A couple of joints?" I thought of the horror stories about American kids on vacation who stupidly tried to carry pot across borders and were thrown into foreign jails for years. But Caroline had been arrested in Michigan, not Thailand.

"Not exactly," Mike said.

He told me that according to the Michigan police, Caroline/Monica had been a big-time drug dealer. And they weren't talking a few nickel bags for her own use. She had denied everything, but the prosecutor claimed that she had a string of employees working for her, mostly young girls. I'd seen Caroline struggle with her own checkbook and Anna had had to dun her for payment almost every month. This was a big-time drug dealer?

Maybe it was all a ruse. Maybe she had been playing the ditzy blonde for so long she didn't know how to stop playing the part.

Mike said that Caroline had originally been arrested with a man and an older girl, who had served two years of her sentence before being paroled. Presumably she'd gotten on with her life, while Caroline had spent decades in hiding. Good grief.

"How's she doing?" I asked.

"Seems okay." Mike eyed the olive oil cake, which had remained untouched since he'd sat down. "Won't see anyone, though. Not even her husband. Poor bastard — he keeps coming by the station anyway. Bringing her food and clothing. Her toilet items. Yesterday he brought a suitcase filled with creams and lotions. We had to go through every onc of those tiny bottles. Is your bathroom filled with stuff like that?"

It was. And I knew what Caroline used. I seriously doubted whether Grant Sturgis could smuggle a file or a poison pill into jail in a flat jar of YvesSaintLaurent eye cream. "What happens next?" I asked. I took a small bite of cake and washed it down with cold coffee.

O'Malley told me Caroline would be extradited to Michigan and a judge there would decide her fate. He'd either send her back to prison to finish her sentence — possibly with a few years tacked on for escaping — or send her home with a suspended sentence. Presumably they'd take into account the way she'd turned her life around, but you could never tell. She could get titanically unlucky and get a judge who prided himself on being a hard case or one who was running for reelection and didn't want to appear "soft on crime." I didn't know what I thought; it was all too fresh. O'Malley was silent and looked longingly at the half-eaten piece of cake on my plate.

"Go on," I said. "You know you want it."

"What makes you think my lean and hungry look is directed at your leftover cake?"

That was as close to a pass as O'Malley had come since I first moved to Springfield. I didn't mind. I never minded, but I kept that to myself. I guess I could sip wine in front of the fire with a man like Mike, talk about our days, laugh at the stupid things that happened, I just hadn't done that for so long. And I wasn't sure I knew how not to be sarcastic and distant with Mike O'Malley.

Just as things were getting interesting we were interrupted by his coffee coming and my cell phone ringing. I fished it out of the bottom of my backpack and froze when I saw the name on-screen: *Caroline*. I fumbled to unlock the keypad and hit answer before the phone kicked into voice mail mode. Would she be calling *me* from the Springfield jail? Why? I waited for what seemed like an eternity. "Who is this?" I whispered.

"It's Grant. Grant Sturgis. I need to talk to someone. Someone I can trust."

Of course. He most have reconnected their home phone and I had saved the number as *Caroline*.

"Will you meet me?

"All right," I said, "where?"

"Your place?"

"No way. Yours?"

"Not a chance. There's an entourage here. I can lose them and meet you. How about Guido's?"

"Yes. Yes. Good-bye." I turned off the phone and shoved it back in my bag.

I slid the rest of the cake toward O'Malley. "It's all yours. I've got to leave. I think it's a new client."

TEN

Guido Chiaramonte's old nursery had been shuttered since his death. The courts had not been able to find any of his relatives in Sicily to claim the property, so it sat there waiting for an out-of-town buyer who either wouldn't know or wouldn't be scared off by its bloody history. There weren't many local takers for the large parcel right on the road and not far from the highway exit. People in town had long memories, and what had happened at Guido's was still fresh in their minds.

Early on, nearby residents worried the nursery would be sold to a developer who'd raze it and put up a multiple-dwelling housing unit, but sewage issues and zoning restrictions put the brakes on that idea. For the last two years nothing much had happened except that a few windows had been broken, some graffiti had appeared, and Guido's remaining stock had either died;

been stolen; or, the way plants sometimes do, burst through their burlap sacks and thin plastic nursery pots and put down roots right where they had been displayed for sale.

About a year earlier, the bank posted a *for sale* sign, fueling rumors that the IRS was selling Guido's assets to claim back taxes — no real surprise — but there were few nibbles. Except from Caroline Sturgis.

The price tag was two million dollars for a house, the greenhouse, and a shop on two acres. That was where Caroline had seen our new partnership taking root. And that was where Grant Sturgis thought he and I should meet, since his house was still being staked out by the media and mine was out of the question.

Springfield had a flinty and very savvy real estate broker named Roxy Rhodes. A tiny woman, she powered around town behind the wheel of a cream-colored Bentley with vanity plates and wore tight suits and lots of jewelry, including a ring with the initials RR in diamonds, which would have looked like brass knuckles on anyone else her size, but somehow she pulled it off.

Unlike Gretchen Kennedy's real estate office, Roxy never needed my quickie curbside face-lifts for her listings. They all had sticker prices of well over a million dollars and they were staged as carefully as movie sets. And Roxy could smell interest in a property the way a dog could smell a slice of pizza. Caroline had reeked of serious interest, so Roxy had given her the combination to the locked box on the door of Guido's main building. She let Caroline go in as often as she liked, to measure things and fantasize, until Roxy knew Caroline was so emotionally invested in the place that she couldn't live without it. I'd passed the place a number of times and seen Caroline's car in the small lot near the main building.

Caroline had written the combination on the massive whiteboard in her kitchen, and that must have given her husband the idea that we could meet there and not be seen.

I'd agreed to meet him that night — less vehicular traffic than in the daytime and less of a chance the neighborhood kids rough-housing on their way from their school bus stop would be nosing around the nursery as they sometimes did. In the meantime I went home to eat, change, and figure out what I was going to say to a man who'd just been told that his wife wasn't the person he thought.

My house wasn't a Roxy Rhodes home. It was a small bungalow well beneath her customary price range and probably unsalable to anyone with serious money or a family because of its small size and quirky layout. But it served a single woman well, especially one who had few pieces of furniture and few friends in the area. And it had a lovely garden that bordered a bird sanctuary on one side and a protected wetlands on another.

At about 8:30 I grabbed an old leather bomber jacket from the closet and headed back out. My place was only fifteen minutes from Guido's, but I parked four blocks away and walked the rest to escape anyone's notice. There was one car in the lot of the deli, diagonally across from the nursery. Probably the deli clerk's. Now that I was one of them, I didn't know how any of these small businessmen stayed alive.

The last time I'd been to Guido's, I'd found the proprietor with a garden tool stuck in his back. It hadn't been pleasant. I took a deep breath and tried the door. It creaked open, the locked box from the real estate office hanging, opened, on a rusty hinge.

The front of the store, about twenty by twenty, held an unplugged refrigerated unit and a small cash and wrap area I remembered well. I flashed back to the way it had looked when Guido Chiaramonte was still alive, with dozens of Styrofoam crosses and funeral wreaths hanging from the ceiling. In color, instead of the black and white created by time, dust, and death.

A few wicker baskets and metal cemetery pots, now covered with cobwebs, still hung on the pegboard walls. The store was dark and smelled faintly of something familiar that I couldn't put my finger on. Sixty feet away at the far end of the barracks-like building, I saw a quivering blue light.

My cell phone rang and I fished it out of my backpack; I didn't recognize the number.

"Hello?"

"I hope that's you out there."

My sentiments exactly. Grant Sturgis was calling from the back of the nursery. I tiptoed over broken pots, weeds that had cropped up through the pea gravel, and the occasional lump of something that felt like a squished pinecone but might have been a dead mouse. My boots crushed some vegetation that blanketed the floor. Then I recognized the smell. It was oregano, covering the ground like a thick carpet and releasing its fragrance every time I stepped on a clump. In the back of the building, Grant Sturgis sat huddled at an old potting table, clutching his phone. He flicked on a

Coleman lantern he must have brought from home. The shadows it threw on his face made him look only more haggard.

"Thanks for coming," he said, pointing to a chair.

"I'm not sure how long I can stay. I'm not really the nervous type, but this place is a little creepy." I pulled out the desk chair and used an old seed catalog I found on the table to brush off the dust as best as I could. Then I sat down.

Sturgis looked as if he hadn't slept since the last time I saw him, rocking back and forth on his family room sofa. I thought of asking how he was, but even in the dark I could see he looked like crap, so it was pointless to ask.

"Why am I here?"

Grant blew out deeply as if emptying his lungs of all air like a leaking balloon. He cleared his throat and began to speak.

"Two weeks ago I had a wonderful life," he said, shaking his head. "People kept telling me I had the best of both worlds. I must have heard that dozens of times over the years."

I bet he had. He had his own successful consulting business, which seemed impervious to the economic downturn; he traveled as much as he wanted, whenever he wanted;

and he had a wonderful family to come home to. A year or so ago Caroline had suspected he was having an affair, but happily it turned out to be a misunderstanding. Their marriage seemed to be a good one. Until this.

He composed himself. "And then something happens that you'd never expect in a million years. You think if something is going to happen, it'll be to one of your kids — heaven forbid, an accident, drugs, some weird Internet business. You never think it's going to be something —" He broke down a little, then shook it off.

I felt for him, I really did. I also felt the dust in the room resettling on my face and in my eyes. I hated being there and ached to get away, but there was no tactful way to do it while the poor man was spilling his guts. And in a perverse way, like the drivers who couldn't help but look at the aforementioned roadkill, I wanted to hear what he had to say. What did he want from me?

"You know how Caroline and I met?" he asked. "We were in South Beach. She was one of those sun-kissed girls in a bikini top and shorts having coffee and reading the paper at a hip café on Ocean Drive."

He told me that she was on her own in Florida, and so was Grant. After three days of furtive smiles and shy waves, he worked up the courage to talk to her and was in heaven when she didn't shoot him down. She told him she'd recently graduated from Bloedell University in Oregon and that she was an orphan, raised by her maternal grandmother who'd just died. The grandmother had left her a little money and she was in Florida trying to decide what to do next — go to graduate school or travel around.

Pretty clever, in retrospect. Oregon was as far away from Florida as you could get, and she claimed to have gone to a small school where not many people were likely to say, "Oh, you must know so-and-so."

And she had her own money.

"She even said something about the Oregon Beavers and I believed her. It was all a lie. She's not an orphan. Her mother is dead but her father and brother still live in Michigan. A town called Okemos."

Half of him was angry and the other half shattered. What must it be like to learn that everything you thought you knew about your spouse was untrue? That you didn't really know her at all? If the rest of Springfield was in shock, what was Grant Sturgis feeling?

"Her father's an alcoholic. God knows

what her brother does, but what kind of guy in his forties still lives with his father?"

"Maybe her father is sick and the brother is looking after him." It was weak, but I wasn't ready to join the chorus of Caroline bashers just yet. "I don't know, Grant, this is personal stuff. I probably shouldn't be hearing it."

"Personal? I may never have anything personal again. My life's been splattered all over the newspapers. Total strangers are *blogging* about me, for God's sake. Morons on AOL are posting comments about my life. Do you know the names they're calling the mother of my children?"

I didn't know, but I could guess. The few times I was dumb enough to read anyone's comments on AOL, I was convinced there must be Internet cafés in every prison and mental institution in the country — the remarks were that irrational, uninformed, and frequently violent and hateful. I tried to calm him down. I slung my bag around to the back of the seat, leaned over, and took both his hands in mine.

"The Caroline we know is a good woman. She's raised two beautiful kids and she's been a good wife to you. Whatever she did in the past, she did when she was young and stupid. Surely a judge will see that."

"That's what we're hoping," he said. "I'm hoping to get Mickey Cameron's firm to represent her. Us."

I knew little about lawyers. I'd started my corporation with a form downloaded from the Internet, but I recognized the firm's name from Cameron's guest appearances on Justice TV and his large white building on the corner of Peachtree and Cummings streets. From the quality of his landscaping, he probably charged his clients a bundle.

"So she's in good hands," I said. "I know it's presumptuous of me to say this, but you have to try not to worry. Think about your kids. Where are they, anyway? Are they here in Springfield?"

He shook his head. "At my mother's in Tucson. I sent them there this afternoon."

"That's good," I said, patting his hands, then pulling mine back to flick away a spider that had dropped down theatrically right in front of my face.

"Okay, I'll get to the point," he said. "I want you to find out who did this. Who wrecked our lives."

"Me? Can't the police tell you?"

He shook his head. "They don't know anything and they have no jurisdiction. All they'll tell me is that it was an anonymous tip. I don't know if they'd tell me even if they knew."

My first thought was, *Who cares? Shouldn't you be thinking of your wife now?* Then I realized he was thinking of her. And he wanted to crush whoever it was that had done this to her.

"I'd like to help, really, but I don't think I'm what you need. I wouldn't know where to begin."

"You found that dead girl, didn't you?"

That girl again. She just wouldn't stay dead and buried. Maybe it was because her fate was unknown for so long that people keep remembering Yoly Rivera, the girl I'd finally sent home and put to rest, closing the books on a local mystery that had baffled members of the Springfield police department for more than thirty years. Two mysteries, really. A missing girl and a mummified baby. It had been in all the papers, even as far away as Boston and New York, and had gotten me a certain amount of notoriety in Springfield. Might have even helped my business a bit. But it wasn't what I did for a living. He needed a professional. And I told him so.

Grant choked his way through a laugh and shook his head. "Where do you think we live, L.A.? It's not as if there are gumshoes on every corner in this town. Besides —

you're smart. I know you're fond of Caroline, otherwise you wouldn't have said what you just did. You're the only new friend she's made in ages and . . . and Caroline trusts you."

So she *had* told him she'd confided in me about his alleged affair. He wasn't wrong, I did like Caroline, but this was serious business, not something for a dilettante. If Grant Sturgis was really going to pursue his hunt for the tipster — and I wasn't sure he should — he needed an experienced, licensed private investigator, not a gardener who knew how to do a Google search. Grant spoke before I could say another word.

"And I'll pay you. *Very* well."

Failing to appeal to my emotional or altruistic side, Grant rushed in with a sneaky move, one that must have served him well in business negotiations: he showed me the money. Dirty lucre — always a powerful motivator. I guess a flicker of interest crossed my face that he read as "How well?" Grant laid it out for me.

"I'll buy this place, put five hundred thousand into the renovations of your choice — my contractor, of course — and rent it to you for a dollar a month, for as long as you like. But we'd need to get started soon. I understand a couple of other people are interested in the property."

It was an insanely generous offer, the operative word being *insanely.*

"You're obviously upset. I wouldn't dream of taking advantage of you by agreeing to something you said under these circumstances. Besides, running a nursery is like being a farmer, weather, pests." I tried to lighten the mood. "Didn't you ever read *The Good Earth?* We could get locusts."

He smiled and then it dawned on me: he didn't care if we would ever make the business work. He wanted to give Caroline something to look forward to. I was almost embarrassed to be in the presence of that kind of love.

What a sweetheart. And what an optimist. She'd already been moved out of Springfield to the county jail and was awaiting extradition to Michigan. Her fate was in a judge's hands. For all we knew, Caroline would remain incarcerated until she completed her original sentence. The authorities in Michigan were under close scrutiny for meting out such a harsh sentence, so they were scrambling to make the nineteen-year-old Caroline sound like the new Pablo Escobar. Why obsess about who snitched when your wife is facing decades in jail? I had the good sense not to mention that, but I didn't have to: it hung in the air like the cobwebs.

"I know I've been flip-flopping with Caroline on this business deal — because of my own financial situation. I'm sorry if I misled her and I'm flattered that you both have such faith in me, but I don't think this is the right time for me. I can't start another business, especially such a risky one, when the one I have is on such shaky ground."

He shook his head in resignation, as if he knew my answer before he'd even asked. I made a move to get up but stopped short when I heard the sound of tires crunching on the gravel outside. And then a muffled voice.

"Kill the lantern," I whispered.

ELEVEN

I prayed it wasn't a tabloid reporter out to snag an unflattering photo of the Fugitive Mom's Philandering Husband! Because that would make me the Mistress and Two-Timing Floozy who betrayed her friend!

We sat still, barely breathing for what felt like twenty minutes but was probably only five. A spider crawled over my forearm and, not wanting to make a sound, I let it despite the fact that I really wanted to scream. I tried to blow it away.

The angled beam from a flashlight moved slowly and methodically over the outside of the building. Grant and I hunkered down trying to appear smaller and less human to anyone who might be peering through the filthy panes. Another vehicle pulled up fast and stopped, spraying gravel on the nursery's glass doors. Great, the cameraman was arriving; if the reporter was a fast writer, we could be on the eleven o'clock news.

The front door creaked open as it had when I'd arrived. Someone stepped on the same debris I'd stepped on, sending a field mouse scurrying, filling the air with the scent of oregano and getting closer to the back of the building. Then, a young and nervous-sounding voice called out to us. "Springfield Police! Springfield Police! Who's back there?"

The tension broke like it does on a close, humid day when it finally rains. Grant and I breathed easier. He even choked out a laugh, and he fumbled to turn the lantern back on, knocking it over in the process. The flashlight stopped moving.

"It's Paula Holliday and Grant Sturgis," I yelled. "We didn't break in. Grant has the combination." I blurted it all out in about five seconds, not wanting to get shot accidentally by one of Springfield's newest cops.

The boy ranger, who'd stumbled upon me and Caroline Sturgis's distraught husband, managed not to shoot either of us, although we did have a scary moment when one of Guido's old wicker baskets fell on his head and he swung around, ready to pounce, as if he'd been attacked from behind.

After six months of classes and the same amount of time spent in field training, the rookie had wisely called for backup before entering the building. That was the second car, which had been on a routine patrol not far away. The two cops made another call once the four of us were assembled outside Guido's nursery. Now that we were outside Guido Chiaramonte's derelict nursery, I could read the name on the young cop's badge, Officer J. Berry, the same cop I'd seen at Babe's.

"My sergeant says there have been a number of break-ins in the area recently, and we should bring you down to the station house *just in case*."

"Just in case *what,* Officer Berry?" I said. "There are some bulbs missing from Guido's?"

"No need to get belligerent, ma'am."

Oh, brother. *Belligerent?* There was that training manual word again. Humor was pointless. Sarcasm was pointless. We were dealing with RoboCop. Was there anything more disgustingly earnest than the newbie — in any field — who had all the rules and regulations freshly imprinted on his brain but none of the logic, experience, or common sense?

Berry and the other officer, a female named Carson, herded us into the backs of the two patrol cars. They had to be kidding.

It would have been comical if it hadn't been so annoying.

Carson drove Grant. I sat in silence, while Officer Berry, who I'd now started to think of as Juniper Berry, drove me through town to the court house/police station complex behind the hospital. The cops pulled into two of the reserved parking spots alongside the building and walked us around through the front entrance, swaggering as if they had just apprehended Bonnie and Clyde.

Grant and I were parked on a bench near a very large soda machine that managed to throw off quite a lot of cold air. Berry and Carson checked us in with a few words to the desk sergeant, then they exited through a back door. We sat there, freezing, for over an hour. I paced and read every flyer on the slatted bulletin board. I learned about National Lock Up Your Meds Day and what ingredients might be purchased if the buyer was planning to manufacture meth, which struck me as a mini-tutorial that you might not want to post in a public place that had a steady stream of criminal types — but, hey, what did I know?

A short, unhappy-looking woman came in and quietly asked for her thirteen-year-old daughter's police report. Good grief, thirteen-year-olds with police reports?

Whatever happened to the good old days when they just shoplifted?

Behind the Plexiglas barrier, another woman, who didn't appear to be a cop but wore an SPD T-shirt, asked what the kid had done.

"She trashed my house."

Tough love or mom from hell? Who can say? I silently thanked my own mother for never having had me arrested.

Just then a young guy barreled through the heavy front doors. He had dirty blond hair flattened over one eye in a style made popular by lead singers from bands I never listened to and only knew about from me-anderings on YouTube. He wore a tan hooded jacket with lots of pockets, and his massive book bag bore the logo from the *Springfield Bulletin.* Grant instinctively looked down, and I pretended to be mesmerized by the age-progressive images of some kids missing since 1994.

"Hey, Sarge. Got anything for me?" the guy said. He looked at us briefly and must have dismissed us as "marital dispute." Not interesting unless one spouse was dead or maimed, hopefully in a colorful way. He ignored us.

Behind the civilian employee, a man I took to be the desk sergeant shook his head and the young man spun on his heel and left before the heavy doors had fully closed. That was a break.

In the space of thirty minutes I'd eaten a very stale package of peanut butter and cheese crackers and downed three bottles of water from the station's soda machine. If they didn't see us soon I'd be moving on to the corn chips. I'd had enough. I approached the desk sergeant.

"Excuse me, Officer."

He pretended I wasn't there for at least two minutes, something I remembered from snooty hostesses in restaurants who sometimes mistook rudeness for exclusivity. But the Springfield police department headquarters was not a velvet-rope joint. There, the tactic might have been used intentionally to make people feel powerless. Which it did.

Not famous for my patience, I tapped my toes, I jiggled the keys in my pocket, I sighed heavily, I turned around to look at Sturgis and made a twisted, eyes-crossed face. Finally the cop acknowledged my presence.

"It's sergeant," he said, tapping the nameplate on the counter with his pencil. "Sergeant Frank Stamos."

"Right. Sergeant Stamos. We've been here for a pretty long time. Are we being charged with something? Because, if not, I'd like to go home. And I'm sure my friend here feels the same way." I waited for Grant to back me up, but he just sat there, forearms on his knees, staring at his shoes.

Stamos looked at me as if everyone he met when he was behind that glass said the same thing: I want to go home. And he answered the same way. "Just be patient, ma'am. Have a seat and the investigating officer should be here any minute."

"Investigating what? Two people talking? A business deal?" I was getting worked up. Not a good thing under the circumstances. I'd already been borderline *belligerent* with the first cop.

Grant rescued me. He came to the desk and without saying a word, clamped a hand on my elbow, and led me back to the wooden bench like a child who'd strayed too far in the playground. The only thing missing was one of those kid leashes that have come back into fashion. Stamos left the counter and went back to shuffling the papers on his desk.

"Word to the wise," Grant said softly. "Don't protest anything in a police station or in an airport. You should have seen me here last week. I pulled a Howard Dean. Everything I said was true, but I came off looking and sounding like a crazy man."

"C'mon," I whispered. "This is Connecticut, not Iraq." Then I realized that to Grant, it probably did feel like Iraq. *Or hell.* His wife had been arrested, his children sent away for their own good, and he couldn't get anyone to help him. Even me, who was supposed to be his wife's friend.

From the back of the station house, two hospital-style doors swung open and Juniper Berry entered the waiting area with Mike O'Malley.

"I might have known," I said, jumping up. "What's going on here? Are you guys having a slow night at the office, or is this the quaint local way of asking for a date?"

O'Malley appeared puzzled and bemused at the same time.

"If I ever do ask you for a date, Ms. Holliday, I don't think I'll send a patrol car to pick you up. I have my own wheels."

Crap, had I really said that out loud? I felt like a prize idiot.

"Mr. Sturgis, you're free to go with our apologies," he said. "Officer Berry was acting appropriately and entirely within the law bringing you both in until someone from Rhodes Realty could confirm that you were authorized to be on the Chiaramonte property. Which they just did."

131

Sturgis nodded but wisely stuck to his game plan and said nothing. He folded his coat over his arm and asked if someone was available to take him back to his car, which was still at Guido's. O'Malley said of course, and chucked his chin at Berry.

"I'll meet you out front," Berry said, and went out through the back, closer to where he'd parked his vehicle.

Grant's red-rimmed eyes bored into my skull. "I'm driving over to see Caroline now. They're sending her back to Michigan tomorrow. Can I tell her you'll do that off-season job for us?" His hand was on the doorknob, but he was rooted to the spot, waiting for my answer. "Just until she comes home?"

I turned to O'Malley. "Do I get to go home, too, or did you want to put me in a lineup?"

"Did anyone say you were being arrested? Were you given a Breathalyzer test? Were you handcuffed? Did we take you around to the back of the station house and beat you with a rubber hose? I just thought you might want to stick around, get a cup of coffee, and tell me your side of the story," O'Malley said. "Why are you so testy? Anyone would think you hadn't —" He didn't finish the thought. He didn't have to. And anyone listening would have known where that crack was going. Stamos coughed to stifle a laugh.

"If I'm testy, *Officer,* it's because I'm hungry — no other reason. I had half a piece of cake and some partially hydrogenated cheese and crackers for dinner. And there is no story, my side or otherwise. Mr. Sturgis was simply hoping to surprise Caroline when she gets home and he asked me to work on a project for her. To do some digging."

"It's *sergeant,* but I think you know that," O'Malley said. "I didn't think gardeners planted at this time of year."

"Well, that's where you're wrong. There's plenty of digging in the fall — bulbs, shrubs." I prattled on, looking from one man to the other — one joking and flirting, the other having the worst week of his life.

Out of the corner of my eye I saw Berry pull up outside in the patrol car. He flashed his lights to let Grant know he was waiting. Grant stared at me, silently begging me to help him.

"There's another kind of digging. And I've decided to do it."

TWELVE

Now that we were no longer deemed a threat to society, Officer Berry drove both of us to the nursery in one patrol car. We rode in the backseat, Grant lost in his thoughts and me lost in mine.

I'd said I'd "do some digging" to spite Mike, to suggest that, once again, I would do his job better than he could; but now I wished the words had never left my lips. Grant Sturgis seemed relieved that I'd agreed to help him, but he didn't need me; he needed a lawyer, a private investigator. Damn it, *a psychic* would be more useful than a freaking gardener.

Once Berry had dropped us off, we were able to talk freely.

"Grant, I'll do what I can, but I can't make any promises. This is really out of my league. I'll give it some thought and be in touch. What's better for you, e-mail or phone?"

"Phone."

I plugged his cell number into my phone and he thanked me profusely. I hadn't done anything, except perhaps given him an ally and some hope, but maybe that was all he needed.

By then, I really was ravenous. I drove to the Paradise, slowing down to check out the parking lot first. No news trucks was good news for me, so I pulled in. Babe was alone behind the counter reading the *Bulletin*. A handful of familiar faces were scattered around the diner, but none bothered to look up as I entered.

"Where have *you* been?" Babe asked.

"For the last two hours . . . downtown at the Springfield police station."

"Let me guess. You're not really Paula Holliday. You're Princess Diana and you've been in hiding all these years."

"That's hilarious," I said, faking the cupped royal wave. "When are you getting your own HBO special?" I climbed onto one of the stools at the counter and reached my arms over my head in a long catlike move. I pushed down on each elbow for a deeper stretch.

"That's a good one. Neil stretches me like that." Babe offered me coffee, but it was too late for caffeine.

135

"Got any herb tea?"

"Sure, indoor plumbing and everything." She swept aside the newspapers and laid out a setup for me — place mat, paper napkin origami-ed around the utensils, and a mug.

"Any of that cake left?" I asked, really wanting food but needing a treat.

"Dream on."

It was after 11 P.M. but I ordered a turkey wrap and looked at the headlines on the *Springfield Bulletin* while I waited for Pete to create his latest culinary masterpiece, Instant Thanksgiving — turkey, cranberry sauce, and a sliver of sweet potato wrapped in a piece of flatbread. One bite and you could almost hear a football game and bickering relatives in the background.

For the last week the *Bulletin* had been all Caroline, all the time. Any brief flirtation the newspaper's management had had with serious journalism left when Jon Chappell departed for the *Denver Post* and his boss, who'd come of age when newspapers were a nickel, retired. Truth be told, even Jon's conversion was short-lived.

Jon and I had gotten to be pals a few years back, and I'd like to think I'd steered him onto the path of journalistic integrity, but, let's face it, the Caroline story was just too good to pass up. A blond suburban house-wife arrested for being on the lam from a drug rap — it was so juicy Jon was probably writing about it in Denver as an insider who'd known the fugitive. And his successors here were milking it. I pushed the papers away.

"I may have just done something very stupid," I admitted.

"Join the club. Most of the people who come in here at this hour have done something stupid."

"What do you mean, it's not *that* late."

"Doesn't matter. Most normal people are home with their families now, or they're brushing their teeth. They are definitely not just about to sit down for a meal. Unless they're in Barcelona."

"Thank you."

"Sad but true." Babe leaned in. "See that guy over there? He got wasted at a business function tonight and hit on his boss — who was all too happy to take him up on the offer. Now he's afraid to go home *and* he's afraid to go to work tomorrow. He's been in the john five times already — probably trying to get the woman's scent out of his hair and off his clothes. He may be here all night if she was wearing Shalimar or something heavy."

I sneaked a look at the guy. He was not much older than me but probably had the wife, the mortgage, two kids, and a dog. And he'd jeopardized it all with one drink too many and one dance of the horizontal hora. He reminded me a little of Grant Sturgis, sandy hair, bland good looks — like a soap star, handsome but not memorable. There were millions of these guys whose regular features would open doors for them and who were, more often than not, confused as hell after they walked through them and didn't know what to do next.

I used to think of Caroline that way, too, with her subdued palette, the sweater tied artfully around her neck, and her Audrey Hepburn ballet flats. I do remember thinking there was something about Caroline that was different — an inner spark. I just didn't know it was coming from an inner hash pipe. I instantly hated myself for thinking that and groaned out loud.

"So what stupid thing did you do?" Babe asked. "We know *you* don't have a boss."

"I volunteered for something."

"Always a mistake," she said, slapping the counter. "Send a check if you must, but don't volunteer. And never let yourself be put on any committees. It's a wonder there isn't more bloodshed at committee and

138

board meetings."

Babe was delivering one of her insightful, Babe's rules monologues, and I let her go on. Buried in her speeches was always something useful, some nugget of wisdom. And it was refreshing to hear chat that wasn't about Springfield's newest arch-criminal. Besides, it gave me time to think. It was too late to back out. I'd told Grant I would find the person who'd informed on Caroline. I just had to figure out how.

It wasn't hard to find someone if you knew who you were looking for, but what if you didn't know? I stared at the counter, waiting for a bolt of lightning or a Saint Paul moment knocking me off my stool and revealing what I should do next. Eventually it came but not from the sky or a religious epiphany. As if coming out of a trance, I heard Babe's voice, first faint, and then louder.

"Hello, are you listening to me?" Babe said. "There aren't any answers in that mug."

No, there weren't, but there may have been one under it. On the place mat, next to the two-inch ads for unpainted furniture, pictures of pets plastered on T-shirts, and gold-tone trophies for your bowling team was a small ad that read "Think the Rat Is

Cheating? Call Nina Mazzo, reasonable rates, discretion guaranteed. Free consultation."

THIRTEEN

With enough time and money you could find almost anyone. You could also trace any call, e-mail, or Web site visit, but I didn't have to make it easy for Nina Mazzo to discover my identity and to figure out what I was doing. If the tipster could be anonymous, I could be anonymous too. I didn't need to burnish my reputation as a snoop. The next morning, I drove to the main branch of the Springfield library and logged on to one of their public computers to check out Nina's Web site without leaving a trail from my home computer. Her home page was a basic template, turquoise and gold, not a lot of bells and whistles. More tasteful than I expected, given her stock in trade. It fit with her credentials as a nonpracticing attorney and former child advocate.

Nina's specialty was tracking down deadbeat dads and getting the goods on spouses who strayed, whatever the goods were. I could only assume she, or one of her employees, was the one who stood in the bushes snapping pictures of couples in flagrante delicto while guys in designer suits made the real money from the subsequent divorce settlements. Like most things, there was a pecking order in the adultery business.

Two or three high-profile attorneys, including Arthur Horowitz, known in some circles as the first wives' best friend, had provided enthusiastic blurbs that Nina had blatantly incorporated into the banner on her Web site.

So why was she advertising on a place mat?

"Same reason we're here," she said in a throaty voice, spreading her arms. She sat opposite me in an overheated barracks-like building not far from the Metro North station. I'd had some trouble finding the place, tucked in as it was between a ceramic tile showroom and a beauty supply distributor. There were two molded plastic chairs, an oversized turquoise desk clearly purchased for a larger office, and the same basic wall clock that you'd see in any hospital or prison.

"Business is off," she said. "Either people are staying faithful, or the still-rich guys have found better ways to cover their tracks. Alarming prospects for someone like me."

Whatever the reason, it had Nina spending, in her own words, far too much time chasing down the imaginary bank accounts and safe deposit boxes of someone's recently deceased granny.

"Half the county seems convinced the old dears socked something away and forgot where they put it, like that women who stashed all her savings in a mattress and then got Alzheimer's and gave it to Goodwill. Don't get me wrong — a client is a client." She cut off her diatribe, her famous discretion finally kicking in.

I unzipped my jacket and unwound the scarf that that been wrapped two or three times around my neck. I swiped at my forehead with the back of my hand.

"I know. I keep it warm in here. I detest the cold. So what can I do for you? It isn't Grandma's jewels, is it? No, you don't have that desperate hoping-for-a-pot-of-gold expression." She searched my face. "You may actually be worried about something, Miss . . ." She glanced at the online registration form I had filled out and submitted from the library's computer.

"Miss Turner, Miss T. Turner?"

All right, I'd been having a musical moment and hadn't wanted to type in my real name on the online form. I smiled weakly. She looked at me as if she thought I was going to say I was searching for the rest of the Ikettes.

"That's right," I said, rearranging my scarf and my thoughts, "Thelma." It was the only T name I could think of on short notice, other than Tina or Trixie — and I didn't think I could pull that one off without pretending that I had a husband named Ed and we lived next door to the Kramdens. "My mother was very old-fashioned." I rambled on stupidly about the name.

Nina Mazzo unstrapped her plain, tank-like watch and put it on the desk in front of her. I got the message.

"I want to find someone," I said at last.

"Now we're getting somewhere. Who?" she asked, sitting up straighter and poised to write on her yellow legal pad. "The father who abandoned you? Child you gave up for adoption? We have a very good success rate with cases of that nature."

"No," I said.

"Someone you need to subpoena? I have an extremely reliable operative who makes deliveries. Very high percentage there as well."

I was encouraged that she had had so

much experience.

"I don't know. I mean, I don't know his name, what he looks like, or if he's even a he."

She put her pen down. The rest of the meeting went like a riff on the old Abbott and Costello routine "Who's on First." I was being intentionally vague, and she wasn't inclined to reveal any of her methods. Why should she until I was a paying customer? She was deciding how much more time to waste on me when a young man as blank and unformed looking as a Secret Service man entered the office.

She said nothing, he nodded, and she buzzed him into a back office. "One of my operatives," she explained. It was all very James Bond. I started to think that I had wasted both of our time. "Now back to you."

After fifteen minutes of circular chat I decided to forgo the rest of my free (you do get what you pay for) consultation and let Nina Mazzo get back to searching for Grandma's hidden millions. She wasn't sorry to see me go, but I felt her eyes on me all the way out to the parking lot, where I had to wait for a forklift full of Italian tile to crawl by before I could drive off.

All I'd learned was that without a name,

driver's license, or description it was difficult to know where to start looking for someone. Most of Nina Mazzo's clients were looking for the money. *Quel surprise.* What was I looking for?

In fact, what was I doing? I was playing with someone's life. Someone's hopes. I got back in my car, determined to get in touch with Grant and call the whole thing off; then I heard the echo of Grant's voice telling me how much Caroline trusted me and needed me. Me. I hadn't been needed for anything other than the perennial beds for a long time. And whether I liked to admit it or not, sometimes even they did just fine without me.

If it hadn't been for Caroline, Dirty Business might have gone under. Our friendship had sneaked up on me when I wasn't paying attention, like those extra five pounds or a bad habit that you don't even realize you're engaging in until you see yourself doing it in a reflection or a photograph. It hadn't been easy striking off on my own. If I admitted it, I would have been lonely in Springfield without her and Babe.

I left the downtown decorating area and took the back roads home to my place, past my new favorite nursery, the pond, and the school where I voted. Not far from the school, I got trapped behind a school bus that had its hydraulic stop sign sticking out. A seemingly endless stream of children exited the bus and the driver waited for each of them to waddle off in their colorful puffy jackets and disappear into their homes.

I put the car in park and sat there thinking. If I couldn't look for a *who,* maybe I should be looking for a *why* that would lead me to a *who.* And maybe it wasn't cherchez la femme as much as it was *cherchez d'argent.* Perhaps I *had* learned something from Nina Mazzo. I called the Sturgis home. Grant answered on the first ring.

"It's me. Listen, was there a reward offered for Caroline?"

I heard nothing, then a quiet "not as far as I know."

Rats. That meant there had been no financial incentive for a stranger or a bounty hunter to track Caroline down and inform on her. On the other hand, that meant it had to be someone she knew, either here or back in Michigan. Grant listened in silence as I explained.

The schoolkids had vanished and the bus drove away.

"Grant, are you still there?'

"I'm here."

"Have there been any new people in

Caroline's life lately? Anyone she might have shared her secret with?"

There was dead silence on the other end; then he answered in a monotone. "Mickey Cameron asked me the same question a few hours ago."

"And?"

"*You're* the only one she would have told. Only you. How could you do it?"

The crash of Grant Sturgis slamming down the phone rang in my ears until it was replaced by the sound of cars honking their horns at me to get moving.

FOURTEEN

It was true. I had befriended Caroline, I'd had drinks with her on more than a few occasions, I was a former television producer (read ambitious, unscrupulous wench), and I was getting a reputation in Springfield as an amateur sleuth and a busybody. And it was no secret I wasn't rolling in dough. No wonder Grant Sturgis thought I'd informed on his wife. He probably thought I had sold her story for big bucks and was already casting the lead for the eventual movie of the week.

But I never had a chance to explain. To him or to anyone. Grant stopped taking my calls, probably on the advice of his attorney, and I noticed a distinct chill in the air at the Paradise Diner whenever I arrived. As we'd all learned when Caroline had been arrested, bad news travels fast in a small town. My phone had stopped ringing. The leaf cleanup jobs had evaporated. No one had said anything — they didn't have to. The suggestion that I'd been the one to drop a dime on Caroline Sturgis had rippled through Springfield. That and the fall weather were enough to make me a pariah.

Some hard-liners must have secretly supported the tipster; once or twice I thought I saw a little smile from people who thought that I'd been the informer. One woman, Althea Tripplehorn, the self-appointed moral compass of Springfield, had even started a petition that all newcomers should somehow be vetted by the real estate agents who sold them their homes. A little thing like the Constitution didn't bother Althea. I knew sex offenders had to register in some towns, but former media execs? Ex–New Yorkers?

It got particularly quiet when I entered the diner and the Main Street Moms were in attendance. Caroline might no longer have been one of their own, but I doubt they appreciated an interloper coming in and shattering their nice neat little world.

After three years of hard work, I'd reverted to being an outsider again, except to Babe, who stuck by me. I took to going to the diner at off-peak hours so I wouldn't see anyone I knew.

"I'm screwed. Not only does Grant Sturgis hate me, but half my clientele thinks I put the finger on one of the nicest women in Springfield. She volunteers, she carpools other people's bratty kids, she does all those craftsy things for charity events. Come gardening season I'm going to be unemployed, broke, and a social outcast. I'm going to have to start a victory garden just to eat."

Babe was sympathetic. She herself was a local who'd returned after a long absence, and even then it took a few years for her to rejoin the fold.

"They don't hate you. They're just nervous," she said. "And that Althea. She hasn't had a good cause to get up in arms about since the seventies. If it was up to her, the whole town would be gated. What about O'Malley? Can't he do something?"

"Please — the man doesn't know how close he came to being throttled the other night, but we were in the police station and a little too close to those benches with the shackles."

Besides, there was nothing the Springfield police could do. They hadn't received the tip, the Michigan police had. The locals had no jurisdiction in Caroline's case and had only been notified as a courtesy less than an hour before federal marshals came to arrest her. The tipster didn't break the law. Caroline did.

"You *are* screwed," she said, "unless you can find out who really did it and why."

"Me? How is that my job?"

"Fine. You can keep avoiding people and coming here for breakfast at nine o'clock in the evening. Doesn't bother me."

Yeah, that's all I had to do — and there weren't any place mats to help me out with that. Just like the cops in Michigan, *I* needed a tipster.

Outside, a vehicle crawled by the diner, disappearing at the far end of the lot. Then it appeared a second time, hanging a U-turn and pulling into a space. I thought it might have been the last of the intrepid reporters, but most of them had moved on to Bridgeport where Caroline, in a orange jumpsuit, had been transferred to a larger facility. It Becka Reynolds, one of the Main Street Moms, peered through the glass door. She surveyed the few other customers in the diner before coming in, and Babe and I waited to see if she was friend or foe.

I'd never worked on her property but recognized her as one of Caroline's neighbors. She came and sat on the stool beside me, even though there were plenty of empty places a safe distance away from Springfield's new least-popular person.

"This is kind of late for you, Ms. Reynolds," Babe said. "What can I get you?"

"Nothing. No, a decaf, please."

"Gotta make a new pot."

"That's fine, I'll wait. And it's Becka." She pulled off a pair of buttery leather gloves and carefully, needlessly, flattened them out on her thigh but still said nothing. The silence was getting weird. Finally we both started to speak at the same time.

"You go," I said.

"No, you."

As nervous as she was, this was more than a how-deep-to-plant-the-bulbs question. What did she want to ask me? Or tell me?

Always perceptive, Babe offered us some privacy. If we wanted to have a less public chat, we could use her recently violated office, an inner sanctum I'd been in only once before when I was showing her gardening Web sites online. Again Becka and I answered in unison. "Yes." Becka gave a nervous laugh. Babe left one of the waitresses in charge of the diner and the three of us walked outside and around to the back of the building. The new key stuck, but finally worked.

Years ago, the diner's previous owner had added a small room onto the back. It had a

153

view of the lake and the Dumpster depending on where you sat, but neither were visible at this hour of the night. A small woodstove provided the only heat. Two loveseats faced each other and were covered with throws and Indian print pillows, a comfortable place to take a break or put your feet up after a long day behind the counter. The tainted mattress had been deflated and tossed in a corner of the room until Babe decided whether or not she could still live with it. She drew the bark cloth curtains together and told us to sit down.

"I'll bring the coffee when it's ready." Then she left.

Becka spoke first. "I haven't known who else to tell. My husband told me to stay out of it, and he's right, of course."

Becka Reynolds looked too young to be so submissive, but I'd been wrong about my neighbors before. She fiddled with her expensive gloves again, matching up the seams. If she wasn't careful she'd stain them with the oil from her long, tapered fingers. She had something painful to spit out and for some reason had chosen me as the recipient.

"Some of the other women are a little uncomfortable around you. Especially now . . ."

154

"Me? I'm a pussycat. What have I done?"

Was that what this was about? Was I being run out of town by a Junior Leaguer? Was this the suburban equivalent of the Old West's tar and feathers?

Becka explained. I'd done nothing, that was it. No husband, no kids, not much makeup, no pearls, no "every strand in place" helmet hair. Half of them thought I would try to steal their husbands and the other half thought I was gay. This was going to be hard to address without putting myself firmly in one camp or the other.

"And now they think I'm the bigmouth who called the cops on Caroline, right?" I said. She smiled almost apologetically.

"Why," I said, "because I'm madly in love with Grant Sturgis and wanted her out of the way?"

"You're not, are you?" she asked, the color draining from her face.

"I was *joking*. How can you think that?"

Then I saw how she could. Perhaps I wasn't the only one Caroline had confided in when she thought Grant was having an affair. I'd been at her place a lot, and until recently Grant and I had been pretty chummy — even being discovered canoodling in the greenhouse by two of Springfield's finest. At least that was the way it might have been described on the bush telegraph. By whom, one of the cops? The civilian office worker? So Grant thought I was a snitch and everyone else thought I was a slut. Excellent. Forget having breakfast at night. I'd have to sell my house, leave town, and get a real job. And what had *I* done?

"Put it out of your head. I don't want anyone's husband and it's not because I'm gay. Grant hired me to try to find out who tipped off the cops about Caroline."

Becka seemed relieved. Maybe she hadn't really believed I was guilty, but she needed to be sure.

"Did *you* know about Caroline before this all happened?" I asked.

"Absolutely not. I knew there were things she didn't like to talk about, but we all have those. If . . . if I tell you something, you can't say you heard it from me." I felt like screaming "get on with it," but Becka had to do this in her own excruciatingly slow way.

"Go on." I nodded and patted her forearm to encourage her, then pulled back so she wouldn't resurrect the gay theory.

"It was last week — no, two weeks ago — when we had our last morning ride together."

156

Becka told me Caroline had been on a roller coaster the entire morning. She'd gotten a ticket for running a stop sign on the way to the stables. Becka was amused that she was inordinately concerned about it, but Caroline kept repeating she'd never gotten a ticket before as if it were the worst thing that had ever happened to her.

"I told her it's a rite of passage. Everyone gets a ticket on Chesterfield Road at some point in time, especially at the end of the month, when the cops have their quotas to make. It's as if they have a roulette wheel and just decide whose turn it is. I was surprised it hadn't happened years ago."

I made a mental note to be super careful on Chesterfield.

On top of that, Becka said, something odd had happened at the stables.

Now we were getting somewhere. "What was it?" I asked.

"Something rattled her. In the lounge area outside of the women's locker room."

"Another rider?" I asked.

"I don't know, possibly."

"Did you recognize the person?"

Becka shook her head. She didn't see who it was, but thought it might have been a new early morning regular. It was unusual for a man to be riding alone at that time, but they'd seen the newcomer from a distance twice and had gotten to the stage of polite nods and waves.

"Something he said troubled her. She wouldn't tell me what it was. Then we came to the diner, met the others, and she was so happy to see you, I assumed she was fine. When she came out, she was pale as a ghost. She made up some flimsy excuse and left right away."

And that must have helped fuel the rumor, at least among the Main Street Moms, that I'd been connected to Caroline's arrest, that I'd said or done something to upset her.

Someone or something was scratching at the door. Finally, Babe pushed it open butt first, balancing a tray with two coffees and a small round of biscotti.

"Pete is outdoing himself," I said, jumping up and holding the door for her. "Are they twice baked?"

"Yeah, he's getting good." Babe bunny-dipped the tray onto the coffee table. "How are you girls doing?" she asked. "Playing nice?"

I didn't want Becka to regret having confided in me, so I kept mum. She did the same.

"Right. Don't leave any food in here, okay? The raccoons are killing me. I'm this close to getting a pellet gun. I've only got one key to the new lock. Just press the button to lock the door when you leave.

Babe left us, and Becka and I picked at the biscotti and used the coffee mugs to keep our hands warm. She hadn't given me much to go on, just one or two details about the new rider's habits and schedule, but I planned to talk to O'Malley about what information could have been gleaned from Caroline's driver's license. Then I'd visit the stables to ask Hank Mossdale about his new customer.

I went to Mossdale's regularly during the gardening season for free horse manure. Hank might open up to me — maybe I'd even get to meet the man who had spoken to Caroline.

"Was there anything or anyone else new in Caroline's life that you know of?" I asked. "Had she signed up for any new classes?" I remembered her telling me about all the craft projects started, then tucked away on her garage.

Nothing. Apart from the ticket and the brief encounter with the man at the stables, Caroline's life had been stultifyingly routine, detailed and color-coded in erasable marker on the large whiteboard in her otherwise pristine kitchen. Soccer, dentist, when to pick up this one, when to drop off that one. As far as I knew, there'd been no new entries since she'd been arrested.

When we finished we locked Babe's office and brought the tray inside. I walked Becka to her car.

"I'm sorry we never talked before," she said, shaking my hand. "We will, I promise. And I can use some help with my garden next season if you have the time. I know how pleased Caroline is with your work. She was so excited about the venture you two were starting. I confess I was jealous. She might have asked any of us to go in with her, but she asked you. And Chiaramonte's is a perfect location for a gift shop and small garden design center. I guess that won't happen now."

"Grant said me someone else was interested in the property," I said, "unless Roxy was just trying to push him into making an offer. I wouldn't put it past her to do that."

"Oh no, it's probably true," Becka said. "I think you met him. Attractive man, around fifty years old? He spent a lot of time at the Paradise Diner the day you worked on the planters. He asked if we happened to know of a nursery for sale. Can you beat that for coincidence? I guess he's the one."

Now I had two mysterious strangers on

my suspect list, so that's where I started
looking for my tipster.

FIFTEEN

It was time to whip out the blow-dryer.

There was an unfortunate truism that the better you looked and felt, the more people gave you what you wanted. Ordinarily I raged against this unfair fact of life and would have protested bitterly if anyone had suggested that I'd ever taken advantage of a situation with a flick of the hair or a well-timed laugh. But these were extraordinary times.

I made a lunch date with Mike O'Malley. I rummaged through the bags of Lucy's cast-off purchases and laid out my clothes more carefully than I had for the wedding we'd attended. Some of my makeup was dried out or clumpy, but there was enough of the old magic left in that neglected basket of tubes and pots to help me look smoky-eyed and full-lipped.

My first stop was Mossdale Stables, located on one of Springfield's many back roads. A series of swoops and rises past a small stream and over a stone bridge led me to Mossdale's, where privileged kids worked on their seats and I occasionally went to collect horse manure to spread around flower beds.

When they've finished sharing their favorite tips on how to keep the deer at bay (human hair, coyote urine, Irish Spring soap), gardeners frequently debated the value of different kinds of manures, bat guano being the most highly prized and most expensive — think how long it must take to get a full barrel. Gardeners discussing manure was as lively a conversation as die-hard baseball fans arguing about the designated hitter.

Cow manure is right up there, but there aren't too many farms left in Connecticut. Most of that product is imported, bagged, and shipped from who knows where. On the other hand, in Connecticut, we had no shortage of little girls bobbing up and down in those cute little riding outfits — the velvet hats preparing them for their velvet headbands. There were more than seven million horses in the United States, and I'd have bet a large number of them were here in the Nutmeg State.

I liked The Black Stallion as much as

anybody, but I'm not much of a rider. Like most things I did once or twice a year — skiing, riding a bike, baking bread — I was a perennial novice, never doing it often enough to get better. When I rode, the horse never had any doubt who was in charge, and it was never me. For me, it was all about the horse poop. Black gold, plentiful and free.

Hank Mossdale was a quiet, capable guy in his forties whom I'd never seen in anything other than jeans and a chambray work shirt. He had thick brown hair, a year-round tan, and a body that looked rock hard from riding and manual labor.

Hank had gotten into the business late and through an unlikely path. He wasn't to the saddle born; he'd been an accountant. At some point in the late 1990s the firm he worked for was recommending livestock as a tax shelter. At the time, you could take a large depreciation on the animals for the first few years and thereby shelter income. And it worked until the IRS changed the rules.

One day on a visit to a horse farm in upstate New York where he was breaking the bad news to the owners that their silent partners were soon to be even more silent, Hank had an epiphany. He realized that *live*stock was *alive.* Horses weren't just items on a balance sheet, they were magnificent creatures, and he became obsessed with the idea of owning a stable.

Most people — if they had the horse fantasy at all — saw themselves at the Kentucky Derby sipping mint juleps, wearing outlandish hats they'd never wear in real life, and paying experts to train their horses. Hank's plan — he was after all an accountant — was more conservative. He would buy one horse and train it himself for the somewhat less elite world of harness racing. No juleps. Less cachet, but an easier field to enter. He'd use the money from purses to buy the stable.

If he'd bothered to ask any professionals what they thought of his idea, they would have told him it was insane. It could take a hundred thousand dollars of care and training to win an eight-thousand-dollar purse. But he didn't ask — he just went ahead and did it.

His first wife, smelling the horse manure but not the potential roses, left him for a more reliable breadwinner, a cardiologist; but she should have had more faith, because eventually Hank made it work.

He and his partner, Karen, a professional horse trainer, bought a horse that went on to win two of harness racing's most prestigious races and, ultimately, more than one million dollars. By that time the ex-wife had unhappily relocated to St. Louis, where she was in the process of getting another divorce. Between the purses and the horse's stud fees, five hundred dollars a, um, pop, they were able to buy a defunct riding academy on eight acres adjacent to the highway and state land, where riders where permitted to go. Hank and Karen were up to their elbows in horse manure for the foreseeable future.

I pulled into the long dirt driveway and parked next to a black Audi. Hank was leaning on the paddock fence, watching a minibus disgorge a load of kids and their teachers, who tried to keep their changes from spreading out in all directions. He waved and walked over to me.

"Karen will have her hands full with that lot. They always ask how fast the horses can run, as if that's all there was to it. The urge for speed. I guess life's a video game at that age."

Hank Mossdale was always friendly, but that day he seemed warmer than usual. And he smiled a lot more. "You're not dressed for mucking out."

So that was it. I'd thrown a barrel and a

pitchfork into the back of my Jeep, but I wasn't kidding anyone. (Note to self: leave the blow-dryer out.)

"Just visiting, really. Got a few minutes?"

"For the woman who hauls away horse apples for me? Of course." We left the horse trainer to her charges.

Owners who boarded their horses at Mossdale's were considered members. I'd heard that was the business model that worked for Mossdale's — not unlike membership in a county club. I guess that was the accountant in him. Horses were available for day use, but it was the members who kept his business afloat. Becka Reynolds had told me the man who'd spoken to Caroline generally rode at around 8 A.M.

There was the tiniest bit of frost of the ground and it crunched under our feet as Hank and I strode over to the barn where his office was located. I waited for one of his workers to lead away the horse she was grooming before telling him why I'd come.

"Only one new rider here on any kind of regular basis," Hank said. "He's in the locker room now, as a matter of fact. Said he had real estate business this morning, that's why he's riding later than usual. Name's Ellis Damon."

According to Hank, Damon was new to

the neighborhood. He didn't ride his own horse. The mare he took out belonged to a older woman who'd stabled her horses here for twelve years, even before Mossdale owned the place. She often let Hank rent the horse to responsible, accomplished riders so the animal would get more exercise than she could give him herself.

"Damon said he moved here for work a few weeks back, but he's just been here three or four times. Doesn't seem to be too entrenched in suburban life yet. Short guy. Pretty good rider."

"You think I could talk to him?"

"I don't see why not. Seems like a sociable guy. Want me to tell him you're looking for him?"

"You mind?"

Hank shook his head and left for the men's locker room. He tucked his shirt into his jeans almost as if he knew that I enjoyed watching the fabric stretch across the V of his back. Five minutes later, Hank came out with tiny, fussy-looking Ellis Damon. The latter was running his hands through his still wet hair, and adjusting his clerical collar.

"She looked troubled. I told her I was the new pastor at the Church on Fallsview Road and that if she wanted to talk to someone I was available." He sounded apologetic. "Perhaps I was too forward, trying too hard. I may have frightened her off. People have said that about me."

Or maybe the speeding ticket had shaken her up and Caroline Sturgis had started to feel exposed, the protective layers falling away. One of my mysterious strangers was in the clear. Whatever had troubled Caroline, it probably wasn't a suburban priest, however clumsy and pushy. Maybe seeing a priest at just that moment made her want to confess. Who knows?

I thanked Father Damon and walked him to his car, a white SUV crammed with his belongings.

"I'm still something of a nomad," he explained, "staying with one friend and then another until I find a permanent place."

"What are you looking for?" I asked. "I have some friends in the real estate business."

"Some place between five and ten acres that we can use as a retreat house. Nothing fancy, mind you. But preferably somewhere with a lot of greenery. Where people can come to reflect."

"Like a former nursery?"

"Yes, do you know of one?"

Sixteen

Why all this sudden interest in Guido Chiaramonte's old nursery? It had been virtually abandoned for years and now there were two interested parties? Right after Caroline Sturgis announces her intention to buy it in a crowded diner? Had the recession ended and Gretchen Kennedy and I hadn't gotten the e-mail? Or was the two men's interest in the property more complicated than a love of greenery and contemplative spaces?

"Rhodes Realty"

"It's Paula Holliday. Any chance Roxy can see me today for a few minutes?"

A few minutes was all Roxy Rhodes would spare unless she smelled the blood of a client with deep pockets. Maybe she had agreed to the meeting because of my relationship with the Sturgises. It wasn't because I was a high roller.

Rhodes Realty was a stone and clapboard building with a wrap-around porch in a good neighborhood and would have commanded a high price itself if it had been for sale. Fat chance. Town lore had it Roxy acquired the house as part of the settlement from her first divorce decades ago and that had sparked her love of real estate. Three husbands later, she owned quite a lot of property in Springfield and even more in neighboring towns, as well as in Boca Raton and San Diego.

Roxy's waiting room was filled with postmodern furniture, meant to impress but not to be comfortable. The walls were covered with plaques honoring her for this or that real estate accomplishment and as many for service to the community. Her assistant had me cool my heels for about ten minutes, presumably so I could read them all, then she led me into a room four times the size of the first. It, too, had a collection of Danish modern furniture mixed with chrome and black leather accents. Roxy sat curled up on a red velvet loveseat behind a sleek glass desk that could have accommodated twelve for dinner. Her leopard print flats were tucked underneath.

"Paula, what can I do for you?" She extended limp fingers in my direction but didn't get up or lean forward, so I had to stretch my upper body over her desk to reach her powdery hand. "Has Grant Sturgis finally sent you to make an offer on the Chiaramonte place?"

I hated it when people put words in my mouth.

"Not exactly. But I am here to talk about the nursery." I took that exchange to mean I could sit down, so I did, balancing my butt on one of the less comfortable spaghetti chairs and trying not to let my butt cheeks slip through. "I understand there's been another offer on the place."

"You're rather well-informed yourself."

"Just doing some reconnaissance for my friends. Is it true?"

Roxy loved competition — it got her juices flowing. Yes, she had shown the property to another gentleman, an out-of-town buyer who had specifically asked if there was a nursery for sale.

"Was he, by any chance, a priest?"

"If this man was a priest, it would be an absolute tragedy. It was a week or so ago. Maybe two, my calendar is so full it's hard to remember. He was looking for a business opportunity. He certainly wasn't a clergyman, but I wouldn't have guessed he'd be a gardener, either. Still, you never know about people."

There was an insult in there somewhere, but I chose to let it pass.

"What did he look like?"

Roxy ticked off the man's assets as if she'd written them down in a ledger. "Elegant, well-spoken, beautifully dressed, but with that broken nose he looked like a gorgeous linebacker or one of those French boxers from the forties."

It sounded like the man at the diner who had charmed the Main Street Moms, not Ellis Damon.

"He said he'd been in sales before, but the nursery property would be a departure for him. He was vague about how he was planning to use the space. I thought it might be as a banquet or meeting facility, not a nursery."

"Did you happen to mention there was another party interested in purchasing the property?" I asked.

"Do I look stupid, Ms. Holliday? Of course I did. I may have even mentioned Caroline's name and yours — at least, your company, Dirty Business. Very provocative, by the way. He was definitely considering the place," she said, fingering a crystal paperweight. "I could see him working out something in his brain . . . *something.* I have a sixth sense for the serious buyers. It's my famous mojo, you see."

To go with her famous ego. I shifted in my seat.

"He didn't ask about financing. Just said he'd be back. And he will." She drove now the point with a well-manicured finger.

"Can you tell me his name?" I asked.

"I don't see why not. It was Brookfield, Kevin Brookfield. Easy to remember because of Brookfield Road."

"Was he the only man you showed the property to? Could someone else have taken out another client? A priest?"

"No one else. It's an exclusive and only I handle the AAA properties. What is this obsession with priests? Is Oxygen airing *The Thorn Birds* again?"

I wasn't obsessed with priests, and if I'd been Meggie Cleary I'd have figured out a way to make it work with the handsome sheep-shearer. But what were the odds that the two newcomers to Springfield would both claim to be interested in purchasing a nursery? Unless they thought that saying they were would somehow lead them to Caroline.

I stood up and thanked Roxy for her help.

"I don't suppose Grant is in a position to do anything now. I can't sit on the property for another twenty years."

Ouch. Did she really say that? Harsh, very harsh.

"Don't go. Who's the other prospective buyer?"

She was still mumbling when I left the outer office and headed for my next stop.

SEVENTEEN

The central police station in Springfield was located downtown at a busy intersection in the shape of a Y. On one side stood a fleet of silver and blue patrol cars; on another was the visitors' parking area. I couldn't see what was in the back.

It never occurred to me they'd have anything as mundane as visitors' parking. I suppose I thought trips to the station house were made by people who were marched in, gnashing their teeth, the way Grant and I had been.

I parked out front and was checking myself out in the rearview mirror when I heard a tap on the driver's side window. I lowered the window.

"You look good," he said. "You're early."

"If you're here, that makes you early, too."

Three blocks away was Sabatini's, the restaurant where Mike O'Malley and I had agreed to have lunch.

"Should I leave the car here, or should we drive?"

"Drive." He walked around to the passenger side door and I popped the lock to let him in. "Good safety measure."

"Habit, I guess, from living in New York."

When I'd invited Mike for lunch, I'd had an ulterior motive. I wanted to pick his brain, and I wanted to do it in neutral territory, not at the police station or the Paradise Diner. Being around Babe didn't automatically make me more sarcastic, but for some reason I always was. Maybe it was something in the coffee, but most of our exchanges at the diner started out fun and wisecracky and then escalated, or descended, depending on how you looked at it. I wanted to have a civilized conversation with Mike that lasted as long as an entire meal and quietly, unemotionally get some answers.

Sabatini's was a good place to do it. Great location, free parking, and nothing to make us lapse into our old patterns of behavior. And the food was terrific. Pete number two was in a class by himself when it came to breakfast and desserts, but he had a way to go before he could touch Sabatini's bucatini con sarde or their orrechiette con broccoli. The waiter brought menus and, in minutes, our drink orders: an iced tea for O'Malley and a pinot grigio for me.

"Imagine my surprise when you called and asked me to lunch," O'Malley said, unfolding his napkin. "And here."

It came as something of a surprise to me, too. But Babe kept telling me I should talk to the cops about the tipster who'd informed on Caroline. O'Malley might share some information in a friendly, nonthreatening setting.

He ordered the linguine with clam sauce, and I went with the orrechiette. At the same time, we motioned for the waiter to remove the bread basket.

"So you *are* watching your weight," I said, starting with a safe subject. He did look a bit slimmer since we'd first met, but I wasn't sure if that was weight loss or my own revised notion of what an average body type was since my move from the city.

"Just a bit. It's mostly an increase in exercise. My dad's doing better, so we've been trying to get out for the odd walk after I get home from work."

"I'm glad to hear it."

We chatted so pleasantly all during lunch that when the waiter came to clear our plates, I realized I hadn't surreptitiously slipped in any of the questions I'd wanted to ask.

I let Mike babble on with mildly amusing anecdotes about the new guys on the force, particularly the one who had nearly shot himself with his own gun. It was going well. I hadn't gotten to my agenda yet, but I was getting there. I persuaded him to stay for espresso.

"I guess things have cooled off for you in Springfield," he said, twisting a strip of lemon.

The phrasing was strange. "What do you mean?"

"If you're reduced to having lunch with me, the rest of the natives must be giving you the cold shoulder."

"Don't sell yourself short. I'm fine. In fact, Becka Reynolds and I have actually gotten closer since this whole unfortunate business with Caroline. I may work on her garden next season. She's got bamboo — challenging but beautiful. She also warned me to watch out for the speed trap on Chesterfield." Now *I* was babbling, but gently steering the conversation in the direction I'd wanted it to go.

"She said you sent the rookies there to write their first tickets — that way they were no longer virgins. Is that true?" Inwardly, I

179

was beaming, proud of the smooth transition I was making to the first question on my list. "I got a speeding ticket once in Virginia. I was driving to Florida with a pal on my birthday. The road was so wide and empty, I didn't realize how fast I was going. I was certain the cop would let me slide when he looked at my license and saw what day it was. He didn't. What do you guys really do with all that information when you check someone driver's license, anyway?" The speeding ticket was the first thing to go wrong for Caroline. Maybe Mike would reveal information that I could use.

I was feeling pretty clever about how I'd slipped that in so naturally. Mike was less impressed with my subtlety. He gunned his espresso, his smile vanishing with the hot liquid.

"You could have been honest and just asked me outright. You didn't need to spend eighty dollars on lunch — because I *am* going to leave you here with the check." Clearly it was not as subtle as I'd thought. O'Malley was pissed. He thought we were picking up on his food-as-foreplay conversation from the diner and instead I was pumping him for information like one of the reporters we'd all been avoiding.

He pushed away from the table and stood

up, wiping his mouth with the cloth napkin and tossing it on the table. The waiter rushed over to see what was wrong.

"She'll take the check. Will you excuse us for a minute?" The waiter backed away. He'd witnessed scenes in the restaurant before.

"If we have any suspicions, we run it through the system to see if the driver has any history — frequent violations, arrests, outstanding warrants, convictions. We can even see if the person has done time anywhere. In Caroline's case, she would have just gotten a ticket. Since officially there is no record of a Caroline Sturgis before her marriage. Had we looked, we would have found nothing. Which in and of itself might have sent up a flare. But we didn't look. Any other questions or have I earned my lunch?"

With that, he pointedly said good-bye to the maître d' and not to me. The waiter brought the faux leather folder with the check. O'Malley was right. Seventy-eight fifty, not including the tip. I pocketed the receipt and shook my head, wondering how my strategy for a nonconfrontational exchange with O'Malley had gone so horribly wrong. Unlike real estate, location had nothing to do with it.

Unless I could talk to Caroline herself — if she'd even agree to it — my plan to help the Sturgises and clear my name would be hopeless. The scraps of information I was picking up seemed to be leading nowhere. May be the newcomers were involved, but may be not. Chances are I was playing P.I. and investigating a man of the cloth and an Eagle Scout, neither of whom had anything to do with Caroline Sturgis. But Caroline was scheduled to be extradited to Michigan some time today; for all I knew, she'd already left.

I'd dropped the data plan on my phone to save a few bucks, so I needed a computer and the latest Caroline news ASAP to help me decide whether to drive to Bridgeport or just go home, where I'd console myself with a large tumbler of cheap but cheerful wine.

The Paradise was the closest place I knew of with a computer I could use, twenty minutes closer than my house and near the highway if I did decide to make the trek to Bridgeport. Two long semis blocked most of the parking spots but I was able to slide in between them, trusting that the drivers were so skilled they wouldn't squish my Jeep when pulling out.

Babe wasn't there. Eyebrow Girl told me

she was on a break, and motioned to Babe's den behind the diner. I sprinted around to the back door and knocked.

"Babe, you in there?" I called.

"Over here."

She stood, arms folded, wearing elbow-length rubber gloves, behind a lattice fence near the Dumpster. She was up to her knees in garbage and papers. "This better not be Countertop Man again. Otherwise, when I find him I'm going to douse him with waste vegetable oil, strap him down, and let the raccoons get him." Babe had a vindictive side — or at the very least a vivid imagination.

I offered to help clean up but told her I needed to use her computer first.

"This isn't a home-shopping jones, is it?" she asked, unlocking the door, peeling off her gloves, and flopping down on one of the sofas. "Because there are support groups for that."

I assured Babe it wasn't.

She logged on and then I searched both Caroline Sturgis and Monica Weithorn. Pages of the inevitable before and after pix loaded — Caroline at a charity function, Monica's class picture. Caroline at the Historical Society gala, Monica's mug shot. There she was, side by side with her doppelgänger. Frisky, yes, maybe even a little slutty for a teenager, but a drug kingpin?

Caroline/Monica already had a Wikipedia page. Astonishing. Who had the time to do this stuff? There was also a Free Caroline page started by a cannabis club that admitted it had nothing to do with her or her family; she'd quickly become a symbol to people on both sides of the drug issue. I scrolled through the rest of the junk items until I saw a article posted a few hours earlier on WTIC, the local news radio's Web site: *Fugitive Mom Returned to Michigan.* Caroline was gone.

Eighteen

How I disappeared. The last driver took me for a runaway, escaping an abusive stepfather. She looked me up and down and decided she knew my story the way people do all the time. I'd done it myself. She assumed my gaunt face was the product of mistreatment at home, not bad prison food, and she thought my calloused hands were the result of punishing household chores, not the harsh chemicals in the prison laundry. I let her think that. For the previous two days nothing I'd said was the truth, and I was getting better at lying. She gave me a bag of trail mix, a pair of woolen gloves, and the best advice I'd gotten in my young life, certainly better than anything from that jerk lawyer.

She said it wasn't enough just to hope that someone couldn't follow you, you had to actively feed misinformation into whatever system you thought they'd use to track you. I had to stay away from everything and everyone I formerly knew or loved. She sounded as if she knew what she was talking about. Maybe she'd left an unhappy marriage or a difficult past. Who knew? But she had me thinking about what I could or couldn't do next.

There could be no tearful late-night calls to my brother, no showing up on old friend's doorstep. No registering for school or doing anything that required me to give my social security number. It was easier back in the eighties. I don't know how someone would do it now.

I was afraid to throw away my driver's license and passport for fear of leaving a trail, so I kept them. Besides, maybe I could use them. I'd already toughened up and learned a lot, but I needed a plan. First and foremost I needed to clean up. I'd been on the road since that first night at the motel in Michigan and I stank.

The ladies' room at the Port Authority wasn't as disgusting as I thought it would be. When I saw my reflection in the cloudy mirror, I teared up but didn't let myself cry. The washroom attendant didn't seem surprised when I took a poor man's bath in the sink with my stolen washcloth and a sliver of soap that had all the weight of a matchbook. I dried off with the hand dryer. The attendant warned me to keep my bags close and wear the shoulder strap across my chest so there was less chance of its getting ripped off. I must have looked like Alice in Wonderland, the only thing missing was the pinafore.

I took my time lingering in the bathroom, because I hadn't a clue as to what I'd do next. Near the diaper changing table there were stacks of flyers — social service agencies, suicide prevention hotlines, employment opportunities from an escort service, and a flyer from St. Ann's Community Kitchen. I took one of each and shoved them in my bag.

"St. Ann's is four blocks south of here. Make a left when you get outside," the woman said. "You don't wanna go to that other place. Go to St. Ann's. They got chicken stew on Fridays." As if I knew what day it was.

The sign on St. Ann's said the kitchen was open from 7 to 10 A.M., 12 to 2 P.M., and 5 to 8 P.M. It was 3 P.M. I heard the rain before I felt it, pelting my brother's cheap nylon duffel that held everything I owned and was already starting to show signs of fabric fatigue from having been dragged on highways and thrown into the backs of trucks. I was showing signs of fatigue, too. Then it really started to pour and I figured no one would mind if I ducked into the church to wait out the storm. Isn't that what they were for? Sanctuary?

A priest was rearranging items on the altar,

moving candlesticks or something. I didn't want him to see me still there two hours later, so when he went behind the altar, I crept into the confessional booth and pulled the carved door closed behind me. Then I fell asleep.

There was no anger or judgment in the priest's voice when he woke me two hours later.

"You look troubled. Would you like to talk?" The same words that other priest had said to me at the stable in Connecticut.

The priest at St. Ann's led me to the church basement, where dinner was being served. I took a tray and waited in a line that reminded me of a school cafeteria, albeit one with a down-at-the-heels student body. I was starving. I loaded up on sides and tried not to be too piggy with the meat, which didn't look that appetizing anyway. Then I sat at a long table opposite a girl about my age. She had a choppy haircut and wore a lot of makeup, and I could see a pack of Marlboros sticking out of the pocket of her denim jacket. Again I felt like a child. We shoveled in the food in silence. She put a cigarette in her mouth but knew the rules well enough to not light it. Finally she spoke to me. "Need a place?"

NINETEEN

I suppose only the wildly optimistic in Springfield were surprised. I saw *Les Mis.* Turn your life around? It doesn't matter. Maybe it shouldn't. I'd never really thought about it before. I just knew Caroline Sturgis and couldn't see what purpose it would serve to have her making license plates in the big house for the next fifteen years.

I turned off Babe's computer. It was time for that drink, and Babe Chinnery obliged, pulling a bottle of Jack Daniel's from a small wooden cabinet under the window in her office. I'd had a Jack night once a few years back. All I remember was that I forgot where I parked my car, and it was a damn good thing, since driving would have been suicidal.

"What do you have for lightweights?" I asked.

"How about a dark and stormy — rum and ginger beer?"

"Maybe just coffee for now."

Babe locked up her office and we took our time walking to the diner's front entrance. If I hadn't spent the time going to Mossdale's and blowing eighty dollars on lunch, maybe I could have driven to Bridgeport and convinced Caroline to see me, but it was too late to speculate.

"Something happened that day," I said. "She got a ticket, saw the priest, and then came here. However startling those first two events might have been, they didn't put her out of commission. She was pretty happy when she got here."

"Yeah, she came in to see you, you talked, she started to leave, and the trucker hit on her," Babe said. "That long-haired guy who tried to help Terry?" I didn't know who she was talking about, then realized the waitress with the bolt in her eyebrow was Terry.

"She flung a tray of coffee cups and nearly decapitated someone? You were there, remember?"

"Right. The guy who said Caroline looked *familiar,*" I said, trying to dredge up a mental image.

"Please, I hear that ten times a day. It only registers when it's one of my regular customers and I'm worried that it's early stage Alzheimer's."

"Maybe he wasn't throwing her a line. Maybe she looked familiar because he knew her back in Michigan when she was Monica Weithorn. Maybe she was upset because he looked familiar to her." Could be. It was right after that that Caroline made her hasty departure, giving some phony excuse to her friends outside.

All I remembered was that the trucker had long hair and wore a baseball hat, but Terry had spoken with him. He'd even gotten a laugh out of her, which was the first time I'd ever seen her teeth. Maybe something about him stuck with her.

"He was with another driver, someone you knew, wasn't he?"

"Retro Joe," she said. "No one knows if that's his real name — that's just what everyone calls him. One of the long haulers. I can almost see the truck, red logo, two letters interlocked. I'll get it but it may take some time. But those guys don't always drive with the same partners."

Inside the diner, we escorted Terry to a booth and sat her down to ask her a few questions.

"What is this, the Spanish Inquisition? You guys are worse than my parents. I don't know. I wasn't paying attention. I dropped the tray and he helped me clean up until

Babe came over. It was two seconds. No great meeting of the minds."

I went into schmooze mode. "Come on, Terry. You're an observant girl. And sensitive. You write songs — you notice things about people." She looked down, working hard to live up to my flattering assessment of her powers of perception and conjure up his image. All three of us were.

"He had long hair and a baseball hat. He said something that made you laugh," I prompted. "What did he say?"

"It was nothing. Something stupid, like I had a nice wrist move. He was a champion Frisbee player when he was in college, so he would know. It just seemed like a dumb thing to say at the time, but it was perfect. Better than asking if I was okay. I hate when people ask me that."

(Note to self: When we're finished, don't ask if she's okay.)

"Did he mention where he went to school?" I asked.

"Man, it was all of two minutes. It wasn't a date. He said it was cold and they jumped around a lot to keep warm." She ratcheted down and gave it some more thought. "His friend called him JW — he was with Retro Joe." Then she made an up-and-down motion with one hand, almost as if she were playing a washboard. "And he had something strange about his lip. You could barely see it because of the facial hair. A scar — like the guy who played Johnny Cash in that movie."

"He had a cleft lip?"

"I don't know what you call it. It's kind of cute, like a little line. And his hat had an ornate D on it."

"*D* like in Dodgers?" Babe asked.

A voice over my shoulder said, "No," and three heads turned in its direction at the same time. It was one of the truckers.

He peeled off a few bills and left them on the counter. "*D* like in Tigers. *Detroit* Tigers," he said.

TWENTY

Detroit was big, but Caroline/Monica's hometown wasn't. The papers had said she was from Newtonville, one of the smaller specks on the MapQuest page, and a Google search made me think people probably didn't go there unless they were visiting relatives or were passing through to get to somewhere else. Blue-collar residents commuted to jobs in the bigger cities or simply packed up and moved when their jobs did. The ones who stayed were rich or old, or just didn't have any other place to go. It seemed like a lot of other towns — nice enough, maybe even wonderful forty years ago, but now still lovely on the surface but quietly dying.

I'd start my Internet research with Caroline's high school. The papers had said Caroline had been a senior at Newtonville High in 1981. How many kids could have been in her graduating class in a town that size? Or were enrolled during the four years she attended? And how many of them could have had a cleft lip? Wasn't that pretty rare?

I found the school online and ordered yearbooks from all four years that Caroline attended. If I wasn't successful, I'd have to eat the cost (and the cost of my eighty-dollar lunch with O'Malley), but if I found out who the tipster was, I knew Grant would reimburse me. And I had my fingers crossed that a pretty and popular girl like Caroline would be in lots of pictures and I'd get a handle on who some of her friends were. There was no guarantee our trucker who talked to Caroline even went to high school with her, but it was the only lead I had from Michigan.

Who knew how long the yearbooks would take to arrive? In the meantime, I took the plunge and said yes to one of the biggest time suckers on the Internet, highschoolmemories.com. I signed in pretending to be Monica Weithorn.

For free, I got the tantalizing "Old friends are trying to find you" page with the names strategically blurred. Of course they are. All those people who ignored you or made your life miserable when you were sixteen really wanted to find you. Why? To make sure that they were still cooler than you? For more specific information, I'd have to upgrade my membership. Fifty bucks got me the whole enchilada and a bag of chips. Every classmate's name in alphabetical order for the four years Caroline had been enrolled, even the old varsity team schedules and records. And updated background info on everyone who'd been dumb enough to enter their current coordinates.

No one I knew used highschoolmemories.com. Well okay, one person, but she was recently divorced and looking for love, or a reasonable facsimile. Why she thought she'd find it among her former high school classmates was beyond me. Most people would rather eat ground glass than relive their high school years.

I printed out the list of Caroline's classmates and planned to search the likeliest candidates on Facebook — athletes, cheerleaders, and those with the same zip codes as Caroline had had. I didn't know the demographics of the average Facebook user, and it was a long shot that there would be a lot of overlap with Caroline's classmates, but it would keep me busy until the yearbooks arrived, and I might trip over somebody with the initials JW. In my former career I had unearthed more than a few good stories by just doggedly pursuing trails that others had dropped.

I had my own dormant Facebook page that I'd started, under protest, three years earlier. Most of my "friends" were old television contacts, and once I stopped being interested in who had his hand in what cookie jar and who had signed what deal, I stopped checking my Facebook page for invitations and new friend requests, but I was still out there in cyberspace with a three-year-old picture and outdated contact info. Just as well — I looked younger and wasn't as easy to find, a winning combination.

Maybe I'd get lucky and locate that one perky gal who considers it her mission to reconnect people whether they want it or not. Every school, business, or organization has one, the person who organizes things no one else wanted to bother with — the uncool activities, the obscure charity events. (Hi, want to volunteer for the National Frankfurter Finger Weenie Roast?)

At my school her name was Rena. She wore an ear-to-ear grin from the first day of high school to graduation. A relative of mine, from the cynical side of the family, claims only babies and idiots are that happy. In Rena's case, she might have been right. Rena always seemed to be cradling a clipboard in her arms as if the sign-up sheet was her baby. She was probably working for a cruise line now, with a steady stream of new people to annoy every week.

I started with the school and the word *cheerleader*. Two female names popped up but no pictures — presumably they wanted to be remembered as they were, ponytailed, flying through the air, no cellulite, eternally young. Perversely, I was glad. Who wanted to think cheerleaders from twenty-five years ago were still as beautiful and limber as they were back then? No male names appeared.

Next I tried the football and baseball teams. The hat was a Detroit Tigers hat. Maybe our man was an athlete and not just a fan. T hat coughed up pages of names to scroll through; either Newtonville's male students were all on Facebook, or every water boy and equipment manager claimed he played a valuable role on some team. And this was interesting: the men were more likely to post pictures of themselves and the women posted avatars or nothing. No matter how saggy, bald, or tubby they got, the males thought they still looked hot. Self-esteem or self-delusion?

I was up to the *F*s and getting a little punchy. There was nothing in the fridge, so I ordered a pizza and a two-liter bottle of diet soda for dinner. Good food was going to take time and mine would be there in less than twenty-five minutes or it would be free. My finances being what they were, I found myself hoping for a tiny fender bender somewhere between here and Armando's Pizza Coliseum, nothing serious, just enough to hold up traffic and make the pizza arrive in twenty-seven minutes.

I stared at my computer screen, wondering how else I might find the man who'd bumped into Caroline if I got to the Zs and didn't see a guy with a cleft lip. The customer who knew his sports teams also knew Retro Joe, and said that these days Joe was driving for Hutchinson Shipping. If my other research came up empty, I'd try Hutchinson, but I wasn't relishing that conversation. *"Hi, do any of your truckers have scarred or cleft lips?" I'd* have hung up on me.

For her part, Babe posted a note on the Paradise bulletin board claiming the man had left something at the diner. Not entirely true but not entirely false either, he'd left a lot of questions.

The bell rang, I snapped out of my blue screen stupor, grabbed my wallet, and headed for the door. I glanced at my watch — shoot, twenty-three minutes. When I opened the door I saw Mike O'Malley standing there holding a pizza box and a paper bag.

"What are you doing here?"

"Delivering your pizza," he said, inspecting the receipt that was taped to the top of the box. "I thought you ate healthy food. Cake for lunch the other day and now this. Has life in Springfield totally corrupted you?"

"What have you done with the pizza man?" I asked, looking down the driveway.

"Ran him off the road and stole his pie." He waited for me to at least smile, but I was too tired. "You used to have a sense of humor. I stopped him for speeding, around the corner."

"And he bribed you with my dinner?"

"Of course not. Technically, I'm off the clock, so he got away with a strongly worded warning. I paid for your pizza and this swill that you're planning to drink. Can I come in or are we going to let this pie get cold? Truce?"

I should have just tipped him and sent him on his way after his less-than-polite exit at lunch, but there was something about him that always made me open the door and invite him in.

Of course, he was one of the few single

men I knew in Springfield between the ages of eighteen and seventy-five. It could have been that. Or maybe it was something else. He was a good man: he looked after his elderly father, he had a dog, he brought me food. He had all the outward signs of normalcy that usually appealed to women, but maybe that was it. I didn't ordinarily gravitate toward normal. I wanted the tortured artist. The driven genius. The explorer with just one more mountain to climb. And here I was, once again trying to picture this pale, thinning-on-top suburban policeman naked on a fur rug in front of a crackling fire. There was no denying it — we had the worst timing since that couple on the *Titanic.*

"What are you smiling at?" he said.

"Nothing. When did you get so health conscious?" I said, shaking off the image. I shooed him in and led him past the door to my office. He peeked in.

"You're working late."

"Actually I'm being interrupted late. Is this supposed to make up for stiffing me at lunch?"

"Yes."

We went upstairs to the kitchen and I dropped the greasy cardboard box on a round oak table I'd scored at a flea market the previous summer. The last time Mike O'Malley was here, my kitchen had been ransacked, with all the drawers and cabinets open and their contents strewn about. Despite that, he knew where everything was located. He set the table as if he lived there and we sat down to dinner every night.

"I think the garlic powder is downstairs."

"No worries, I can do without it."

We were being very careful with other, not wanting to get into another of our volatile and incomprehensible dustups. The tiptoeing generally lasted about three minutes. According to my kitchen clock, we were at two minutes and forty-five seconds.

"What were you doing around the corner?" I asked. "Am I under surveillance?" I meant it as a joke, but it came out sounding too snippy. He let it slide.

"No. The pizza delivery boy was speeding on Longview Road. I just happened to catch up with him here. Fortuitous, since I'm now off duty and strangely in the mood for one of our pizza dates." He separated a slice and deftly wiggled it away from the others without adding too much extra cheese. Was this a date?

We agreed that drivers on my street were reckless fools and it was only a matter of time before some poor soul, driver or pedestrian, was sent flying into the wet-lands, never to be seen again, body parts scattered by foraging critters. We discussed the renovation of the one and only Chinese restaurant in a twenty-mile radius and the latest exhibit on Polish immigrants at the historical society. What was next? The weather? The merits of the Mets' newest acquisition? Caroline was the eight-hundred-pound gorilla in the room with us, whether we said her name out loud or not. As usual with O'Malley, I blinked first.

"I'm sorry if you think I asked you to lunch only to pump you for information."

"Well, didn't you?"

"Grant Sturgis asked me to find the tipster. That's the digging I said I'd do, and it kind of backfired."

O'Malley picked the pepperoni disks off his slice and stacked them like poker chips in one corner of the cardboard box. "I take it that was before he thought it was you who informed on her?"

"Yes, wise guy. Before everyone thought it was me." Stay calm, I told myself. If you're going to ask someone for his help, try not to call him names first. "I know it's not your case, but isn't there anything you can tell me?"

O'Malley added to what I'd already

learned. Caroline was arrested for attempting to sell drugs to an undercover cop. That much anyone with a newspaper or an Internet connection knew. Her attorney claimed it was entrapment — the cop was a young woman and they were at a party. Apparently, Caroline offered the woman a joint and the woman insisted on paying. The next day the police came to the football field and arrested her in the middle of practice.

"I don't know anything about the law, but that sounds like a trap to me."

"Harder drugs were found in Caroline's gym bag, as was forty-seven thousand dollars in cash. She'd been under surveillance for some time. Seems like half the student body was on speed at one time or another, and what better way to distribute than through one of the most popular girls in school?"

I couldn't believe it. Our Caroline?

"But why would she do it?"

"There could have been any number of reasons — money, wanting to look cooler than the other kids, boredom. I'm a bachelor. I don't know why kids do the things they do. I'm just telling you what I heard and read."

"Where?" I asked.

In the police report. O'Malley had seen it

and I needed to. I didn't know about the past, but police records were public these days. In Springfield, all I'd have to do was walk into the station house and ask for it, like the mother of that unruly thirteen-year-old. A decades-old report in another state where I'd never been and didn't know anyone was going to be harder. Certainly for a gardener, but maybe not for a journalist. I thought of asking Lucy for help, but I'd have to tread carefully. In this instance, she was one of them. I didn't want her contributing to the feeding frenzy surrounding the Sturgises, although it was naive to imagine I could stop it.

At least now I had something tangible to look for, and who knew, maybe my online research would turn something up. I couldn't wait to hustle O'Malley out of the house and get back to the computer.

I inhaled three slices of pizza and washed them down with copious amounts of diet soda guaranteed to ruin my teeth and the lining of my stomach.

"You were hungry," O'Malley said, working on slice number two, pacing himself and peeling off excess strands of cheese.

Not really, but I hoped that if the food was gone, O'Malley would leave soon after. He finally took the hint.

"I can't stop you from looking for this person, but I don't see what good it will do anyone."

He didn't, but I did. It was my reputation and my new life, almost as much as it was Caroline's.

Soon after Mike left I resumed my Facebook research. The *M*s were promising because there were just so many, but no one looked remotely like the trucker I'd seen at the diner. Nothing at all until the *W*s, someone named Jeff Warren. I'd assumed the name JW referred to his first and middle names. The picture he posted was of a Tigers shirt and hat. I reedited my Facebook profile and became a Detroit Tigers fan. Then I friended Jeff. Within four hours he'd confirmed me as a friend and I learned that he worked for Hutchinson Shipping and was currently on some mind "making a dead-head run on some mind-numbing stretch of highway between Maine and North Carolina." Which would mean he'd recently driven through Connecticut.

TWENTY-ONE

Before I even brushed my teeth I ran downstairs and turned on the computer to check for Facebook messages. Had Jeff Warren posted something? Did he say where he was? It was ridiculous — I felt like a fifteen-year-old girl waiting for "Billy" to ask me to the prom. I showered and dressed but punctuated every morning ritual with a return to the computer and my Facebook page. It was as if I were tethered to the damn thing and some unseen force was reeling me back in every ten or fifteen minutes.

When I was in the television business, my company had an account with an online outfit called Background.com. It was pretty scary that something like Background.com even existed. I hadn't thought of it that way in my previous life when I had different notions of the definition of privacy, but the fact that anyone, anywhere could simply plug in your name and get your phone number and vital statistics made me want to close every credit card account, shred every piece of paper that had my name on it, and become a survivalist somewhere in Montana.

The production company used it to vet possible hires and to confirm the reliability of story sources. It wasn't a given that you'd get all the info you needed on a source, but often you could find out if someone who'd been spilling his guts to you had any hidden agenda or ax to grind. Once I'd learned that a so-called witness to improprieties at a day care center had himself spent time in jail on a lesser but similar charge. It had saved me days and an embarrassing story, but more important, it had saved his potential victims a lifetime of having to repudiate untrue allegations. They never learned how close they came to being ruined.

Instead of checking Facebook for the umpteenth time, I went to the Background Web site. Our passwords used to be changed monthly but were sometimes repeated since Betsy, the department head, wasn't quite as paranoid as management thought she should be. And it wasn't easy to keep coming up with memorable words or names every four weeks when you'd been doing it for years and had passwords for just about everything.

When I had left the company the password was Pyewacket1250. Betsy was an animal lover, and Pyewacket was the name of the cat in a movie she was crazy about. The twelve fifty was a constant, a required numerical addition to the password. That part was easy to remember — it was our address. I took a chance and tried to sign on with the old password. No luck.

I considered looking through the newspapers, trying to find a more recent film with animals in it, but how would I know? — They rarely got top billing unless you went back to *Marley & Me,* and Betsy was more of a cat person than a dog lover. I knew it would mean tipping my hand, but it was a heckuva lot simpler to call Lucy Cavanaugh.

Lucy and I went way back. She'd have liked us to go way forward, too, but I was still committed to my five-year plan for Dirty Business. If I couldn't make it work, then maybe I'd see about a return to the big city and the career I'd left behind. *I can get us a production deal. We'd be a two-woman team and just use the freelancers we liked and only when we needed them. Our lives will be a write-off.* I could hear her sales pitch even as I dialed.

The company we'd both worked for had flirted with hard-hitting news stories during my tenure, but I couldn't take credit for that. I left during the embryonic stage of non-news news. Now there was more money and ratings in missing coeds, baby bumps — real or imagined — and celebrities misbehaving. Those were the things people seemed to care about, and it was one of the reasons I was not unhappy to get out.

Lucy's assistant, Courtney, always sounded disappointed when she heard it was me on the phone and not a colleague or source about to drop some bomb that would make them all famous. Courtney might have been nicer to me if she knew that I was on the fringes of one of those salacious stories, but I resisted the urge to impress her. She put me through.

"Luce, I need a favor." I was interrupting her, of course — I could hear her keyboard clicking. It was nearly impossible to get her undivided attention.

"What's up?" she asked. "I'm checking on a chocolatier who's being accused of using less cocoa in his candies than he claims. I think we got him."

I felt so much safer knowing that someone was tracking down the real evildoers. "I'm calling about Caroline Sturgis," I said.

The clicking stopped, and for a moment I wondered if I had crossed over to the dark side.

Lucy knew Caroline had been extradited to Michigan; everyone who cared to, knew. It was what I would have considered junk news if I hadn't been tangentially involved. A judge there had scheduled a hearing to be held in three weeks. Until that time Caroline would be making her home in a Michigan jail. I tried to imagine her in a cell instead of in her pristine kitchen with its whiteboard tracking everyone's activities. What would her new bulletin board read? Walk around courtyard, make hand-carved shivs, design tattoos, join gang?

"They confiscated her knitting needles," Lucy told me. I could tell she was reading from a screen. "I guess they didn't think she was a threat to herself or anyone else in the Bridgeport jail, but things are more formal where she is now. Maybe they'll let her crochet. How much damage can she inflict with a plastic crochet hook? Although I suppose you could kill someone with a sharpened pencil if you stuck it in that right spot." An interesting theory. I'd have to bring my pencil case the next time I went out at night.

"I need to use Background. Do you guys

still have an account?" I whispered, as if someone other than Lucy could hear me.

"You're wasting your time." The keyboard clicking resumed. "I already plugged her name in. Just a few old phone numbers under Monica's name and five under Caroline's — her home number and four cells which look like hers, her husband's, and the two kids'. I did get the criminal records, though, and the original arrest report. You want them?"

Sure I did. Lucy sent them and the phone numbers as an E-mail attachment. The police report had been copied so many times it was probably six generations away from the original and nearly impossible to read, but I printed it out anyway.

"Caroline was arrested with two others, Kate Gustafson and Edward Donnelley. I checked them out but nothing much came up," Lucy said. "She's dead and he's out of prison. Gone."

"I need to look up someone else. Betsy will never know and it won't cost the company a dime. Can you give me the new password?"

Silence.

"C'mon, it's five hundred dollars to open a Background account — you know I can't afford that. Just this once?"

The clicking stopped.

"You know I'm not supposed to. Why don't you tell me who you're looking for and let me do it?" she asked.

"I can't tell you just now. Later, I promise. If I'm right I don't want to scare anyone off with major media coming in."

"Flatterer. And do I get to use any of the info at some point in the future?"

"Absolutely."

After a pause she spoke.

"Do we?"

"Do we what?" I asked. "Have a deal? Yes, we do."

"*Dewey*. Dewey1250."

TWENTY-TWO

Warren. It had to be Warren. It couldn't be something less common like Wozniacki or Wittgenstein, so he would be easier to find. Background.com had phone records for fifty-three men named Jeff or Jeffrey Warren. Seven of the fifty-three were Michiganders. I didn't know the Upper Peninsula from Upper Volta, but three of the seven had zip codes that were reasonably close to the one I'd found for Caroline, and luckily there were only two high schools in her town.

I reminded myself that when I searched my own name, I found nothing except entries about Billie Holiday and Judy Holliday, so I wasn't optimistic, but it was a place to start.

All I had to do was to call three total strangers. Easy, right? Except that electronically invading someone's privacy was one thing. Given the anonymity of the Internet, it was simply a matter of pressing keys on a keyboard. If the information was available online, people had somehow made the decision to put it out there for all to see, hadn't they? That's what I told myself anyway. I was less sure I could pull off this level of snooping on the phone. *Hi, I was just wondering if you ratted out my favorite client?* Ugh, I was starting to sound like a character from *The Sopranos.*

I tried to channel the telemarketers who routinely and breathlessly interrupted my dinners and at-home movie nights. Two seconds of silence and then a friendly voice suggesting they were someone I knew before they launched into their pitches: "This is Heather?" as if they're asking you, waiting for you to commit yourself by continuing to listen or, worse still, asking "Heather who?"

What was it that kept people on the phone, as opposed to automatically hanging up the way I did when I answered the phone and heard those first few seconds of dead air? How do the good ones hook people? Bank error in your favor? You may already have won? We're calling about the warranty on your car? It had been a long time since anyone I knew had been taken in by one of those ploys.

A lost item was a possibility. Babe had used it on her bulletin board, but on the phone I'd have to say what it was. It had to be something most people owned that you could conceivably be without for a day or two without missing or freaking, so anything like a wallet or driver's license was out. Terry had said the guy was wearing expensive sunglasses, Oakley's. I'd give them a shot. If it sounded ridiculous when I said it out loud, I'd come up with something more inventive for the next call.

Telemarketers generally sounded as if they were smiling — like they were drugged or lobotomized (less like babies or idiots in this instance). I smiled. I dialed. A woman answered the phone. Expecting a man to pick up, I hadn't thought that far ahead. Astonishingly enough she didn't buy my story about having found old Jeff's sunglasses.

Somewhere in between being called a skanky ho and a heartless home wrecker I considered stopping her, but it wasn't really me she was trashing and she obviously had buckets of venom inside her, so I let her vent. Given some of the details she was throwing out, I'd have been very surprised if this Jeff Warren hadn't been cheating on his wife, so maybe she had a right. She had dates, locations, and all the particulars of a tryst in Milwaukee that her Jeff and I were supposed to have taken together. Then she got personal. She made disparaging remarks about my hair and my alleged cup size. It went further south from there, to my butt and hips and the problems I undoubtedly had with them. How she knew this was beyond me. Still, I stayed on the line. I was fascinated by her lung capacity. Perhaps she was a swimmer?

My family was scum. She could tell by my voice that I, too, was trash. (I'd liked to have asked, "How exactly?" but didn't see how I could fit it in.) I was dangerously close to switching allegiance. No wonder her Jeff fooled around — the woman was a harridan. I gave her thirty seconds to come up for air. If the confirmation of Jeff's infidelity had driven her crazy, it had been a short drive and I'd done enough penance for it.

"Excuse me, ma'am?" I said. How many adulteresses called their lovers' wife *ma'am?* "I think I must have dialed the wrong number." It stopped her cold — but just long enough for her to fill her tank and start again.

"Like hell you did. Don't give me that ma'am crap — and don't think you're the first —"

I put the phone back in the cradle and prayed she didn't have the star 69 option on her telephone service.

The next call was marginally better. This time I did my best to sound sweet and wholesome. But according to this Jeff's roommate, Jeff was touring with a production of *Jersey Boys* and always wore Oliver Peoples's prescription sunglasses with dark blue lenses. They were his trademark. It was unlikely that he was the man I was looking for.

"You didn't really find a pair of sunglasses, did you?" the roommate asked. Jeez, was I that transparent? "Listen, you sound like a nice person. If he's hiding out from you, honey, it's probably over. It's time to move on. I know from whence I speak." I let him tell me the story of his breakup with Ethan and thanked him for being so supportive. Jeff was lucky to have such a sensitive and understanding partner.

So far I'd been excoriated for being a slut and pitied for being a dumpee who was all but stalking a former lover. If I didn't have such a positive self-image, I might have let those two calls discourage me.

There was one number left. I didn't know what my next step would be or how I'd search the other forty-nine states if all the Michigan calls were as unsuccessful as the first two.

The phone rang ten times. I was just about to hang up when an older woman answered. Yes, her son was always misplacing things. The old sweetheart gave me a laundry list of the things this Jeff Warren had lost since grade school, including a jersey signed by his coach and the five starters on his high school basketball team, two of whom went on the play for the Spartans. I was impressed that she knew who they were, but obviously she was a hoops fan. He'd lost a collection of commemorative first edition stamps given to him by his uncle Lou, who'd spent forty years working for the post office, three jobs — one that the aforementioned Uncle Lou had had to pull strings to get him — and two wives. So she wasn't surprised that he'd lost his expensive sunglasses and wasn't I a dear for trying to return them. But Jeff wasn't home now. He was on the road, driving a truck up and down the East Coast. He got the job through one of his ex-brothers-in-law, Leroy, who worked for Hutchinson Shipping. Bingo.

Mrs. Helen Warren clearly didn't get many phone calls. Jeff's ex-wives never stayed in touch, but that was probably a good thing because they were worthless gold diggers and never really appreciated her boy. Her daughter Abby had moved to Northern California and rarely came to visit, not even for her high school reunion — just came the one time when her dad passed. Helen and Abby's relationship had been reduced to twice-yearly baskets from Harry & David on Christmas and Mother's Day, and the twins' annual class picture slipped into an envelope with just the date on the back, not even a note. It was so sad I almost hung up on her to call my own mother.

Jeff had moved his few possessions back home after the second divorce since he was now driving for a living (better money), and he was on the road so much these days it didn't make sense for him to pay rent. Especially since he was still supporting those two floozies whom she'd never liked, who had never given her grandchildren, and who'd taken him to the cleaners or, in Jeff's more modest circumstances, the launderette.

I hated to stop her; it was like stream-of-consciousness reality television. I started to picture them all standing in front of a retired judge, pointing fingers and shouting at one another until they broke for a commercial. Even though it hadn't worked the last time, I thought it time to resurrect "ma'am."

"Excuse me, ma'am?"

"Yes, dear?"

"Do you know where I can find Jeff now? Is there a cell number you can give me?"

Somehow that convinced her I was a girlfriend. She'd love to see her boy settle down with a really nice girl and I sounded like a nice girl. She asked if I had a job and I mumbled something about my own small business. My stock was rising. Twenty minutes earlier I'd been treated like a whore and then a pathetic discard. All of a sudden I'd turned into a good catch. Mrs. Warren asked what church I went to, and I struggled to remember the name of the parochial school where I had spent the worst two months of my six-year-old life.

"Sacred Heart, ma'am."

Dead silence. Obviously, Catholic wasn't as good as Protestant, but at least Jeff wasn't dating a heathen. Mrs. Warren regrouped quickly. It was okay — she was sure I was nice anyway. If I stayed on the phone with her much longer, she'd have me converted and us engaged.

She didn't know if the number she had was his latest. Jeff changed numbers a lot, and Mrs. Warren hated to cross any of them out, as if doing so was erasing a part of his life. My guess was that changing numbers was less about his adventurous lifestyle than it was about staying one step ahead of the bill collectors and his ex-wives.

"I suppose the best way to reach him right now is through Leroy." I could hear Mrs. Warren flipping through a phone book that I imagined looked like my mother's, pages falling out, slightly sticky from being in the kitchen for the last thirty years, with numbers and addresses written in blue ballpoint ink in beautiful copperplate script, except for their children's, which had been crossed out and changed over and over while everyone else's stayed the same. (Note to self: Call Mom!)

"Here it is, Leroy Donnelley."

Suddenly, my heart was racing. "Leroy Donnelley? Any relation to Edward Donnelley?"

I scribbled notes as fast as I could while Mrs. Warren gave me the extended family tree of all the Donnelleys and their kin. Off the top of her head she recited a veritable Book of Donnelley — who they'd married, who their kids were, and where they'd gone to school. If she had used the word *begat* it could not have been more biblical or more complete. It was as if I had stumbled upon the town historian.

Now, the pieces of the puzzle were falling

into place. Jeff Warren had bumped into his old high school friend, Monica, and accidentally or intentionally mentioned it to a relative of one of the people she'd been arrested with. I still wasn't sure how they found her. Warren knew she was going by the name Caroline and had been seen in Springfield, but as far as I knew, that was all.

Kate Gustafson, the other woman in the case, served only two years. After she was released, she'd been killed in a suspicious fire. The man, Eddie Donnelley, served his entire sentence, all twenty years. Could you carry a grudge for that long because one of your partners in crime had gotten away? It's been known to happen.

Mrs. Warren was still rambling on, but I felt sure I'd already gotten the lion's share of the story. Somehow I didn't think the health issues of the current crop of Donnelleys was going to help me, Grant, or Caroline; but, as is often the case with seniors when they're on the phone, if they sense you're ready to hang up, they dig in their heels and tear into another long-winded anecdote, frequently about the azaleas, the garbage-man, or something equally mundane just to keep you hanging on.

"Of course, they never did find all that

money they said was missing," she said, wheezing, daring me to hang up.

I had to hand it to her: Mama Warren knew how to tell a story. I switched my phone to the other ear, sharpened my pencil, and got comfortable. This anecdote I *did* want to hear.

Two hours later Grant Sturgis called me from a hotel room in Michigan. Caroline had told him I hadn't been the one to give away her secret, and he was calling to apologize.

I had a lot to tell him about Caroline and Jeff's accidental meeting in the diner and what I thought had happened afterward.

"But why?" he asked.

"Grant, Donnelley served twenty years in prison. Not even time off for good behavior." (I had thought everyone got time off for good behavior.) "Caroline walked away after eighteen months. And then to learn that she's been living a pretty cushy life in suburban Connecticut, it might have ticked him off. I mean, he wasn't one of life's noblemen before he went to jail. Something tells me he didn't see the error of his ways while behind bars. The man was angry."

And then there was the missing money. Mama Warren wasn't sure how much, but the police had suggested the forty-seven grand found in Caroline's gym bag was just the tip of the iceberg. Over seven hundred fifty thousand dollars was unaccounted for, the drug money having funded an extensive college sports gambling ring. A tidy sum then and not too shabby now. Maybe Donnelley had reclaimed it when he got out of prison, or maybe he couldn't find it and was looking for the person he thought still had it. Or had used it to buy a nice big house in Connecticut once she thought no one would be looking for her.

Grant was quiet. Had I gone too far? This was, after all, the woman he loved. What had he called her in a tone that suggested sainthood — "the mother of his children"? He took a deep breath.

"Except for one thing," he said. "Even if the judge and the jury didn't know it, Eddie Donnelley did and I do. Caroline was entirely innocent."

TWENTY-THREE

If half of what Grant Sturgis told me next was true, Caroline had lived through a succession of nightmarish events equaled only by Jean Valjean; right out of *Les Misérables.*

Caroline started dating Eddie Donnelley when she was a senior at Newtonville High School and he was a sophomore at Nixon County Community College. She was flattered by his attentions. He was an older man, relatively speaking, and the town was so small that, as pretty as she was, she'd already been through all the interesting boys her own age. Not in a slutty, town pump kind of way — she just had an idea of what she wanted and was quick to realize when she hadn't found it, so she kept looking.

Kate Gustafson was Eddie's ex-girlfriend, who was surprisingly cordial to her replacement. At least it was surprising to me. Where I grew up, you didn't want to be in the same time zone with your boyfriend's ex, much less hang out with her, but Newtonville, Michigan, was a far cry from Brooklyn, New York.

Attractive and popular, Caroline was a capable student but more interested in creative pursuits than academics — painting and dancing were two of her passions. Beyond the Twinkletoes ballet classes which she'd outgrown by the age of twelve, there was no dance studio in town, so Caroline turned to cheerleading. And she pursued it with a vengeance. They said she was fearless and would cheerfully and accurately fling her body into whatever formation the coach asked, landing with her trademark happy face without even breaking a sweat.

As the school's head cheerleader she went to all the varsity events on the road and was invited to every postgame party. Eddie and Kate went everywhere with her, Eddie following the school bus that carried the team and the cheerleaders, driving to the games and meets that were out of the city, with Kate tagging along, as a pal and chaperone. At least that was what they told Caroline's dad, who by that time was consoling himself for the loss of his wife every day with a quart of scotch and a six-pack of beer and every night with a hairdresser named Rita.

At first, the invitations were just for Caroline. After all, who wouldn't want the prettiest girl in school at their party? But later all three were invited because Caroline's friends could pretty much get you anything you wanted. According to Grant, unbeknownst to Caroline, they'd used her to open a whole new line of distribution for the drugs they were selling — mostly speed, some pot, and eventually heroin, at schools all over the county. Place your orders now for next week's postgame party. It didn't take long for interested parties to get involved in betting on the games. That's when the stakes were really jacked up.

When the three of them were busted, witnesses and former clients testified to the damning truth, that Caroline had been present at virtually every drug sale or buy; if she hadn't actually taken the cash and handed over the drugs, she had, in fact, introduced Eddie and Kate to most of the buyers, thereby helping them make the transaction. On paper it was hard to dispute.

Caroline's court-appointed attorney was a recent grad, two years out of law school and clearly out of his league. With all the evidence stacked against her, and Eddie and Kate pleading guilty, the lawyer convinced Caroline's dad that she should plead guilty, too. At her age and with no previous convictions, he was sure she'd be put on probation or sentenced to community service; she should throw herself on the mercy of the court.

But there was no mercy. With the help of Eddie's and Kate's well-paid attorneys, the prosecutors successfully argued that Caroline had masterminded the entire business. After all, she was the charismatic one with all the connections. And who were the others? Eddie was a troubled underachiever in his fourth year at a two-year college, and Kate, five years older than she'd originally claimed, identified herself as an actress and model, which in those days was code for *prostitute.* Caroline was the only one smart enough to have planned it all. Caroline, Eddie, and Kate were each sentenced to ten to twenty years at the Henderson Dade Correctional Facility. At the sentencing Caroline passed out.

Grant was still processing all this new information about his wife of twenty years. It was hard enough for me to believe. I couldn't imagine what he was going through.

If Caroline really was innocent, Grant needed a good attorney to reopen the case, otherwise it could be a very long time before any of us ever saw her again. At least this time she could afford the best. And an attorney could hire a professional to look for Donnelley, not a gifted amateur like me.

Grant thanked me for sticking with the job even after he'd treated me so shabbily. He insisted on paying me for my time and the yearbooks, and I made a show of protesting but not too hard. The offer was more than enough to cover my expenses and keep me in soup and big breakfasts until gardening season rolled around again in March, and I was grateful for it. Before he hung up, we talked about meeting at Babe's when he returned to show the folks in town that I was once again one of the good guys.

I decided to call Lucy or Babe to share my news, even though it wasn't really good news, simply one piece of the puzzle leading to a different, bigger puzzle. Just as I was about to dial, the phone rang. I assumed it was Grant, who'd forgotten to tell me something.

"Grant?" I said.

There was silence, but not a robodialer's silence: someone was there. I could hear breathing.

"No."

I looked at the phone to see if I recognized the caller's number. I didn't, but it was a familiar area code. One I'd recently dialed.

Michigan.

"I hear you've been looking for me. My name's Jeff Warren."

TWENTY-FOUR

I froze. Of course. How long would it have taken Mama Warren to call her boy and congratulate him on his new girlfriend and imminent nuptials? She probably called the minute we hung up to ask him where we were registered and what colors we were featuring.

"I think we should talk, don't you?" he said.

I wasn't so sure.

Warren said he was calling from Massachusetts. He was headed south with another driver and they'd just made a pit stop at a service station about three and a half hours away from Springfield.

"I want to explain," he said, "about Monica."

"Go ahead, explain."

"I can't talk now. I'm still on probation with the trucking company and the fella I'm with today is being a real hard case. He's been busting my chops about being on the phone so much."

Right. I bet he'd spent a lot of time on the phone with Mom. "What about tomorrow morning?" I said.

"We have to be in Virginia by then."

They had an official two-hour rest stop planned not far from Springfield. The other driver had a girlfriend nearby. The plan was for Warren to catch some z's in the truck while his colleague had a conjugal visit. Instead, he offered to come to my place, but there was no way I was giving him my address. I suggested a more public venue, the diner. I'd feel safe there and he knew where it was.

With any luck someone would also be at the police substation across the road, and the Dunkin' Donuts in that same strip of stores was open late. And even if they were both closed, the Springfield police department sign might be enough of a deterrent if Warren had anything on his mind besides talking.

"The owner of the diner has an office at the back," I said. "We can meet there if the place is closed." We agreed to meet in three and a half hours.

If I hadn't lost track of the time when I was online and then on the phone with

Grant I'd have realized that three and a half hours from then was 1 A.M. I wasn't stupid enough to meet a total stranger in a parking lot at that hour. I hit star sixty-nine on my phone but was unable to connect. Either Warren was in a dead zone or the other driver was still hassling him about the calls and had made him turn off his cell. I drove to Babe's.

Three or four small parties were crammed into booths, laughing and finishing up with dinner. One guy sat at the counter nursing a soft drink and staring into space.

"Look what the cat drug in," Babe said. I knew she'd said *drug* to be funny, but *drug* had assumed a whole new meaning in the last two weeks, and I didn't laugh. She pursed her lips. "One of *those* days?"

"Guess who I just got a call from," I said, climbing on a stool a safe distance from the others. Babe brought over two coffees, one for me and one for her.

"Let's see, Sir Paul McCartney — he wants you to redesign the gardens for his new castle?"

"Funny. No, Jeff Warren."

"I give up. Who's Jeff Warren?" she asked.

One bleary-eyed day and I had lost touch with all the humans I knew. I brought Babe up to speed on my online research and marathon phone call with Mama Warren.

"Dang it, girl, you do have a *knack* for this stuff," she said. We clinked mugs. "So some guy gets a new job driving a truck and everything changes for two towns and one family. This is like that butterfly-wings-on-the-other-side-of-the-planet thing isn't it? You're not seriously going to meet him, are you?"

I shook my head and handed her a note I'd written for Warren. If he had time to meet me tonight, he'd have time to answer some questions, and I didn't want to forget anything. I asked Babe to tack it to her back door when she closed up.

"Can I read it?"

"Sure."

Surprise, bewilderment, and finally concern registered on Babe's face as she read the note with my questions. "Caroline Sturgis *knows* these people? Whodathunkit? Two weeks ago I would have bet the most dangerous thing she'd ever done was try the new aesthetician at the day spa." She let out a long low whistle.

"These sound like some nasty characters," she said, refolding the note and slipping it into her back pocket. "How do we know our truck driver friend isn't one of them?

235

Or that he isn't working for this man Donnelley?"

I didn't know. That's why my plan was to leave the note on her back door. I'd return at around 12:30 and hide in the shopping strip across the street to see what happened when Jeff Warren arrived and realized I wasn't coming. My note said something had come up, but wouldn't he please help us out by answering some questions. Babe didn't like the plan.

"Why do you have to come at all? Why not just leave the note and see what happens?"

I'd thought of that. But if Jeff really sat down to write the answers like the good boy his mother thought he was, I'd run across the street and tell him I'd just been detained. If he got pissed off and left, then he knew more than he'd suggested and had another reason to want to meet me.

"Can't you just call O'Malley?" Babe said, still trying to talk me out of it.

"And tell him what? I'm meeting a man, does he want to make it a threesome? Jeff Warren knows something. By accident or design, he's the reason this whole thing started. I'll be careful. Besides," I said, coming around the counter to refill my coffee mug, "he's a hardworking guy — even his two gold-digging ex-wives admit that. And his mother says he's a good boy. Aren't you always after me to find some nice guy?"

Babe was not amused.

"What did you find out about this Donnelley character and the woman who was arrested with them?" she asked.

After Warren's call, I did an online search for Kate Gustafson and the charming Mr. Donnelley. It didn't take long. Kate had been paroled after serving two years of her sentence. She died in a fire at a bar not long after that. Eddie's digital trail seemed to end a year and a half ago, right after his release from prison. Disappeared like a puff of smoke.

But how does someone intentionally disappear? No doubt, like everything else, things were easier if you had money. Caroline had done it, but that was years ago before everything we did left an online trail like the silvery tracings of a slug. Now it was harder. We might just as well have microchips placed in our necks like some suburban pets.

I never knew how they reckoned amounts from years ago versus current dollars, I just knew whatever the number was then, it would be worth more now. In 1986, I was a fine judge of Cabbage Patch dolls and

Strawberry Shortcake merchandise, but I didn't know what any of it cost.

"Pete and I bought the diner around then, for a helluva lot less," Babe said. "If someone invested that money wisely for him, Donnelley could have been sitting on quite a pile when he got out. With that much money he could have bought a new identity and gone anywhere in the world."

Except something told me Donnelley hadn't left the money with a trusted financial adviser who'd invested it soundly on his behalf. More likely he'd hidden it or given it to a compatriot who didn't spend twenty years in jail. Was it possible Caroline knew where the money was, or had it, and she was still lying to Grant, to all of us?

If Caroline's parents and grandmother didn't die leaving her well provided for, where had she gotten the money she was living on when she met Grant? My head was swimming with different scenarios. I had to find out what really happened and Jeff Warren could fill in some of the blanks.

"I don't like this," Babe said, handing over her spare key. She made me promise to call her after Warren and I met, just in case.

"I'm not going to do anything stupid," I said.

"You're already doing something stupid."

TWENTY-FIVE

Babe was wrong. People met strangers all the time, didn't they? On airplanes, blind dates, hookups in bars. I dropped that train of thought when I realized I was making her case for not meeting him instead of my own for keeping the appointment.

I drove home and prepared to meet Jeff Warren, even though it was hours before the appointed time. I must have changed clothes half a dozen times. It wasn't about making a fashion statement. Unconsciously, I was practicing defensive dressing. Sneakers would be good if I had to run, but cowboy boots would be better if I had to deliver a good, swift kick. Nothing in my closet would stop a bullet, but why make it easy for someone to grab, stab, or throttle me? I opted for boots, jeans, and my leather jacket over a thick but loose hoodie.

It reminded me of October 11, 2001, the first time I flew after 9/11. I dressed for the flight as if I was preparing for an undercover SWAT mission: heavy denim layers, steel-toed work boots, and a hardcover copy of *The Corrections,* which I figured I could use as a weapon if necessary. I'd seen a man killed with a pair of eyeglasses in a movie once, but I was wearing contacts and I didn't think they'd do much good. I knew I was being ridiculous, but I couldn't stop. I'd let Babe give me the heebie-jeebies.

If I really thought it was dangerous, why would I be going? And Jeff Warren would hardly call his sweet old gray-haired mother before he planned to rape and kill someone. Would he? Unless this was one of those twisted Ma Barker or honeymoon killers-type scenarios . . .

I needed to ratchet down. I made a pot of green tea and sat in my kitchen all bundled up, tapping my toes, watching the clock, and sweating it out until 11:45, when I convinced myself it wasn't too early to leave.

The shopping strip across from the diner was almost dark; one streetlight a football field away was the only public lighting. I turned into the lot on the far right side of the strip, adjacent to a nearby gas station, where I hoped my Jeep would look like any of the other vehicles in for repairs and overflowing from the station's own small triangular lot. It was also as far away from our meeting place as I could park and still be within walking distance.

The temperature had dropped considerably and the wind was kicking up. That made me feel a little less foolish for all the layers — although they were so loose, the cold air blew up my cuffs and down my collar and sent a chill right down my vertebrae to the base of my spine. I could see my breath. I zipped up, flipped up the hood of my sweatshirt, and buried my hands deep in my pockets. Should have worn gloves.

Even walking fast, I took almost ten minutes to get from my end of the lot; down a few short steps; past the shuttered nail salon, karate school, and liquor store; past the police substation and dimly lit Dunkin' Donuts all the way to the other end, where I'd planned to crouch down and give myself an unobstructed view of Babe's and the door to her office.

I scoped out my surroundings. Two cars in the lot probably belonged to the Dunkin' Donuts employees. Across the street, the Paradise was closed, nothing visible except the pale blue light from the Snapple fridge. Next to the diner was an ATM, the last vestige of a bank branch that had shuttered its doors five years earlier, and a gas station that had also gone belly-up and was await-ing demolition to make room for a piano showroom, which had to be a front for some other more questionable activity, since why would anyone build a piano showroom on a quiet stretch of road like this? And it *was* quiet.

During the day, inside the Paradise Diner, the air was warm with the mingled fra-grances of cinnamon, bacon, and comfort foods; and this was an idyllic spot with ducks and geese fluttering over the lake or waddling onto the shore. From my new vantage point it was as cold and lifeless as a postcard.

On my side of the road, the police substa-tion had one light on. It no longer fooled any of the locals, but it was a gentle re-minder of the long arm of the law, especially for anyone coming off the highway and not knowing any better. Inside the donut shop the employees were cleaning up, getting ready to close.

Shoot. If I'd arrived earlier I could have bought a coffee to stay warm. I checked my watch — plenty of time before Warren ar-rived. I was still more than an hour early. I jogged back to the shop and banged on the door with the heel of my hand. The two Indian kids inside looked at me, then each other, warily. Was this a setup? Were my confederates lying in wait, looking for my signal that they should rush the doors, duct-tape the employees, and empty the cash register? Or was I simply a chowhound desperate for caffeine and her next fatty, sugary fix?

One of the kids leaned his mop against the counter, wiped his hands on his apron, and came over to check me out. I pushed my hood down to look a little less gangsta and a little more suburban lady. He squinted, said something to his colleague, and unlocked the door, opening it just a crack.

"Great one, skim milk, no sugar," he said, nodding.

Those words would probably be chiseled on my tombstone. Between the cold and my covert mission, I smiled a smile I didn't really feel. That was me, harmless caffeine addict with a six-word bio.

"Got any coffee left? I'm supposed to meet someone here and I'm going to freeze my keister off if I don't get something warm inside me. Even the dregs." I tried to sound like an upbeat gal with an appointment, not a woman on a stakeout. "I don't care, I'll take anything." I did want the coffee, but in the back of my mind I thought it wouldn't hurt to let someone else know my where-abouts. *That's right, Officer, we saw her at around midnight. . . .*

The kid in charge told me they'd already closed out the register and made their bank drop across the road at the ATM — either to reiterate that they were closed or to an-nounce that there was no cash on the prem-ises, just in case one of their innocent-looking customers who ordered the same thing every time she came in also knocked over convenience stores in her spare time.

I offered them twenty bucks for a thermos of whatever hot liquid they had left and the two almost stale cinnamon crullers they were going to throw out anyway. Beggars couldn't be choosers. They conferred, then accepted.

"Eh, if there's ever something I can do for you . . ." My meant-to-be-amusing line from *The Godfather* fell on deaf ears and they tensed up, wondering if they'd made a colossal mistake and had, in fact, let a crazy woman into the store late at night. Now I felt like Babe, bemoaning the younger generation's lack of a complete cultural education that should rightly include *The Godfather* saga, even the much-maligned number three.

The kids finished closing, locked up, and

drove off in opposite directions, the only vehicles I'd seen on the road since I'd arrived. Now there were no cars in my end of the lot. I went back to my somewhat smaller blind, taking cover on a stone slab in between a spirea hedge and a U.S. mailbox with an elongated front for drive-by mailings. The coffee was still too hot to drink, but it made a nifty heater. I poured some into the thermos cup, trying to calculate how late that much caffeine would keep me awake. I sat cross-legged on the curb, nestling the thermos in between my thighs, blowing on the steaming coffee.

I pushed the light button on my watch: 12:25. Cripes, I didn't have to worry about Warren harming me, I'd be dead from exposure, sitting on a Belgian block curb for thirty-five minutes in this weather, which was gradually worsening. They'd find me in the morning, butt frozen to the ground, huddled around my Dunkin' Donuts thermos like some suburban bodhisattva.

I was muttering to myself when I heard something behind me. Probably the wind, whistling through the shrubs, blowing soot and leaves in my eyes and making things even more uncomfortable. I flipped my hood up again and tried to find the cord to tighten it around my head but it must have come out in the wash or the end was floating around inside the seam. I grabbed both sides and held them tight under my chin with one hand. I heard more leaf crunching behind me and exposed one ear to hear better. The noise stopped.

Deer were faster and squirrels didn't move around much at night. Wild turkeys? Raccoons, maybe. Hadn't I seen them rummaging around at Babe's? I was shifting position to get the circulation back in my legs when someone yanked me by the hood of my sweatshirt and pulled me to my feet. The sweatshirt was so big, I was temporarily blinded as it partially covered my face and my eyes.

My assailant grabbed me by the wrist and swung me around, knocking my coffee out of my hands, burning my fingertips. All I could make out before I was twisted around again inside the voluminous sweatshirt was a man with a pair of panty hose over his face. He wrapped his arm around my neck, and I tucked my chin down to keep him from choking me. I tried to wrest myself away from him, and in the course of struggling I kicked the thermos of coffee on the ground. I picked up my right foot and kicked back as hard as I could into his right knee. He loosened his grip and doubled over. I bent down, picked up the container of coffee, twisted off the top, and threw the scalding hot liquid, aiming for the man's eyes. I must have scored, because he cursed, his hands rushing to his eyes. My cowboy boots turned out to be a fashion do. The creep was a little too tall and I was too far away to reach the number one spot where no man wants to be kicked, so I aimed for his other knee, letting fly with as much power as I could. He cursed again and crumpled to the ground. Now I *could* reach the good stuff. I hauled off and gave him another kick, with my pointy boot seriously jeopardizing his ability to reproduce. He fell backward.

If he got up fast, I'd have less than a minute to get away. I got lucky: an eighteen-wheeler came by and slowed him down just long enough for me to run across the road, through the parking lot, and to Babe's back door. The key was in my hand, but I could barely breathe and I fumbled for a few seconds, putting it in upside down. I looked across the street and saw the man staggering to his feet. I took the key out and tried it again. This time it worked. I locked the door behind me and called the cops as I heard him cursing and banging on the door. Then the banging stopped.

TWENTY-SIX

"Is this your edgy New York way of asking for a date?"

I suppose I deserved that, but I didn't like it much. I'd just been attacked by a masked assailant. I'd twisted my knee, aggravating an old ACL injury. My wrist was still sore from being jerked around, and a thick purplish bracelet had come out on it in the five to ten minutes it took the cops to arrive. I didn't think it was an appropriate time for verbal foreplay; I needed a bandage more than I needed badinage.

Mike O'Malley stood in the doorway of Babe's office with another cop who looked so young I thought I could smell the milk on his breath. When did everyone start to look so young?

"Come in," I said, showing him into Babe's den.

The note I'd asked Babe to tack on the door for Jeff Warren was still there, flapping in the wind that had made the night seem colder than it was. I opened the door wider to let the cops in and tried to casually pluck the note off the door and shove it in my pocket without catching O'Malley's eye.

"Are you all right?" he asked.

I cataloged my physical complaints out loud this time, then gave Mike the broad strokes without exactly telling him what I'd been doing hunkered down in an empty parking lot well past my usual bedtime. He noticed I left that part out.

"My coffee machine is broken," I said, jumping in with an explanation too fast. Tactical error. Never volunteer anything when you're lying. Take a breath, fidget with something, wait until they ask. It gives you more time to make up something believable.

O'Malley was polite enough not to raise his left eyebrow, the diplomatic response I'd seen him deliver far too often that spoke volumes and was loosely translated as "That's a crock."

"Let me make sure I have this. Someone accosted you in the parking lot after you got your late-night coffee and crullers and instead of running to your car and locking yourself in and driving away, you sprinted across the street to an obviously closed diner, hoping that Babe had left the back door open — even though she'd recently had a prowler?"

I'd forgotten about that. Were they officially calling him a prowler now? I thought he was still a trespasser. At that moment I hated Countertop Man, O'Malley, and Jeff Warren, my presumptive attacker. And I hated the word *accosted.* It was like *alleged.* It somehow qualified my experience.

"Yes," I said defiantly, as if it was the most logical thing in the world to do. Sometimes short and sweet did the trick.

O'Malley closed his eyes and rubbed his forehead, knowing there was more to the story. "Show us where it happened," he said.

I followed the cops into the parking lot and locked the office door behind me. From where we stood, it was obvious there were no cars in the parking area near the Dunkin' Donuts. The three of us unnecessarily looked both ways, crossed the deserted road, and entered the lot.

During one of our periodic truces, Mike had told me that in the Springfield police department it was customary for newbies to ride with the more experienced cops for at least six months. O'Malley had been on the force for more than ten years, so it wasn't unusual to find him baby-sitting one of the newer guys. Most of them moved on to bigger departments elsewhere, where they could actually use the sophisticated forensics training that was standard these days, but they got their starts in small departments like the one in Springfield.

Up until that point, O'Malley's charge hadn't said a word, but he was chomping at the bit to prove his worth to his superior.

"Excuse me, sir. Carjacking?"

It was a logical assumption for Milk Breath to make, since my car was nowhere in sight. They looked at me, waiting for an explanation. I told them my car was at the other end of the lot and took my time concocting a legitimate reason for something that, in the suburbs, was tantamount to lunatic behavior, i.e., not parking as close to your destination as humanly possible. Nothing was coming; the well was dry. I paused, picking up the now empty thermos while something halfway reasonable sprang to mind.

"I wanted to burn a few extra calories," I said, trying not to look up and to the left, which I'd read somewhere was a sure tip-off that the speaker was lying.

O'Malley's eyebrow lift was barely perceptible. That time he couldn't control it, but it was definitely there, even if he spared me the full drawbridge-raise treatment. I was grateful.

The cops left me briefly and made a show of investigating. The young one did most of the talking. I knew I hadn't given them much of a description. A man wearing panty hose. Suntan, looked like control top from the way his features were distorted and his lips were pulled back like a woman with a bad face-lift. He was five foot ten or thereabouts, average weight. He didn't try to rob or rape me, and didn't say anything to reveal either an accent or a manner of speaking, just the one expletive, repeated twice, referring to an activity he wasn't likely to be engaging in that night or any time soon thanks to my extremely pointy Lucchese cowboy boots.

"Anybody else see this guy? Maybe the kids from Double D?"

I shook my head. "They were gone by the time he attacked me."

"Funny you'd still be here so much later after they closed." I'd forgotten that he used to work at the police substation and probably knew their routine almost as well as they did. Mike told his partner to go back to their patrol car and wait for him. He'd walk me to my car.

"Is your car really here?" O'Malley asked

when the other man left.

"Of course it is." I pointed to the far end of the lot near the gas station, and we started walking.

"My young partner is suspicious. He thinks your boyfriend roughed you up, and you're protecting him. He's not right, is he?"

I didn't feel like announcing that I had no boyfriend. We both knew it. "Of course not. Your partner should be a novelist, not a cop."

"You're up to something, aren't you? You, Babe, maybe that whack job friend of yours from New York?"

And to think Lucy was always asking how he was. "Hey, she's *my* whack job friend. Just leave Lucy out of it." I wasn't looking forward to the sermon I knew was coming, so I said nothing more and just kept walking to my car.

"Who was the note for?" he asked. Aaayy. My oh-so-subtle sleight of hand had worked on the kid but not O'Malley; I'd never make it as a magician.

I wasn't used to telling so many lies in one night; it was exhausting. How in hell had Caroline done it for so long? I looked around for inspiration. All I saw were the patrol car's flashing red lights reflected in the windows of the closed shops and my own Jeep a hundred yards in the other direction. I unlocked it with the automatic button on my car keys. The lights turned on and instantly I could see something was different.

I'd slid right in next to another car, larger than mine, one of those I assumed was in the gas station's lot being repaired. Now it was gone. I tried drawing a mental picture of the car but all I could remember was that it was a dark-colored SUV with unfamiliar-looking license plates, not Connecticut, New York, or Massachusetts.

Just then, O'Malley and I heard a screech of brakes. An eighteen-wheeler slowed down, then blew by us. I couldn't see much from where we stood, but I thought I could make out the silhouette of a baseball hat and longish hair flying out the open driver's side window. Leaving the scene of the crime? Or maybe Jeff Warren hadn't been my assailant. Could he have gotten to his truck and back so fast if he had been the one to attack me? And why would he come back?

Then it hit me: Warren had passed by earlier to drop off his randy coworker, unwittingly giving me time to get away from my attacker. Thanks, Jeff. When he returned for our appointment, he saw the cop cars, freaked, and hauled ass out of there.

"Shoot," I said, louder than I meant to.

"You expecting a delivery?"

"Sort of." I watched as my savior barreled toward Virginia. Then my phone rang, breaking the silence.

"I guess city folk and the rich really *are* different. I never realized you were such a night owl," he said, folding his arms and looking at me as if he'd never seen me before.

Yeah, that was me, party, party, party. I gave him a weak smile. The phone continued to ring.

"You gonna answer that?"

I worried that it was Warren phoning to curse me out for calling the cops and maybe even siccing them on him as he sped across state lines until I saw the number.

It wasn't Warren: it was Babe checking up on me, right on the dot at 1 A.M. I repeated her name loud enough so O'Malley could hear who I was talking to. She peppered me with questions until she overheard Mike's voice and finally believed that I was okay.

"All right, missy, what's going on?" he asked.

I said nothing, but he wasn't going to let me off that easily.

"There's nothing to tell." And there

255

wasn't — not yet anyway. Maybe Warren *was* the hapless, accidental catalyst of this whole Caroline Sturgis business and maybe *I* was the hapless, accidental victim of an opportunistic mugger. Maybe. But somebody I knew once said that there was no such thing as a coincidence.

"Why are you cross-examining me?" I said. "I'm the victim here, remember? I'm not supposed to go out after dark? What is this, Victorian London? Is Jack the Ripper on the loose stalking women?"

"I'm not cross-examining you; I simply asked a question. It's what I do for a living."

I hated that he was being so rational, and I, tired and irritated, was not.

O'Malley insisted on following me home and sprinted back to Babe's to join his colleague in the patrol car. As soon as his back was turned, I dialed Warren's number. No answer. I was leaving him a long-winded message when the cops returned. I abruptly hung up and pretended I'd been fidgeting with my seat belt. O'Malley pulled parallel to the Jeep and pointed straight ahead, telling me to go.

I drove well below the speed limit to annoy him, hoping he'd get frustrated or take the hint that I didn't appreciate a police escort, but he stuck to my rear bumper like a trailer hitch until I turned into my driveway — where the motion-sensitive security lights were on. Someone or something had just been there.

I stopped short, and only O'Malley's quick reflexes kept me from getting rear-ended. Now I was glad they'd followed me home. I parked at the base of my driveway as far to the right as I could to let the patrol car pass. O'Malley hopped out and came over to my side of the Jeep.

"Stay put, roll the window up, and lock the doors. We'll take a look." This was the side of O'Malley I rarely saw during our bantering matches at the diner. It said something that a few words from him made me feel safe, and even more that I hadn't realized I *didn't* feel safe before he'd said them.

At the top of the driveway O'Malley went left and the other cop went right, their elongated searchlights scouring the shrubs and dense foundation plantings. Then the two men disappeared behind my house. After a few minutes the timed security lights went off and my driveway was plunged into darkness. No light pollution in the sticks. I couldn't see their flashlights anymore. I turned the car back on so my headlights would illuminate the driveway. Fifteen long minutes later, both men returned, once again setting off the security lights.

"All the doors and windows look secure. Nothing seems amiss. Coulda been deer. How long do the lights stay on after they've been activated?"

I hadn't a clue. The security lights had been put in by the previous owners, who'd also installed an alarm system. In three years, I'd only set the alarm twice and the security lights had gone on twice that I knew of, both times accidentally tripped by me as I was leaving. O'Malley and his young partner entered before me, and searched the garage and all the rooms. Once they left, I double-checked the windows and doors and unearthed the alarm system's manual from under the sink to remind myself how to turn the damn thing on.

TWENTY-SEVEN

I was in that warm drowsy state when the switch is just about to flip that takes you from half awake to half asleep when the telephone rang. It was 3:18. No one called at this hour with good news.

"Yeah?" Silence on the other end. I raised myself on one elbow. I thought I heard breathing. I was about to berate the prank caller when someone took a deep breath and blurted out, "You mean it? You really didn't call the cops?" It was Warren. He'd played my abbreviated voice mail message.

"I didn't. Well, I did. But not for you. I was mugged while I was waiting for you." I sat up then, fully awake and thinking how ridiculous the whole thing sounded.

"Oh lord. I am so sorry." Jeff Warren sounded like he meant it. Like his mother, he was a stream-of-conscious talker, rattling off a series of transgressions that started with his stabbing his little brother George with a pencil on the first day of school and ending with his accidentally breaking his ex-brother-in-law Leroy's thumb when they were fooling around in the cab of Leroy's truck two weeks ago. On one hand, it was astonishing and almost admirable that the man could remember and relive the anguish of every affront he'd ever committed; on the other, it was like speed-dating the worst loser on the planet. Once I assured him that he needn't add my name to the extended list of people he'd unintentionally wronged or maimed, he told me what had happened. It was as I'd suspected.

He'd dropped off his amorous pal and then come back to meet me. When he saw the cops he figured it was a setup and put the pedal to the metal. He was calling from a weigh station, where he sat chain-smoking — by the sound of it — and waiting for a text message from his buddy letting him know that his "date" was over and he wanted to be picked up.

Warren had flip-flopped for the last two hours on whether or not to call me, whether or not he believed the voice mail message I'd left for him. I just wished that he had flopped about two hours earlier.

"I think I still have about an hour," he said, trying to suggest another meeting.

"I've already had a pretty exciting night. Can we do this on the phone?"

Warren didn't say anything for a while, but even in my semiconscious state I could tell he had something to spit out and he did. I swung my legs over the side of the bed and stood up.

"Okay, let's try this one last time," I said, getting dressed in the same clothes I'd flung around the room earlier. "Thirty minutes. There's an all-night deli at a strip mall near the Merritt, just off Wave Hill Road." Even at that hour, I thought there'd be traffic. Hell, by that time, they'd be serving breakfast

"I'll be there."

This time I resolved to stay in my car until I saw Warren and got a reality check. Was he as safe and as aw-shucks innocent as he and Mama Warren wanted me to think or not? I thought so, but I still wasn't sure.

There was no time for a hot caffeine jolt, so I grabbed a diet Red Bull from the fridge, hoping the buzz would clear my head. I pulled on my jacket in the entranceway and stepped down to the door that led to the garage. Just as I turned the doorknob —
"Burglary! Burglary! Step away from the house!" An earsplitting shriek ripped through my brain. It was me, screaming. I

261

dropped my keys and my bag. The two horrendous sounds — the siren and the taped warning — continued alternating until I scrambled back up the stairs to turn off the alarm. All I could think of were World War II documentaries and ambulances during the London Blitz.

I finally found the alarm code, entered it, and the hideous noises stopped, although the vibrations seemed to hang in the air for a few seconds like the aftereffects of a fireworks display. Then the phone rang. Cripes, what was it now?

"Alarm Central. We have a report of the alarm going off at your residence." It was nice to know someone was paying attention, since I hadn't noticed one light go on in any neighboring houses.

"It was me." I leafed through the instruction manual, looking for some language or jargon to put the caller's mind at rest. "I'm the *homeowner*. It was an accident."

"We understand. We just need your password."

My password? I had so many passwords they were recorded on multicolored notes stuck all over my office. My bulletin board and the side of my computer were feathered with them, but none was the password for an alarm system someone else had installed at least three years ago.

"Uh, I don't think I have a password. It was the previous owner's system. But I can assure you, I'm fine."

"We understand, ma'am," Cheerful Clerk said, "but we still need your password. After all, you could be the burglar. You could be holding the homeowner hostage." This speech was delivered in a singsong manner and with all the sensitivity and concern of someone reading it off a plastic card hanging in his cubicle while he text-messaged his girlfriend. *The homeowner could be hogtied on the kitchen floor. . . .*

"Okay, okay, I get it. I'll look for the password."

I searched through the manual again. Nothing scribbled on the back, no dog-eared corners in the booklet to give me a hint what the damn password was.

"I'm sorry. I don't know what else to tell you," I said. "I didn't install the system and I've never even been sent a bill for the service." That got his attention.

I heard keyboard clicking. "Let's see . . . the system was installed four years ago and that fee included five years of monitoring at no additional charge. That period ends in seven months."

"So what does that mean? Can I change

the password?"

"Yes, ma'am. You can go on our Web site, but you'd have to sign in with your original password. Otherwise we need you to do it in writing and send it to us along with a copy of your deed."

My deed? I looked at the clock. I didn't want Warren to drive off again and I could still be on time if I got off the phone in the next thirty seconds. "Great, you know where I live. Send me the form. I'll make a copy of my deed. Gotta go, thanks." I hung up and dashed out the door to my car.

Not long after I turned onto Lakeview Road, I saw red flashing lights in my rear-view mirror. I slowed down, not wanting to attract any more attention, and I was relieved when the patrol car made a left a few blocks behind me.

I pulled into the strip mall and parked about a hundred or so feet from the deli's entrance. It was still open, but it was not the teeming hot spot I'd read about in the *Bulletin.*

I was still visible from the road — that couldn't be helped — but at least I was out of the direct light of the streetlamp. I killed my lights but left the engine running to stay warm and to make a quick departure if necessary.

I've tried to re-create what happened next, but it's something of a blur, a weird permutation of what had happened earlier. Just as Warren pulled in, he must have seen what I'd seen in my rearview mirror not long before — the red flashing lights of a Springfield police car. This time Warren tore ass out of the lot, knocking over a bank of free newspaper stands on his way to the highway. Something told me his truck driving partner would be hitching a ride to Virginia in the morning.

Seconds later the police car screeched into the lot, stopping at an angle, just shy of the overturned newsstand. Two cops jumped out and started running toward my Jeep. I turned the lights on to show them I was all right.

O'Malley stopped running first and walked the rest of the way. He did not look amused, but I was.

"You just can't stand the thought of me meeting another man, can you?"

TWENTY-EIGHT

"You mean to tell me after all that, you never even met the guy?"

Babe Chinnery snatched back the menu as if she were going to withhold food because I'd failed to accomplish my mission. "I'm disappointed in you."

"Hey, I have an absolute rule about how many times per night I'm going to arrange to meet a strange man in a deserted parking lot." I said it a little too loud and got a few puzzled looks from the other diners at Babe's.

I was disappointed, too. I'd given up an entire night's sleep and had gotten only two useful words from Jeff Warren on the phone — Eddie Donnelley. How useful they were remained to be seen. Was Donnelley behind all Caroline's troubles — old *and* new? That was the suggestion Warren had made, and it was what had gotten me out of bed a second time when common sense should have dictated that I stay put. Some people were like ticks — they just couldn't let go of things — and I was turning into one of them.

Babe didn't bother listening for my order. She brought me a tall glass of orange juice, coffee, buttered toast, and three scrambled eggs, well done, a meal that would have been anathema to me two years earlier, before I knew that a little bread and butter wouldn't kill me. Her only acknowledgment of my formerly restricted lifestyle was that she didn't heap a mountain of Pete's parsleyed potatoes alongside the toast. A side dish fondly referred to as the 3Pete, Pete's parsleyed potatoes were so good, they were all some diners had for breakfast, but I needed protein — and that wasn't one of the *P*s in the secret recipe.

Babe set the plate down in front of me and cast a quick eye around the diner. She decided she had a few minutes before the only other customer in the diner asked for the check, so she settled in on her side of the counter to wheedle the rest of the story out of me as I ate.

"This Donnelley creep must really hold a grudge. I myself don't believe in holding grudges," she said. "Stresses you out. Bad for the digestion, the skin. I knew a girl in the Collins Band whose hair fell out because she was stressed over not being named lead tambourine. Although she may have pulled it out herself. We were never really sure. Either way, it was stress related."

I could feel another rock and roll flashback coming on.

"And if you do get some satisfaction," she said, stretching her arms over her head, "that period of elation is fleeting. More likely you'll regret it. I remember being ticked off at a roadie once. The guy promised to get me backstage to see Jerry Garcia after a concert. He got me backstage all right, but everyone was already gone. No Mr. Garcia, only Mr. Johnson."

Babe's revenge had been swift. She let the roadie keep drinking while she spilled her own wine in a bucket of sand meant to be used as an ashtray. When the guy was good and plastered, she led him out onto the empty stage, telling him she wanted their first time to be something special. Instead, he was so falling-down drunk she was able to tie him to a set of drums, where he passed out with his pants down around his ankles.

"The whole crew knew about it in the morning. It's amazing what some guys will let you do when they think they're going to get some. Coupla years later, he got religion and wound up traveling all the way to Decatur, Georgia, just to apologize to me."

It warmed my heart that Babe was no longer inclined to seek revenge, but not everyone was as highly evolved. Something told me Eddie Donnelley wasn't one of the enlightened. If he was in town, I didn't think it was to give Caroline a big old bear hug and to have that cathartic "closure" conversation.

I hadn't called Warren back. What for? The way the previous evening had gone we would have only missed each other again. And he'd have had to have the innocence of Charlie Brown to show up a third time for a rendezvous with a woman who claimed to have never called the cops and yet always seemed to have a police escort.

Instead, after a final round of verbal sparring with O'Malley I'd gone home and crawled into bed thinking how close I'd come to getting answers — if only the police hadn't shown up again.

"The police," I said, thinking out loud and shaking my head.

"Excuse me?" Babe was horrified. She was still reliving the revenge memory. "Jerry Garcia was a member of the Dead, the Grateful Dead? Sting, Stewart Copeland,

269

and Andy Summers were the Police."

"Give me some credit, I know that. I'm not one of your little acolytes. I've owned *vinyl*. I was just thinking how happy I was to see the police the first time last night, then how unhappy."

Babe was relieved — she didn't take kindly to too many disappointments in one day. "Has it occurred to you that O'Malley may have appointed himself your guardian angel?" Babe said.

It hadn't. Over the last few years the snappy dialogue between O'Malley and me — even when it bordered on the frisky — had built up a kind of scar tissue. We couldn't touch nerve endings if we tried. And I think we did try every once in a while, but never, it seemed, at the same time, so we never made that complete circuit required to turn on the lightbulb.

"Speaking of the angel . . ." Babe jerked her chin in the direction of the police station across the road, where a now ubiquitous patrol car sat idling and O'Malley stood leaning against it, on the phone. "The angel's lookin' good. I think he's dropped a few pounds," she said, sizing him up. "You take him out of that blue polyester uniform, put him in a pair of black jeans, black T-shirt, leather blazer. I bet he'd look mighty fine, with that salt-and-pepper hair and blue eyes." Clearly she'd given this some thought. I hadn't and I had a hard time resisting the urge to raise myself up off the counter stool, peer out the window, and visualize Mike O'Malley's proposed make over.

Babe left to seat a couple of women with two toddlers and I peeked at O'Malley while pretending to be reaching for napkins. Not bad, but was he really date material? What was it Lucy and Babe were seeing that I wasn't? Maybe all these near misses meant we were just supposed to be friends.

"You're busted," Babe said over her shoulder.

"I just wanted to see if he was coming this way."

"You are such a bad liar. If you're going to survive in a small town, you're going to need to hone those skills."

O'Malley headed toward the diner. He sprinted across the street easily, and moments later the screen door opened, then jingled shut with a smack. Babe was still with the newcomers, helping one of the women strap an obstreperous kid into a wooden seat that had all the appeal of a vintage electric chair. No wonder the kid was screaming.

"Hello, ladies. Okay if I serve myself?" O'Malley needn't have asked for permission. Babe adored him and he knew the diner's setup better than some of her employees. He poured himself a coffee and slid onto the counter stool beside me, a smug look on his face.

"Okay. What?"

"State police didn't need to chase your friend too far — he drove straight into an overpass on the Merritt. Sheared off the top of his rig.

"Oh, and there's something else. Caroline Sturgis is coming home."

TWENTY-NINE

Home. Was it here in Michigan where this cell was; Oregon where my fictional grandmother lived and died; or Springfield, where everyone knew me as Caroline Sturgis? Bland, boring, stay-at-home, faintly amusing and to-be-pitied Caroline Sturgis, who drank a little too often and rarely finished her crafts projects but was otherwise just like any of the other suburban moms who spent their days chauffeuring kids from one structured activity to the next with only the occasional break for spa treatments or Wednesday matinees in New York City.

The last weeks had been a far cry from soccer matches and afternoon theater dates. I no longer knew or remembered how I'd managed to keep track of all the lies for so many years. It was as if I'd kept an internal bulletin board just like the slick white one in my kitchen that told me where everyone was. Some days the schedules were as complicated as the landing at Normandy, but the bulletin board gave me

273

the illusion of order — Molly at soccer, Jason at hockey practice, Grant gallivanting all over the world, Caroline in Connecticut, not to be confused with Monica in Michigan. Never to be confused with that girl I used to be.

They put me in solitary confinement for my own safety. No one seriously thought that I'd hang myself with an Hermès scarf, but they'd never had a resident like me before and frankly didn't know what to do with me. Oddly enough, I might have welcomed the company of the other women. As it was, I heard them only once a day when I was let out for my forty-five-minute exercise break. Some jeered and some cheered as I was led past their cells. I heard everything from "skinny bitch" to "hockey mom, can you hook me up with some blow?"

I tried to focus on Grant and the kids. Was Molly keeping up with her piano lessons in Tucson? Was Jason wearing his helmet for the pickup hockey games he'd be playing in? I didn't imagine anyone else in the building was thinking about hockey pucks, and it was difficult for me to do it. I kept drifting back to the path that had led me here.

Sherry, the girl I'd met at the soup kitchen, had been around the block at least a couple of times. She was a user, and I knew it, but I learned a lot from her — good and bad. We spent two weeks together, my total-immersion apprenticeship into a life of petty crime. She and I took full advantage of all the social services agencies in the city, offering different names and different sad stories to each and moving on before too many questions were asked. We stayed away from personal details, even with each other.

On her own, Sherry inspired others, inside the shelter system and out, to grip their handbags and backpacks as if she was about to snatch them and make a run for it. It was an understandable reflex. She had the look of a female Artful Dodger, eager to give them the pitch, slick and practiced and knowledge-able of which buttons to push for maximum, sympathetic effect.

With my cherubic face, we made a good team. I gave her credibility. People were more trusting of us. As a duo, we got the benefit of the doubt, until one day she did snatch someone's bag while waiting for her turn at a communal shower. She ran off and left me, her presumed accomplice, to face the music alone. It took all the vestiges of my Midwest charm to convince the others at the shelter I'd had nothing to do with the robbery.

But it was a sign I should move on before I slipped up and gave something away. I'd lost my cicerone, my guide to the strange city, where every ten-block neighborhood was larger than my entire hometown.

I was sitting on a bench in Central Park, eating a bologna sandwich on squishy white bread for breakfast, when Sherry reappeared, jumping out from behind the statue of Balto, a hero dog who'd saved a bunch of people during a diphtheria outbreak.

"Ta-da!"

She laughed and boogied around the statue as if we were two friends who'd planned to meet for a movie or an afternoon in the city and she'd been a few minutes late. I tightened my hold on my bag and kept eating, eyes down. The sandwich was rubbery and tasteless, but I'd been happy to score four of them last night when the do-gooder truck made its rounds circling the park. I made them last for two meals.

"C'mon," she said. "You're not really sore, are you? I knew they wouldn't call the cops on you. Look at you. You're clean as a bar of soap."

That's what she thought. Where was she when my crap attorney was looking for jurors? I almost blurted that out but bit my lips. If Sherry knew I was wanted and there was any kind of reward for my capture, I'd be in

custody before I finished my bologna sandwich.

"What do you want?" I said, trying to sound
tougher than I felt.

Sherry reached into her stash and pulled
out something that looked frighteningly familiar
to me. My passport. I dropped the sandwich
and fumbled around in my bag to see what
else she'd stolen. Squirrels miraculously appeared to make off with the few scraps of
bread and bologna at my feet. I kicked them
away as if they were rats.

She held her hands up. "Nothing else, I
swear. Take it," she said, flapping the passport
up and down, "before I change my mind. I
could have gotten a nice chunk of change for
it. It's a testament to your good influence on
me that I brought it back." She gently placed
the passport on the wax paper my breakfast
had been wrapped in, trying to avoid the mus-
tard.

I was in shock. After my experience with
Kate and Eddie, I knew enough not to trust
anyone completely, but apparently I was still a
stupid kid from Michigan who could be suck-
ered into any setup and left holding the bag.

A discarded newspaper fluttered underneath
the park bench. Sherry pulled it out and tore
off a corner of the masthead. She scribbled a
name and a number on it with a pencil stub

she fished out of her pocket.

"Max will offer you a thousand dollars for it, but tell him I sent you." She handed me the scrap of paper. "Hold out for two; he's going to sell it for four anyway. And make him give you a fake driver's license for free. He's got tons of them. Pick a name you like. Pick a state."

She walked away swishing the bag she'd ripped off from the other girl. "I'd love to stay and chat," she yelled, "but if I spend any longer with you, you'll have me going straight. And that would be a terrible waste of talent. One last piece of advice. Wise up, trust no one."

That was the last time I saw her.

Max did offer me $1,000, but, as instructed, I negotiated and got him up to $2,500. He fanned out driver's licenses like a deck of cards. When I saw Oregon, I knew I had the beginnings of my new life story. It was perfect — I'd lied about it so many times I already felt as if I was from Oregon. I tapped it with one finger and Max plucked it from the stack as if he were doing a card trick.

"You have to come back tomorrow with a passport-size picture, chica. Then I give you the money."

"No. Money today and picture this after-noon."

"Okay, okay, I tried. How do you know Sherry?" Max asked, his nose running from who knew what substance he'd just inhaled. Sherry had said he was a dealer, but she didn't say in what. Whatever it was, he managed to stay under the radar of most law enforcement types. According to Max, they hassled him only when things were really slow.

"The cops don't bother me. I don't kill nobody. I don't sell drugs near schools. I don't pimp out no little girls."

Yes, I bet they loved him. I bet even now some civic group was naming a park after him near the Port Authority.

I sat in the back of a coffee shop on West 54th Street as he cut and pasted my picture into the fake driver's license and then sealed it with a portable laminating machine.

"This gizmo, best investment I ever made. You gotta think about a revenue stream, chica, an IRA. I can help you get work." He looked at me and then shook his head.

"Nah, I don't think so. You too sweet. You look so sweet you could be like that girl in the Neil Diamond song, 'Sweet Caroline.' " He pumped his fist in the air in time to the music in his head.

So a grubby guy who dealt in black market

IDs and fake food stamp booklets gave me twenty-five hundred dollars, a new driver's license, and a new name. On the bus ride to Florida I fleshed out my new past and hurtled toward what I hoped was a new future.

Three years later when I met Grant Sturgis he gave me another new life. Over time, I allowed myself to think that I might really have buried that other person. The one from Michigan who did a stupid thing so long ago she really did seem like another person.

THIRTY

Babe's Paradise Diner looked the same as it did most mornings, with one exception. In the past if there had been a cluster of people hunched around one other person, it would have been around Babe. That morning people were huddled around a ten-inch computer screen in the corner booth.

"I'm standing outside the Connecticut police station where just weeks ago the suburban woman known as the Fugitive Mom was held when it was discovered that she was escaped convict Monica Jane Weithorn. Weithorn escaped from a minimum security facility in Michigan more than twenty years ago and today she returns to sleepy Springfield, Connecticut, to the shocked neighbors and friends who for decades knew her as Caroline Sturgis.

"After surrendering her passport, the convicted drug dealer was released on one million dollars bail. What she does next and what she'll call herself is anyone's guess, but one thing is certain. Authorities in two states will be keeping a watchful eye on her until December 6, when she returns to Michigan to hear the judge's decision on whether she'll be forced to serve out her original sentence or be returned to the privileged upper-middle-class lifestyle she's been enjoying for these last two decades. Back to you, Dave."

"Stop screwing around on the Internet, Harry. Aren't you supposed to be working on that thing?"

The man in the corner booth grumbled but complied. That news report was as much as most people had seen or heard that morning anyway. Caroline was coming home. The crowd dispersed as he turned off the sound on his netbook.

"Something in the tone of that reporter's voice made me hate her," Babe said.

I knew what she meant. As vague as it was, the report made it seem as if Caroline had been selling crack in school yards and buying bling and driving big cars over the backs of small children and hopeless drug addicts. The true story was more complicated. Of course she did have a pretty sizable bling collection and a couple of big cars. It was a confusing situation. Even Caroline's friends

282

didn't know exactly where they stood.

I'd caught the early news at home, and it was a little more complete than the web video clip. According to the TV news, she and Grant would be landing at the Westchester Airport at 7 P.M. Journalists and cameramen were already camped out, ready to pounce.

But I knew better. Caroline was already home, having arrived at Bradley Airport, outside Hartford late the previous evening. I knew because we'd talked this morning. I was on my way to see her.

I'd take a private unpaved road to the back of the Sturgis house. Caroline and Grant would leave the inside garage door open for me and I'd be able to enter that way.

They waited for me in the mud room, looking pasty and drained. I guess that was to be expected. He had cavernous circles under his eyes, and she had dark roots, edgy if you lived in the East Village but a major no-no for suburban Connecticut. She tried unsuccessfully to cover them with a scarf folded over many times to serve as a wide headband. Her usually buffed and ovalled nails were rough, and she'd torn at her cuticles, bloodying a few of the fingers.

"Welcome home," I said, trying to sound

chipper. "Everything's going according to plan. I heard from Lucy last night."

The three of us hugged. Then, as previously arranged, Grant left for Hartford to lead any reporters on the merry chase we'd orchestrated with help from Lucy Cavanaugh. Eager to be a part of the story, Lucy had come up with a cloak-and-dagger scenario that would buy Caroline some time with Grant and the rest of her family and the Sturgises had agreed. Lucy had flown to Detroit the previous night and would return on the flight that Caroline would reportedly be taking. Lucy would be in an obvious disguise and when Grant met her at the airport they would lead any intrusive reporters on as long as chase as they could. If it gave Caroline a day of peace to reconnect with her children and meet with her lawyer, that would be enough.

Caroline led me into their immaculate kitchen. The only thing that was incongruous was a mountain of unopened mail on the credenza opposite the central island. There were no mimosas this time, only a pot of herbal tea. She brought out a blue tin of Danish butter cookies that I'd seen stacked up at the local Costco.

"Grant's been amazing. But look at this," she said, fingering the top of the tin. "He's been living on the pantry. If I hadn't gotten out, when I did he would have been down to the cocktail onions and foil packets of coffee and cheese from last year's holiday gift baskets." She pointed to the spotless kitchen. "He's trying so hard to be normal, he even wrote 'Mommy home!' on the whiteboard."

There was a catch in her voice as she said it, but she was remarkably composed for a woman who'd been through the ordeal that she'd had.

"We'll survive this," she said. "Our marriage may even be stronger after the dust settles. If it wasn't for the kids, I'd be glad this came out. You don't know what it's been like, keeping it in all these years. Thank you for finding out how it happened. I wouldn't have cared, but Grant *had* to know who was responsible. It would have driven him crazy."

She shook her head and smiled. "Jeff Warren. I recognized him immediately, even with the beard and mustache. He was always a nice boy."

"That's what his mother says. Did you recognize anyone else who was new in town? Someone at Mossdale's, perhaps?"

"No," she said. "I usually just go out with Becka and we rarely see anyone. You mean the priest, don't you?"

I nodded.

"Never saw him before in my life. He just scared the heck out of me. He used exactly the same words another priest had used years ago when I went to the St. Ann's shelter. I send them a check every year for their Holiday Fund Drive."

"What are you gonna do now?" I asked.

"Wait until the judge decides. Until then, whatever *they* let me do. The people who used to be in my life. You, the moms, my book group."

"I'm here, aren't I? Give the rest of them time," I said. "They don't know how to process this." Privately I thought all it would take was one well-connected person to step up and welcome her back, to remind the rest of the pack that she was still Caroline, the woman they all loved a month earlier. For goodness sake, we forgave Nixon, didn't we?

I was betting that person would be Becka Reynolds. She had a good heart and had helped before, but I made a mental note to give her a little nudge if she needed it.

"Is there anything else I can do?"

"Yes." Caroline looked quite serious now. "That's really why I called."

She pulled a light blue bubble pack mailer

out of the stack of mail on her credenza, hidden in plain sight. It had been stapled closed but was now just folded over. There was no postage and no address; it had been hand-delivered that morning.

"Grant doesn't know about this."

Caroline had turned into a light sleeper; perhaps a week in prison did that to a person. She'd heard a sound in her driveway around 6:30 A.M. when Grant was in the shower. She didn't dare open the door but peered out through her bedroom window and noticed the envelope on her doorstep leaning against a cedar planter. In her peripheral vision she saw a car that had been parked across the road take off, but she couldn't be sure the two actions were connected. And it was still too dark to identify the car or the driver.

"You shouldn't have opened it," I said, staring at the envelope but not touching it. "It could have been dangerous."

"Like what, a dead rat from one of my neighbors? Anthrax?"

"Who knows?" I started to say you never really knew people, but thought better of it.

Caroline slid something out of the envelope and onto the table. It was a glossy blue jewelry box. Inside was an item wrapped in tissue paper. And a note typed on ivory card stock.

It's not over till it's over.

"Well, looks like someone has a problem with your release."

"There's more to it than that. *It's not over till it's over?* That was a cheer we did when our team was down toward the end of a game. Whoever sent this knew me when I was Monica."

And despite what a judge in Michigan might decide, that person didn't think anything was over. Caroline unwrapped the tissue paper. It was a silver megaphone charm with the letters NHS on it. Newtonville High School. On the other side were the initials MJW, Monica Jane Weithorn.

Caroline's cell phone rang, announcing she had a text message: *Want it to be over? If you can pay one million dollars in bail you can damn well pay back the money you stole from me.*

THIRTY-ONE

I put the water on for tea and made Caroline go over the story she'd kept to herself for years and had undoubtedly repeated out loud and to herself a dozen times in the last month.

"I guess I was pretty, but who thinks she's pretty at that age — only the most confident girls, and I wasn't one of them. I was the poor girl, pretty enough to make out with but not presentable enough to bring home to your parents. Until I met Eddie and Kate. They made me feel special. Kate even gave me some of her clothes and convinced me to try out for cheerleading. She knew the coach. Cheerleading made me popular, at least I thought that's what it was. Once I started dating Eddie, I had lots of friends. Coach Hopper even encouraged Eddie and Kate to come along to games. He gave them credit for bringing me out of my shell.

"I never knew what they were doing, and

I didn't steal anything," Caroline said. "Honestly."

"Caroline, I'm not going to judge you and I'm not sure that's the hot issue right now. Someone I would characterize as one of the bad guys thinks you did. And knows your phone number and knows where you live. He may even know that you're holding this thing right now." As I said it, the two of us looked out the sliding glass doors into Caroline's backyard and the reservoir behind it. A beautiful spot. Peaceful. Wooded. Remote. She pushed a button under the island and sun shades rolled down, allowing us to see out but obscuring the view from outside. Then she went into her living room to retrieve a bottle of vodka.

"I don't think that's such a good idea. Let's have some more tea, okay?"

"Tea is not going to do the trick. I'm screwed. My life has been unalterably changed, my kids must think I'm a hypocrite, my mother-in-law wants custody of my children. Lord knows how Grant's clients will react. What else can they do to me?"

What they could do, and she'd realize it once she calmed down, was to make her look as bad as possible so that a judge in Michigan would *have* to send her back to prison to complete her sentence, otherwise risk being thought of as too liberal.

"You have to call the police," I said.

She shook her head vigorously and I couldn't blame her. The last time she trusted them, she was sentenced to twenty years in jail for a crime I still wanted to believe she hadn't committed.

"No," she said. "We just have to find this man and see what he wants."

"Caroline, we know what he wants — money. Some measure of revenge. And from the tone of that note, scaring the pants off you would be a nice little bonus for him."

"You have to help me. You found Jeff Warren, you can find this guy."

I had to admit I was getting good at locating things and people. I found myself wondering what Nina Mazzo charged for this line of work. It had to be more than gardeners earned, and the work was a lot less strenuous, if occasionally risky.

"Okay, let's narrow down the possibilities. We keep saying 'he.' Are we even sure it's a man?" I asked.

There was only one other woman who'd been involved with the case, and she wasn't talking. Unless it was from the grave.

"I can't tell you anything about Kate," Caroline said. "The subject is off-limits."

THIRTY-TWO

Apparently, only a few people had shown up for Kate Gustafson's funeral. Even her mother hadn't gone, although maybe she was too heartbroken to watch her only child being put in the ground. Kate and Caroline were seven years apart in age, but had had a lot in common. They were pretty, smart, and from single-parent homes where there was never enough supervision.

Kate had always wanted to be on the stage, ever since her first beauty pageant at age six. She hadn't won, but she'd stayed on the local pageant circuit until her late teens, when being named Miss Atwell Air Filter was about as much fun as being named Miss Jiffy Lube. Some people just didn't respect the beauty pageant community. To hell with them. The Atwell prize paid for six months of tuition and they couldn't laugh at that. In contrast to what her lawyer tried to claim at the trial, she did well in school and finished college in three and a half years because she had calculated exactly when her financial aid would run out.

Originally, she had hoped to be a teacher, but there were no jobs available since residents were leaving Newtonville and insisted on taking their kids with them. One of the public schools had even shut down and the overflow of teachers were subbing and waiting for their colleagues to either retire or die.

Kate had had a succession of part-time jobs including tending bar. She was reading the obituaries, looking for job openings one night when Eddie Donnelly came in.

She went back to bartending after her release and was found dead in the bar's basement after a fire caused by faulty, non-licensed wiring on a neon sign. Arson investigators were suspicious but found nothing.

"Kate was a good person," Caroline said. "People thought it was odd that we became friends, but she was like an older sister to me. There was no jealousy over Eddie. We were all friends."

Friends who were all criminals, or two friends who set up the third one? Caroline knew what I was thinking.

"You don't understand. Kate tried to protect me." Caroline fiddled with her tissues and looked longingly at the bottle on the table. Clearly she was deciding how much to tell me and I wondered how much more there was to tell.

"Three months into my freshman year, I sensed something was going on. I didn't know what it was. I thought Kate had started seeing Eddie again. There had been a lot of big parties after the games. Sometimes they'd get lost in the crowd and leave me to fend for myself. We weren't the Three Musketeers anymore, the way it had been the previous year. I confronted her and she denied it, but I knew they were hiding something."

One night, Caroline overheard the two of them arguing. Kate said she was tired of sneaking around and hiding things from Caroline and the coach. That confirmed Caroline's worst suspicions. Her mother was gone, she had no other female friends to confide in; by then Kate and Eddie had become her surrogate family. She was devastated.

"I went to Kate again. This time she swore to me that she and Eddie had no romantic connections anymore. She even laughed at the suggestion. She told me they were working for someone, and the less I knew the better."

Kate had told her once football season ended, she was getting out and would make sure that Caroline was no longer involved either, but for the time being she should just keep going to classes and to the games and try not to think about it. That's what she did until the day Kate and Eddie were arrested. Hours later, Caroline was arrested, too.

"I thought it might have to do with betting on the games. I wasn't much of a football fan, but there were a few games we lost that everyone thought we should have won. Kate would never do anything to hurt me."

"She would never do anything to hurt you? And you know that how?"

Caroline reached for the vodka and this time I let her. She poured us each a stiff one. I took a tiny sip and stared out at the woods through the shade, wondering what to do next.

"Let me ask you something else," I said. "Do you get a lot of deer around here?"

"No. The reservoir and the dirt road are privately owned by a water company. They use some sort of organic deer repellent. I don't know what kind. I had to sign an approval form, but it was so long ago I don't remember what it was. Why?"

Now my eyes were glued to the shades. "Because if you don't have a deer problem, there's another large mammal prowling around outside that just ducked into those hemlocks."

THIRTY-THREE

"Reporters? Kids?" Caroline said. "No matter how many signs the water company puts up, teenagers do trespass. They outgrow it, it's just kids' stuff."

"Kids' stuff — trespassing — let me guess your name . . . *Monica?*"

Caroline asked if I was all right.

"I have a hunch I know who is out there. Some weird guy was in the diner recently asking a bunch of questions. He took a picture of Babe with his cell phone and then broke into her office later that night. He claimed the door was open and he just crawled in to sleep off a drunk, but I don't think the cops believed him. I know I didn't."

Then I remembered what the man had been yelling when he was arrested — something about Babe being the one the cops should be taking in. What if Eddie Donnelley sent him to the diner to look for a blonde named Caroline or Monica, and he thought it was Babe? And after he sent her picture, Donnelley told him to keep looking until he found her?

"I'm calling the cops."

Once he knew it was me, O'Malley took his time getting to the phone.

"Let me guess," he said. "You'd like to have dinner? Sorry, I'm busy."

"Mike, I think Countertop Man is trespassing again, this time on Caroline Sturgis's property. I think he's involved with some of the people Caroline knew in Michigan." Mike told me to lock the doors and set the alarm. He'd be right over.

"Countertop Man?" Caroline said, pouring another one and wondering how much of the story she'd missed with one glass of vodka.

"It's a long story."

But it made sense. Jeff Warren sees Caroline at the diner and casually mentions it to a few people, including Leroy Donnelley, who must have told his cousin Eddie. Eddie sends C-Man to Springfield to find out if it's really her.

"How could this man mistake Babe for me if he knew me in Michigan?"

"Maybe he's a friend of Eddie's or someone Eddie met later who owes him a favor.

Eddie might not want to scare you off by coming himself."

Ten minutes later, O'Malley was in Caroline's kitchen, the shades were up and I was telling him what I thought I knew. I thought I laid out my evidence beautifully, but O'Malley was not convinced.

"That's why he was yelling that Babe was a criminal, remember?" I said, my voice rising an octave. "He thought she was *Caroline.*"

"People say a lot of stupid things when they're being arrested. Or when they're agitated." He eyed the bottle on the island. "Or when their senses are impaired."

"We are not impaired. Can't you at least confirm that the guy was in prison in Michigan at the same time as Eddie Donnelley?"

"No, I can't."

"Well, why not?"

"Because he wasn't."

The main real man was Thomas Chase McGinley. According to the mandatory check of his Michigan driver's license he'd never been convicted of a felony. He didn't even have any outstanding traffic violations. Okay, he had bad teeth and stringy hair, and there was the faint whiff of *Deliverance* about him, but maybe that was just me being snobbish. Other than those grooming defects, he appeared to be an upstanding citizen who had until recently worked as a shipping clerk in a sporting goods store in Michigan. Perhaps he *would* know the difference between a countertop and a kayak.

"The only remotely criminal activity McGinley's been engaged in was two years ago" — O'Malley leafed through a tiny spiral notebook — "a tussle at a Big Boy restaurant in Tipp City, Ohio, when management said he tried to walk out with someone else's larger order and McGinley claimed it was all an accident. That's why no bond was set. We let him go with a promise to appear."

"Why would he lie about being in prison? To brag?"

"Men have been known to say stupid things. Perhaps he thought it would impress Babe."

"He's from Michigan, though. What about that?"

"Lots of people are from Michigan, Paula. Magic Johnson. Eminem. Madonna."

Caroline's fingers were playing on an invisible keyboard. She was aching to reach for another drink but didn't want to fuel O'Malley's assumption that she was loaded.

A month earlier she had helped to organize the library fund-raiser and had baked brownies for the Unitarian church rummage sale. Both were big successes. Now she was out on bail, hiding from the media, and listening, bewildered, as two people in her kitchen argued about Madonna and a guy they called Countertop Man. Wanting a drink was perfectly understandable.

"Where's Grant?" O'Malley asked.

"He's in Hartford," I said. "With Lucy."

Now O'Malley looked like he wanted a drink.

THIRTY-FOUR

O'Malley refused to let me go with him. He and his partner searched the woods and came back to the house to report. All they found was a flattened area where someone had knelt down and had a cigarette, a can of Bud, and a pee. No way to tell how long ago any of those activities took place.

"Can you really tell about the pee?" Caroline asked.

"No. I'm making an educated guess based on the number of beer cans. Someone was there, but who knows when? It could have been last summer during the fireworks."

"Were the cans rusty?" I asked.

"Aluminum cans don't rust, Sherlock, they oxidize."

"Was it flattened grass or something else? Grass would have sprung back up after a day or so, especially if it had rained."

His look said it all. Maybe I was letting my imagination run wild. Caroline lived near the woods. All sorts of animals probably trespassed on her property with nothing more on their minds than eating, eliminating, and making babies — and some of them sat down flattening the grass.

"I'll have a car swing by the house regularly for the next few days," Mike said. "As annoying as they are, when the press gets wind that you're home, they'll probably camp out in front and keep away anyone who might have mischief on his mind. Set the alarm and if you see anything, call us right away."

Caroline was close to tears. "Mike, I didn't do anything."

How could he respond? He was a cop. She was a convicted felon and a fugitive out on bail. He said nothing, just squeezed her arm and left.

I didn't know what else I could do for her. As long as Lucy was out there pretending to be Caroline, the genuine article would have some peace. She could get in touch with her lawyer and try to explain things to her kids who were still in Tucson. The next day would be a totally different story. And she'd had lots of them. So many it was possible she no longer knew which one was the truth. I picked up my backpack and got ready to leave.

"I should go, too," I said. "Besides, you probably want to be alone."

"I don't want to be alone. I've just gotten out of a ten-by-ten cell. You can't leave me here. If the reporters don't think I'm arriving until later, and Lucy and Grant take the back roads trying to ditch them, I'll be all by myself. What if he *is* out there? Corian Man?"

"Countertop. He didn't specify stone or composite. Caroline, much as I hate to admit this, O'Malley was probably right. It was a raccoon or a turkey."

"Turkeys don't throw off five-foot-tall shadows, and if there is one that big outside I'd rather not be here." she said quite sensibly. She grabbed an erasable marker and scribbled a cryptic note on the whiteboard letting Grant know that she was all right and would be in touch. I waited while she rummaged in her hall closet.

An hour later, we were on the road. Caroline Sturgis was crouched down in the backseat of my car, under a tarp wearing one of her son's hockey uniforms. Every once in a while, she'd peek out from under the tarp.

"Where are we going?" she asked.

"Toward New Haven," I said. "More places to stash you." That was our plan, I'd check Caroline into a hotel or motel for the night and head home. Then I'd call Grant and tell him where to pick her up in the morning.

"I should have made sure this was Jason's clean uniform," she said, sniffing the armpits of her son's jersey. "I think I took the dirty one." She popped up again like one of those carnival games where the mole keeps bobbing up and you're supposed to whack it on the head. "Stay down," I said.

"Between the stinky uniform and the dirty tarp it's hard to breathe under here."

"That's not dirt on the tarp, it's soil. Do you know there are places in the world where people eat dirt?" I said.

"Kids do it, too. They call of pica — eating stuff that isn't food. I hope that's not on the menu tonight, I am the tiniest bit hungry."

We passed an exit whose only claim to fame was cheap gas, something called the Famely Restaurant, and a motel, the Hacienda.

"Famely with an *e,*" I said, thinking ahead to dinner. "If they can't spell can they read recipes?"

"Oh, Grant and I stayed at a place called the Hacienda on our honeymoon in Zihuatenejo." She sounded wistful and looked pathetic. Her face *was* dirty, and after all she'd been through, I thought, why not? Something told me it wouldn't be the romantic Mexican hideaway she and Grant had found, but if the sheets were clean it would do for the night. And hopefully the cook at the Famely restaurant was better at his job than the sign maker was.

I got off at the next exit and made my way back, snaking along the road that ran beside the highway until it didn't and then did again and finally we reached the Hacienda.

The place looked about as Mexican as your average generic bag of nachos — cardboardy, some orange, some red, very little spice. I parked around the back so the car couldn't be seen from the lobby.

"Is there a hockey mask in that bag?" I asked.

Caroline looked through her son's duffel bag and pulled out a face and throat protector. She put it on. Her face was covered but her hair stuck out.

"Here, use these." I tossed her a scrunchie and a baseball hat, my "don't leave home without them" kit that I always kept in the compartment between the seats. "Put the hat on backward. It'll cover the stubby ponytail." With Jason's sweatshirt thrown around her shoulders, Caroline could pass for a boy, if someone didn't look too closely.

"I'll go to the front desk, you walk around the lobby like you're not interested."

"I have a teenage son," Caroline said, fidgeting with her disguise. "I know what 'not interested' looks like."

We needn't have worried. Peyton, the desk clerk, couldn't have cared less. It was a little strange to see a grown man, wide-eyed and baby-faced, in an orange vest festooned with yellow rickrack and pom-poms, guzzling diet soda and reading a vampire book so close to Halloween, but probably no stranger than seeing a nervous-looking woman and her sullen, hockey fanatic son checking into a dumpy highway hotel this late on a weeknight.

"Reservation?"

He must have been joking. Did anyone ever stop here intentionally? I'd assumed only the prospect of driving oneself into a ditch would induce anyone to check into this dive.

"No," I said.

We checked in under my name, as mother and son; we'd be staying for one night and we'd need two beds and two keys. My "son," wacky kid, insisted on wearing his face protector and waving his stick around when we entered the building.

"Teenage boys — what can you do?" I said, plucking the card keys from the counter and hoping I sounded like a typical suburban mom. I tried not to let it bother me that the desk clerk didn't bat an eye at the idea that I was the mother of a teenager. (That was the last straw. Microdermabrasion, here I come.)

Caroline was in the breakfast area of the lobby where she'd probably be having bad coffee and chemically preserved muffins in the morning while I was home sleeping in.

"Jason, Jason." It took a while for Caroline to realize I was calling her. She was transfixed by the local news report on the lobby television. It was her own smiling image. Blond, blunt-cut hair, velvet headband, no dark roots.

"C'mon," I said, tugging on her sleeve. "No more television tonight. Didn't you watch enough in the car?"

Caroline said nothing as we walked down the narrow hall all the way to the end. Our room, number 104, was on the left, next to the pool and spa, and smelled faintly of bleach or whatever it was they used to clean the Jacuzzi. At least they cleaned it. Inside the room, Caroline pulled off the mask and sucked air.

"No wonder Jason has zits." She tiptoed

to the bathroom and dampened a scratchy washcloth to wipe her face while I hurriedly pulled the curtains shut.

The bathroom was a toilet and a tub that Toulouse-Lautrec would have felt cramped in. Outside the closet-sized bathroom was a sink with a square of mirror bolted to the wall, and underneath the sink a rectangle of curling plastic tile on the floor to catch the drips. The rest of the room was just as basic with a microwave; a boxy tweed Herculon loveseat; and the one incongruous item, a giant flat-screen television, which probably cost more than all the other furnishings combined. Priorities, I supposed. I turned it on for background noise.

By this time Caroline and I were starving. I was ready to give the curiously named Famely Restaurant a try, so I told Caroline to make herself as comfortable as possible while I went out to get us some dinner.

"Can't we order?" she asked.

"I'll ask at the desk, but I don't think they have room service here, and I doubt that the Famely Restaurant delivers. Barring any unforeseen circumstances, I'll be back in thirty minutes with something reasonably healthy to eat. Bolt the door after I leave; don't open it for anyone but me. Don't call anyone and don't answer the telephone.

And don't walk around barefoot on this rug. My shoes are sticking to it. Not a good sign." Clearly, I was taking my role as "mother" seriously.

True to my word I returned in under thirty minutes. While I was waiting for our order to be ready I learned that Famely was not a typo, the restaurant was actually owned by a couple named Famely, which I'm sure caused their children no end of embarrassment and may have even resulted in early, disastrous marriages as offspring tried to escape the Famely family moniker.

Although good, healthy food was foreign to the Famely family, they made up for it with quantity. Back in our room I laid out our feast on the fake wood coffee table — fried chicken, coleslaw, biscuits, and applesauce. The only things that were green were the straws for our sodas.

"All the basic food groups: grease, mayo, bread, and sugar," I said.

"Don't knock it. You'll be amazed at how easily it all goes down," Caroline said, opening the Styrofoam boxes. "It's better than it sounds. We eat this way all the time when Jason has an away game." Her face darkened and I wondered if she was thinking of her previous life or all those away games long ago that had gotten her into this mess.

My dining standards having plummeted in the last few years, I inhaled the food but swapped out my biscuits for her applesauce. We said little while we ate, just listened to the buzz of some inane low-budget reality show now turned up loud to drown out the shower noises and toilet flushes we could hear through the hotel's cardboard walls.

"Want to tell me about Kate?" I said after we finished eating. I thought that's where she was heading when we fled her house.

"Not really," she said, with a laugh. She told me anyway.

"As soon as Kate got out of prison, she got in touch with my brother. She didn't ask if he knew where I was, just sent him money. A lot of money. He used some of it . . . mostly for my father, but he put the rest of it away for me."

So that's why she still considered Kate a friend.

"You stayed in touch with him while you were on the run? Wasn't that risky?"

"Not really," she said again. "Another lesson learned from Sherry, the girl I met in New York. I wonder what happened to her."

In Florida, Caroline had gotten college kids to mail postcards for her when they returned home from spring break. They'd be sent from all over the country, even from the UK, and wouldn't have a Miami post-mark. Eventually, three and a half years after she last saw him, she thought it might be safe and sent her brother an unsigned postcard asking him to meet her at the Delano in South Beach.

"He came to Florida and brought me the money. That's what I was living on when I met Grant."

"What did you live on the first three years?"

"Don't ask."

Holy cow, and I thought this woman just stayed home and did needlepoint and baked cookies.

"That's why I don't think Kate would do anything to harm me. If she didn't expose me then, why would she do it now?"

"Does that mean you think she's still alive?" I asked.

"I don't know and I don't care. I just know she wouldn't hurt me."

THIRTY-FIVE

If Kate was off our list, as Caroline had insisted, she was the only one we'd been able to eliminate so far. Who had hired Countertop Man to track down Caroline? Who had come after me in the parking lot? Who had sent the threatening note with the charm? It was close to midnight and my brain was getting fuzzy, probably from all the poisons coursing through my system from the crap food, which did, as Caroline predicted, go down far too easily.

We still hadn't heard from Lucy and Grant, and I was getting worried — then I realized it wasn't likely Lucy would call my cell. She knew how bad I was about remembering to turn it on. She probably would have called on the landline. I checked the cell anyway. There was only one voice mail message. From Roxy Rhodes. Did I know how to reach Grant Sturgis? Kevin Brookfield was close to making an offer on the nursery and she wanted me to see if Grant was still interested. Especially since Kevin and I were friends, too.

"What's the matter?" Caroline said, looking adorable in her son's oversized, albeit smelly, hockey shirt. "You look puzzled."

I was. Why would Roxy think I knew more about Kevin Brookfield than she'd told me? I'd only met him once, that time at the diner when I was planting false lamiums for Babe. We'd barely exchanged words.

Despite the hour, I called Lucy and she picked up on the first ring. After pretending to be Caroline, she and Grant had driven in circles for hours trying to elude the press and had decided to stop for the night. She hadn't seen anyone at the dumpy motel where they'd pulled in and felt they were in the clear. Lucy sounded exhilarated over her adventure; I doubted Grant Sturgis was having as much fun.

"Can I talk to him?" I said.

"He's in the shower and I'm waiting for a pizza. That's the only thing they'll deliver to this extremely humble establishment."

There was a bizarre echo on the phone, the repeating sound of traffic and bells, like those on a vehicle that was backing up.

"What's that noise?" I asked. "Where are you?"

"It's a dive, but Sturgis got all weepy when he saw the name. Some fleabag called the Hacienda."

Ten minutes later Lucy and Grant joined us in our room, two doors from their own. After their tearful reunion, I hated to break it to them that if there had been any reporters following them they'd soon be at the Hacienda, but Grant and Lucy were positive they had evaded any cars that might have been on their tail.

"Early on I saw a Civic and an SUV following us — couldn't tell what make because he was behind the Honda." Lucy was good with anything that had a label. "Both cars were light colored."

"Out-of-state plates?"

"Yeah, but I couldn't recognize which state. Remember when each state had one type of license plate and you could play name-that-state on long driving trips? Now there are three or four to choose from. I'm pretty sure the plate was dark blue and white."

"Maybe we should leave," I said.

"C'mon, we lost them. No one's here. Can't we at least wait until the pizza comes? It's Frank Pepe. It's supposed to be wonderful." Lucy said. "I had to give my credit card, so I've already paid for it. And I haven't eaten all day."

We took a vote. If there was no activity outside the hotel in the time that it took the pizza to come, we'd stay. By morning Caroline would have to surface somewhere, and when she did it wouldn't take long for whoever wanted to find her to find her, but we'd deal with that tomorrow.

Lucy, sans wig, and I went to the front desk when the pizza arrived and we went to her room to let Grant and Caroline have their first private visit in weeks.

And that's what would have happened if ten minutes later the cops hadn't burst into both of our rooms.

Props to the desk clerk who I had dismissed as a nerdy loser, so unobservant that he checked in two women as mother and son. When Lucy and Grant arrived, ordered a pizza under a different name than they registered under, and then switched partners with us, the clerk — who probably watched a lot of true crime stories on television — decided I was a madam who'd brought a teenage boy to a motel for an assignation with a man while I ate pizza with the guy's wife. Lord knows what he thought we were doing. It was the stuff of supermarket tabloids.

Once the cops discovered Caroline was not a young boy but a middle-aged woman dressed as a boy, they reckoned it was simply kinky sex, none of their business, and they left the four of us alone. Hey, if consenting adults wanted to play the house-wife and the UPS man or the contessa and the chauffeur, what was it to them? Needless to say, for Grant and Caroline, the moment had been ruined.

THIRTY-SIX

Unlike their first blissful stay at the other Hacienda, Caroline and Grant couldn't leave this one fast enough. The Sturgises declined to spend the night and fled north to a house they sometimes rented in Wellfleet, Massachusetts. It would be shuttered for the season, but they knew where the key was hidden, and they would call the owners in Baltimore as soon as they arrived so the Wellfleet police wouldn't think they were squatters. Having already had run-ins with police in two states and despite the hockey outfit, Caroline and Grant weren't looking to score a hat trick. And there was a TJ Maxx nearby, so the next morning Caroline could buy warm clothing and get out of her son's smelly sports gear. No phone in the house, no cell service, no Internet. It was just what they were looking for.

"There's a general store fifteen minutes away from the house where I can get a cell signal. I'll call you from there tomorrow," Caroline said, rushing to her husband's car in the dark.

Bone-tired, I suggested to Lucy that we spend the rest of night at the Hacienda — after all, we had no fewer than two rooms at our disposal and instead of preservative-laden muffins at the free breakfast bar we could have leftover pizza — but she said something about preferring to take the pizza, chug an energy drink, and get on the road, so we left shortly after Caroline and Grant. Lucy insisted on wearing the wig again and readjusted it several times before we were allowed to leave the room. (*Ah yes, room 104, so many fond memories.*) She said the wig was in case anyone was following us, but I think she enjoyed being in disguise. How often do grown-ups get to play dress up?

"It's one thing to stay in a place like that for a story. Quite another if I have a choice," she said, giving the room a once-over before we left.

"Later when my brain is functioning properly, I'm going to ask you about that 'story' part," I said. "No, let's do it now and get it over with. What the hell are you talking about?"

She stalled for a bit, not wanting to risk

my disapproval, then blurted it out. After spending all day with Grant, she'd gotten his consent to write about the experience, "I Was a Fugitive," by Lucy Cavanaugh.

"What about Caroline? Doesn't she have a say?"

She assured me, as she had probably assured Grant, that it would be tasteful and respectful. I had my doubts whether any story entitled "I Was a Fugitive" could be tasteful and respectful. I wondered which tabloid would be the highest bidder for the classy piece.

In the hour or so it took us to drive home, I brought her up to speed on the note and package that Caroline had received what seemed like days ago but was really only that morning.

"You think it was sent by this guy Eddie?" she said.

That was the obvious assumption. Dead or alive — and I was beginning to suspect that Caroline hadn't told me everything — if Kate Gustafson was not a suspect, who else even knew about Caroline except Donnelley? Warren? O'Malley had told me that he was in the hospital. Her brother? He was an unlikely candidate for villain. Caroline had only spoken of him in glowing terms: *my brother.* I realized I didn't even know his first name and wondered if that was an unconscious habit Caroline had picked up from years on the run. Why would he reveal her identity now after all this time? If he had needed money, Caroline would have simply given it to him as he had given it to her.

"And you think Donnelley is passing himself off as this Kevin Brookfield?" she said.

I wasn't sure what I thought anymore. Brookfield was one of the few newcomers in town. Newcomers were always suspect. I'd been there myself. "That's what I think today. Last week I thought it was a guy who turned out to be a priest." I told Lucy about my trip to Mossdale's stables and my chat with Father Ellis Damon.

"Ellis Damon? E.D.? Same initials?" she said, turning in the passenger seat to face me. "Isn't that what people do when they make up fake names? Use the same initials as their real ones?"

"E.D. also stands for erectile dysfunction. Do you think Bob Dole was involved? For pete's sake, Lucy, the guy was a priest."

"Oh, and I'm a natural blond? You can buy *gladiator* outfits online. How hard can it be to get one of those little white collars? I think I have one from a silk jacket I bought in Chinatown."

"If he'd been Eddie Donnelley," I said, "Caroline would have recognized him when she saw him at Mossdale's that first day. He couldn't have changed that much in twenty years. She recognized Jeff Warren right away, but she didn't even mention the man at the stables. I think she just saw judgment day coming toward her. She was already spooked by the traffic ticket and the fear that her personal information was being fed into a law enforcement computer system. All Father Damon had to do was say 'good morning, my child' and she'd have freaked. Poor guy. I think her reaction caused him to question his calling."

Lucy fell silent. Neither of us had seen any pictures of Donnelley online, and now that Caroline was hurtling toward Cape Cod, the one person who could give us a description was temporarily unavailable. Correction, the one woman. There was always Jeff Warren. And once he got out of the hospital I might ask him. Maybe I could try him anyway. Plenty of people who'd had car accidents could still talk on the phone. I asked Lucy to get my cell from my backpack. Dead.

"This is aggressively antisocial behavior," Lucy said, shaking the phone at me. "You do realize that."

"Chill out." I plugged the cell into the car's cigarette lighter to recharge it and heard the snippet of classical music that told me I had a message. It was the one from Roxy I hadn't deleted. I'd forgotten about it.

"Listen to this." I replayed the message for Lucy.

"What the hell does that mean? Have you spoken to her?" Lucy asked.

I shook my head. "No idea. Just picked it up a few hours ago. I don't think even Roxy stays in the office that late. We'll see her tomorrow."

Warren's number was in saved contacts, and I scrolled through to find it. I autodialed but was kicked into voice mail. Now I started to wonder where McGinley was. Was he back in Michigan, having made his report? Or was he still in Connecticut waiting to finish the job he'd been sent here to do? Or was he — long shot here — really crashing at his friend's place so that they could get an early start hauling those countertops?

I checked the rearview mirror obsessively.

Lucy noticed. "I'm not the nervous type," she said, "but you're making me jumpy. No one is following us. Why would they? Let's just get back to your place."

We pulled into my driveway at around 3:15. We should have been tired, but we'd both gotten our second winds, or maybe it was nervous energy, and instead of collapsing in bed, we decided to pull an all-nighter just like in the old days.

"What's the flashing light — radon levels reaching red alert?"

"Pay no attention. Something to do with the alarm system. I haven't been able to clear it since it went off, and I'm afraid to touch any more buttons for fear it'll go off again. I found out I'm going to be fined a hundred bucks for having a false alarm that the Springfield police had to respond to and I don't want it to happen again."

"Ouch. Can't you get your cop friend to fix it? Like a ticket?"

Did everyone know how to do that except me?

"I'll get around to reading the manual one of these days when I have some time, like in December." I dumped my things on the sofa and headed into the kitchen.

"Let me try." She pushed the reset button and I held my hands over my ears, gearing up for the sirens, but they didn't go off and surprisingly the flashing red lights disappeared.

"Excellent."

We sat on the living room floor with our reheated pizza and I powered on the laptop to google images of Eddie Donnelley. Like Warren, it was a relatively common name and until we added the state and the crime we got nowhere. Even then all we got was a grainy black-and-white mug shot from twenty-five years ago that had been reproduced many times, and had only been resurrected because of Caroline's recent arrest. It could have been any dark-haired male with a long face and brown eyes. The aviator glasses, long hair, and beard didn't help, I guess. When you're a drug dealer or undercover cop, it's an asset to be able to change your looks quickly. Enlarging it only further distorted the image.

"Could this be Brookfield?" Lucy asked.

It could have been Kevin Brookfield or it could have been Kevin Bacon. I wasn't prepared to hang the man based on such a sketchy photo.

"I don't know. I don't think so. There's a lot of hair obscuring his face. But the nose looks different."

"He could have broken his nose in jail," Lucy said. "Rival gang? Power struggle?" She had an even more active imagination than I did. Maybe she *should* turn her fugitive story into a screenplay.

"You've been watching too much cable," I said. "I don't know. I can't say it's him, I only saw him briefly."

While I was at it, I googled *Kate Gustafson.* And sent the images to my downstairs computer — the one hooked upto the the printer.

We'd bring the pictures to Roxy's tomorrow and see what she thought. Babe's, too. Brookfield had camped out at the diner for a while — she might remember him better than any of us.

Tomorrow started four hours later when, sleep-deprived, Lucy and I shuffled into the Paradise Diner.

"Hey, look who's here. You two girls look like crap. You here to give our girl a make over or to get one? I heard she did some shopping in your closet after that wedding, but I haven't seen any new outfits." Rats. That reminded me of the bag full of Lucy's hand-me-downs, still in my entrance awaiting my next trip to Goodwill. I hoped she hadn't seen them.

"No," Lucy said after they air-kissed. "I'm here on a story — 'I Was a Fugitive.' " She slipped onto a counter stool and spread her hands wide, envisioning the headline and the layout.

"Should I assume you're no longer a fugitive if you're announcing it in a public place?"

"That's correct. Paula, tell Babe what happened last night."

"Later. Keep it down. We still have a few private issues to discuss." I robotically ordered two Paradise specials and two coffees and asked Babe to join us at the farthest empty booth when she had a chance. She brought our food and slid into the seat next to Lucy.

"Much as I love to see you, you really should consider keeping a box of cereal in your house for emergencies. Don't you ever eat at home anymore?"

I shook my head, then pulled out the photo of Eddie Donnelley and showed it to Babe. I watched for a glimmer of recognition in her eyes, but none came.

"Who's this? He looks like some guy I picked up in a bar in Greenwood, Indiana, in 1984."

"That's Eddie Donnelley," I whispered. "One of the people who was arrested with Caroline. Does he look familiar?"

"You gotta be kidding," Babe said, "at my age any long-haired hippie in a grainy photo looks familiar."

I told her who I thought it might be.

"That guy looking for real estate? No way. This guy's eyes are closer together and he has finer cheekbones. And the nose is totally different." She'd make a good witness if ever called upon to identify someone in a lineup.

I was starting to feel better about Kevin Brookfield.

"Did he ever come back?" I asked.

Babe had to think. "Yeah, one other time." I could see her piecing together the scene. "A day or two after you saw him. I thought he was planning to camp out here again, the way he did that day, when the Moms were falling all over themselves to give him real estate advice. He sat down at a table outside with a coffee and those damn brochures again, like he was waiting for someone. I thought it was a real estate agent. Then something happened and he left abruptly. His coffee cup was still warm when I cleared." She replayed the event in her brain, rewinding like an old videocassette.

Just then two cops entered the diner. Babe got up and handed them a gray cardboard box that was stashed under the counter. It was filled with three dozen donuts. One of them opened the box and inhaled deeply.

"Can't survive the weekly community

328

meeting without a little help from Pete."

"Standing order every Tuesday. Come to think of it, Brookfield was here on a Tuesday. Same time. As soon as the boys came in, he left."

"You think he doesn't like donuts?" Lucy said.

Or he didn't like cops. I wanted to hear what Roxy Rhodes had to say. I still had a few reservations about Kevin Brookfield before I was ready to jump on the welcome wagon.

THIRTY-SEVEN

Forty minutes later, we were at Rhodes Realty with Roxy Rhodes demanding to know what I'd said to Kevin Brookfield to put him off buying the nursery. Without even asking us to sit down she launched into her assertion that I'd poisoned the waters by leaking information about the former owner's murder.

"It's not exactly a secret," I said. She didn't threaten legal action but came close. I thought I heard the word *ruin* mixed into her rambling, apoplectic message.

"Roxy, I don't know what you're talking about. I only saw the man once. Maybe the Moms told him. Maybe he read about it online. Maybe he was full of baloney and was never really interested. Lots of people look at places and have no intention of buying. They're real estate junkies. Window shopping."

She calmed down briefly. She knew I was right.

"And who is this?" she said, pointing a bony, reaperlike finger at Lucy.

"She's a friend. Can we sit down and talk like civilized people? Like neighbors?" (Thank you, Mr. Rogers.) Roxy collapsed onto her designer throne, and Lucy and I pulled over two stylish but decidedly uncomfortable wire chairs. "Thank you."

All Roxy knew about Kevin Brookfield was that he specifically came to her office to see about buying the Chiaramonte nursery. No other property interested him.

"I should have known he wasn't for real. He didn't even try to get the price down. But he was so simpatico. He said he was making a fresh start and he had that wonderful smile."

Good grief, did he flirt with her, too? I showed her the picture, but she was noncommittal.

"It's this economy," she said, tossing it aside. "Or perhaps I've just lost my mojo." Suddenly Roxy looked old, as old as she really was. This was more than the loss of a 6 percent commission.

"That's not it," I said, trying to make her feel better. "Your mojo is fine. But there's a possibility Kevin Brookfield may not be who he says he is."

She wilted, seeing her commission, and perhaps a budding romance, flying out the door. "Brookfield suggested you and Caroline and he might go into business together."

"Highly unlikely, especially given Caroline's situation."

A door in the outer office slammed and Roxy's assistant tapped gently on Roxy's for permission to enter.

"I'm so sorry, Ms. Rhodes. The documents you requested? You wanted to know as soon as they arrived." The assistant maneuvered her way around the enormous desk and placed a light blue bubble pack envelope in front of the slumping Roxy. Then she turned on her kitten heels and left.

"What are you women staring at now?" Roxy said. "Is there some other deal you'd like to put the kibosh on? Some other area of my business that you'd like to involve yourself in?" The outside door slammed again.

"Just one," I said, rising out of my seat. "Can you tell me what delivery service you use?"

"This isn't from a delivery service. It's a personal matter."

As if on cue, Lucy jumped up and ran to

the window.

"A blue Civic," she said. "Connecticut license plate 485 SMK. It could even be the one I saw last night." She grabbed a felt pen from Roxy's desk and in the absence of any paper, scribbled the license plate number on the palm of her hand.

"Will you two fruitcakes please get out of here?" Roxy sank her head into both of her hands. "Natalie," she yelled for her assistant, "get my calendar. I need four days at the ranch and a stop at Dr. P's on the way up."

"Save us some time, Roxy. Unless that envelope has something to do with Brookfield or Caroline Sturgis, we don't really care what's in it. We just want to know who delivered it."

She closed her eyes and made circles with her head in a stress-reducing ritual I imagined she performed many times during the course of a morning like this one.

"It doesn't have anything to do with either of them. I do represent a great many properties apart from that decrepit, blood-soaked nursery. It's from an agency we sometimes work with. Nina Mazzo's."

I called Nina and made an appointment to see her that afternoon. This time I didn't pretend to be Thelma Turner.

THIRTY-EIGHT

Lucy stared at the image we'd printed out from my computer. "Kevin Brookfield must be a helluva lot better looking than this picture if every woman in this burg would be so all-fired happy to see him relocate here."

"We don't know that Donnelley *is* Brookfield. You may be looking at a picture of someone else. But Brookfield has something. No denying. It's something else," I said, trying to figure out what it was. Lucy and I had time before our meeting with Nina Mazzo, so we doubled back to the Paradise to pick the brains of the town's resident expert on men. Maybe Babe could put her finger on it.

"It's true. I am generally acknowledged to be an expert on a great many subjects — movies, music, and men included," Babe said. We'd parked ourselves in a rear booth and made our guru join us.

"What makes a woman gravitate toward a man?" Lucy asked.

"She kidding or is this some Sphinxlike riddle?" Babe said.

"We're serious."

"You mean if he isn't wealthy, famous, or powerful and doesn't look like Johnny Depp, act like Mr. Darcy, and make love like Don Juan?" She gave it some thought. "Okay, he's got a sad story. How's this? He's a single parent whose wife died young — and tragically — and he nursed her until the bitter end. Could be his mother dying but not as effective as the wife. The kid's not necessary; in the absence of a kid, a dog would work. Dogs are chick magnets, but best for generating one-night stands, not lasting relationships."

Lucy and I were extremely impressed. "Where do you get this?" she asked.

"*Soap Opera Digest,* 1994. Classic story line. I think it was on *Another World*," she said. Babe continued spinning her hypothetical situations. "Hoping to reconnect with a childhood sweetheart is another good one, but the dead wife story works really well. Shows he's a romantic and will stay faithful — even after you're in the ground." She stood up to go back to work.

"Did Brookfield say anything like that to you?" I asked.

"He suggested it. Single guy, not too handsome, not too neat, so probably straight, looking for real estate in a new town, to start a business. To start over. Charming, no ring, or ring line, as if he'd just taken it off. A little flirty but nothing overt. Screams 'you can trust me, I have a broken heart.' "

Even if she was wrong, it was a damn good answer on the fly and something to be filed for future reference. Oddly enough, apart from the wife and the part about being new in town, she had also just described Mike O'Malley — romantic, faithful, looking after an aged parent, and a dog owner, always a plus. And just at that moment entering the diner.

"Oh, this looks a mite scary. Three beautiful women conspiring? Or is it gossiping?" O'Malley said. He sat at a counter stool a few feet away and waved off the young waitress's efforts to bring him a menu.

"Why is it when men talk, they're *discussing,* and when women talk, we're *gossiping?* That's very misogynistic of you," Lucy said. "Very disappointing. I'm going to stop telling Paula and Babe that you are the cutest guy in Springfield."

"This conversation is taking an intriguing turn, but I'm afraid I don't have the time for verbal foreplay. I just came in because I saw your car and thought you might like to know. You can tell Caroline that she doesn't have to worry about Countertop Man anymore. He's dead."

THIRTY-NINE

"Did I miss something?" Lucy said.

Babe, Mike, and I replied as one, "Yes."

"Catch her up," Mike said, getting up to leave. "I've got to go."

"Wait a minute," I said. "You can't go now. Was he . . . murdered?"

McGinley and his car were found in a ditch in Macedonia, Ohio. The local police got in touch with O'Malley because he'd made the most recent inquiry into McGinley's record, and as a courtesy, the cops in Ohio thought they'd inform him.

"What do you think happened?" Babe asked.

"Fell asleep at the wheel, got drunk, and drove — who knows? Pretty bad accident, though. Gas tank caught fire."

"Does that usually happen when a car goes into a ditch?"

"Apparently this ditch led to a twenty-five-foot drop from a two-lane bridge."

"Could he have been run off the road?"

"Yes. He also could have had an Elvis sighting or been abducted by aliens. I didn't ask."

"Why not?" I said.

Because he was a cop in Springfield, Connecticut, not Macedonia, Ohio. But that didn't mean that I couldn't ask. And I would, but first we had an appointment with Nina Mazzo.

"*You* could be a private investigator," Lucy said. "Seriously."

"I think not."

"Look at how good you are at this stuff."

"That's what Babe said. Maybe if the gardening thing doesn't work out."

When I had researched Nina the first time, I learned a little about the profession. Most PIs came from a background of law enforcement. Who knew? It was the image of them standing in the shrubbery snapping pictures that made the job seem faintly cartoonish and not quite legitimate, but it was. Fewer than 40 percent of their cases were related to infidelity and divorce (I would have guessed more), but that's all most people ever thought of when they heard the words *private investigator.* That or Humphrey Bogart in *The Maltese Falcon.* Hopefully, Nina would tell us if tracking down missing persons and delivering unmarked packages like the one Caroline Sturgis had received made up the other 60 percent of the business.

We drove downtown and saw the property values drop sharply from one block to the next until we passed under the railroad tracks.

"This isn't much of an area," Lucy said.

"Depends what you're looking for. If you're a contractor, this is as good as Decorator's Row in New York." We passed antiques alley, the flagstone and paving center, and the kitchen and bathroom remodeling district and I made a right onto the stretch of road where Nina's building was located. As we pulled into Nina's parking lot, I told Lucy about Mazzo's recently reduced circumstances and her fervent wish that the economy would bounce back so there would be more philandering husbands.

"That's the most twisted logic I've heard in a long time. It would make a very salable feature film."

"You two are gonna get along just fine."

We had to wait for three men balancing a massive slice of soapstone on a dolly to pass before we settled into a spot around the corner from the Mazzo Agency.

"What was that?" Lucy said, watching the hunk of rock go by.

"I hear the apartment dweller in you coming out. That's a slab of stone which will be cut into a countertop."

Lucy had been wrong about Ellis Damon, but she wasn't wrong about something else — when people lie, they frequently use or say something familiar because they think it will make the lie more plausible. McGinley may not have been in Springfield to help his friend The Countertop King get his business off the ground, but perhaps he got the idea after a visit to Nina Mazzo. I remembered how hot Nina kept her office, so I peeled off my jacket.

"Are you expecting to come to blows?" Lucy asked as I locked the car.

If Nina was surprised to see me, she hid it well.

"How about that — you know I have another prospective client who looks just like you, I think she said her name was Thelma Turner. And who might you be, Etta James?"

"I'm Paula Holliday and this is Lucy Cavanaugh."

She motioned for us to sit down.

"We're helping a friend and would like to

ask you a few questions."

"That's very admirable. Tell me why I should care."

"We think you or someone from this office delivered an unmarked blue bubble pack mailer to 197 Chelsea Road yesterday morning. Is that true?"

"I have a very busy practice. I really can't say." The famous discretion from her place mat ad was kicking in again. "Unlike you, I'm not in the friend-helping business. I do this for a living."

"Do you know a man named Chase McGinley? He may have used an alias — scruffy guy, plaid shirt, down vest, bad teeth? He would have come in about a week ago."

Nina's face was so stony, she had to be holding something back. "Ms. Holliday, you don't really expect me to answer these questions, do you? Why would I?"

"Because you used to be a cop and presumably cared about the law. Chase McGinley is dead. And the envelope delivered to that address contained blackmail. I think the two incidents are related."

She closed her eyes briefly. "When can I go back to the halcyon days of CEOs cheating on their wives?"

McGinley had visited Nina Mazzo — he'd

probably gotten her name from the same place mat that I had. He said he was looking for an old girlfriend who dumped him when she was carrying his child. She was blond, about forty to forty-five, and would have a son about fourteen.

"I gave him some basic information on how we'd try to find her. Of course I didn't tell him everything. I wanted him to come back, but he never did. I may need to redo the *free consultation* wording on that place mat ad. This is getting ridiculous."

"And the package?"

"Totally different case."

Without revealing details, Nina told us was the item to be delivered was a pendant, a gift from a married lover. The client wanted to end the affair and make a clean break of it, but she knew it had sentimental value and didn't want to just throw it away or trust it to the mails.

"How thoughtful," Lucy said.

"She?" I asked.

FORTY

Nina Mazzo's physical description of the woman who'd hired her to deliver the package to Caroline's home was next to useless. It wasn't that she was not perceptive, she was — but the woman did her best to appear as bland and nondescript as possible.

"She was a big girl," Nina said, "slim but tall, that is."

With thick, dyed blond hair blunt-cut in a chin-length bob. She wore a plain navy suit with a striped silk blouse. Dark sunglasses. Not much jewelry, a ring with a tiny jewel-toned stone and a heart-shaped pendant. She didn't speak much; she just stated the reason that she had come and produced the small white jewelry box in a mesh pouch. She showed Nina what was in the box, but Nina gave it just a cursory look before the woman enclosed a note and sealed the box.

"Her voice was raspy and she coughed into her hankie a few times," Nina said.

"I'm a little germophobic, so I hurried her out and kept my distance when we parted." She said her name was Brigid O'Shaughnessy, "but I'm an old movie buff so I knew she was lying. I didn't believe her about the name, but I believed her three hundred dollars, as the saying goes."

Didn't anyone tell this poor woman their real name? Not-Brigid left the item and paid in cash. Mazzo never saw her again.

"Did you know the item was going to Caroline Sturgis's home?" This was the first time I'd mentioned her name, and from the ashen look on Nina's face I don't think she did know.

"I checked the zip code. When I saw the address was in the high-rent district, I took the gig."

"Did your man return later for any reason?" I asked.

"Woman. But, no, she didn't."

Lucy and I arrived back to my place with more new questions than answers.

"Can I open this wine?" she asked. "I think we deserve a drink."

"Go ahead. I have to think."

She poured herself a glass of red and flopped onto the sofa opposite me, kicking off her shoes and stretching out her legs on the leather ottoman. She flexed and pointed her toes as if she were in an exercise class. "I'm really sorry I have to leave tomorrow morning. This is getting good."

The way Lucy saw it, Kate Gustafson had to be alive. What other woman could it be? Eddie Donnelley's mother? A girlfriend? A homicidal former cheerleader?

"All those bitter girls who didn't make the squad," I said. "Now that's an avenue we haven't explored."

Suddenly I wished that Caroline and Grant hadn't escaped to Wellfleet. Until *she* called *me*, I couldn't get answers to any of the questions that were stacking up like books in my to-be-read pile. She hadn't given me a straight answer. Did she know if Kate Gustafson was alive? She'd *never* given me a straight answer. I willed the phone to ring.

And it did.

"Holy — I made the phone ring!"

"Uh, you did not," Lucy said, circling her ankles and listening to the bones pop. "The person who's calling you made the phone ring. Are you going to answer it or shall I?"

I ran to the kitchen. I didn't recognize the number on caller ID.

"Hello?

"Is this Paula Holliday? I'm Kevin Brookfield. I think we may have some business to discuss." I turned on speakerphone so that Lucy could listen in.

Brookfield wanted to meet. He suggested Chiaramonte's nursery. Lucy shook her head furiously, but no problem, I'd already done that once and wasn't interested in a return engagement. From now on any meetings with strange men, remarkable or otherwise, would occur in crowded, brightly lit locations.

"How about the Springfield Town Center?" I said. It was an enclosed mall that I'd been to once about three years back. "Seven thirty?" Click.

"You think it'll be safe?" Lucy said.

"The man hasn't done anything here except drink coffee. Maybe we've been too quick to think he's involved in all this. Besides, we're meeting in an enclosed mall, after dinner, in the fourth quarter. It'll probably be packed with type-A shoppers who want to get all their gift-buying done before Thanksgiving. You'll be there to protect me. What can happen?"

She brightened. "Can I wear the wig again?"

The Springfield Town Center was about five minutes from the train station. Brookfield and I planned to meet in front of the

Crate & Barrel store on the lower level. Lucy would be on the lookout from the upper level. She'd be outfitted in her Caroline-in-disguise disguise and carrying bags to look like a real shopper. I rummaged under my sink looking for bags.

"I'm not carrying a Walmart bag. Don't you have anything else?" I remembered the clothing she'd given me and resurrected the Victoria's Secret and J. Crew bags filled with her own unworn purchases; she was much happier with her look, which she insisted was more believable.

"You didn't even take the tags off."

"I've only had them for a few weeks. How long did you have them?"

"Good point."

At the shopping center, I grabbed a bench and waited in front of the furniture store. Lucy hovered upstairs pacing back and forth like a nervous talent show contestant.

I scoured the crowd. Everyone looked normal; then in the distance I saw a man smiling and walking directly toward me. Brookfield was more attractive than I remembered, but then I'd been busy and hadn't paid much attention. It was his walk more than anything else. He stopped in front of me, the tiniest bit closer than I was comfortable with.

"I'm Kevin." I stood up and we shook hands. From somewhere I heard a noise and out of the corner of my eye saw Lucy bending over to retrieve the phone she'd dropped. Ten bucks said she was trying to take his picture and couldn't figure out how to do it. I pretended not to know her.

I understood his appeal and instantly felt a kinship with Roxy Rhodes and the Main Street Moms. One thing was certain: he wasn't the man who had jumped me. With those arms he could have inflicted a lot more damage than just a bruised wrist. And he wasn't limping. As hard as I'd kicked my assailant, I had to think he'd still have a little bit of a limp. Things were looking up.

"Want to go someplace?" he said, hands on his hips.

"Let's just stay here, okay?"

He seemed amused by my security precautions, but after my first few ill-advised meetings, I thought it best to stay out in the open.

"Suit yourself."

He sat down and we danced around the subject of Caroline and the nursery. If he wanted something, he was taking his sweet time getting around to it, so I decided to strike first.

"What exactly do you want from Caroline?"

"Well, that's straightforward. Straightforward is good. I'd like her to end this."

"End what?"

We stopped smiling at about the same time. Lucy stopped pacing upstairs; she must have sensed the tone of our conversation had changed.

"Let's not play games. She's been stringing us along for long enough. I want what she's been holding on to. It's what I need to make a new start. Then I'll never darken her door again. I promise."

Omigod. It was him. "Like you did twenty-five years ago," I said, I slid farther away from him on the bench, and he pretended not to know what I was talking about.

From the upper level of the mall a cell phone came crashing down to my feet. Lucy had either dropped it again or thrown it to get my attention. I looked up and saw her struggling with two men.

"Help!" she screamed.

"Leave her alone, you assholes!" I sprinted to the escalator and took the moving steps three at a time, pushing shoppers aside. When I reached the top Lucy was being strong-armed by two men and I slogged

through the crowd that had gathered to follow them.

FORTY-ONE

Ordinarily, Mike O'Malley didn't concern himself with shoplifting busts — that was left to mall cops and the junior men in the Springfield police department. In Lucy's case he made an exception. I'd called him as soon as I realized she wasn't being kidnapped — she was being arrested by undercover security.

True, Lucy did look suspicious with a crooked wig and dark glasses and two bags full of clothing with tags and no receipts, but mall security took O'Malley's word for it that she was probably not a thief, simply another New Yorker with hard-to-fathom habits. That seemed to satisfy them and they let her go.

"Doing a little shopping, are we?" he said outside the security office. Lucy hugged him, and, if I wasn't mistaken, he returned the favor.

"Martinets," she said. "I could sue them.

I haven't been arrested for shoplifting since I was fifteen."

"You mean you haven't *shoplifted* since you were fifteen," Mike said.

"Right. That's what I meant." Lucy caught her reflection in a Williams-Sonoma window and straightened her wig.

"Anyone who didn't know better might think you two were up to something."

"Not us," I said. "Just doing a little comparison shopping. In fact, Lucy . . ." — I paused to organize my thoughts — "is doing a feature on secret shoppers, people hired by stores to check up on their employees. That's why she was wearing the wig." My explanation drew puzzled glances from both of them and I couldn't tell who looked more skeptical at my stream-of-consciousness tale spinning.

When we parted, Lucy was effusive in thanking Mike for coming to her rescue. "Thanks for helping me beat the rap." He left us in the mall's garage. Then it was my turn to look askance. "Beat the rap? Is that wig too tight? Are you back in fugitive mode?"

We spoke little driving back to my place. The meeting with Brookfield was a bust, literally; but, as Lucy pointed out, at least she hadn't been hauled off to jail. But I hadn't learned anything either. Could I have misinterpreted what he said? What had he said that was so awful? For all I knew, Kevin Brookfield really was a handsome single guy who wanted to buy a nursery. Not that I had a chance to find out because he was long gone by the time mall security released us.

The red light changed to green and then back to red but my foot stayed on the brake as a very depressing thought came to me. "I may have totally alienated the perfect man for me."

Lucy patted my arm. "I wasn't going to say anything."

FORTY-TWO

By the time Lucy and I got home it was nine-thirty P.M. Half a bottle of wine was left, and soon there would be none. I made a fire and we sat on the floor in my living room, drinking.

Mike O'Malley was Lucy's new hero and she inundated me with questions about him that made me think she was more interested in him than she'd let on. Surprisingly enough, I didn't mind. Maybe that was the real reason Mike and I had never gotten together. Maybe we weren't meant to. I was still thinking about Kevin Brookfield.

The phone rang as it had a few hours earlier.

"Don't answer it," Lucy said. "I'm not getting into that wig again!"

It was good advice. I'd had enough drama for one day. I let the call go to voice mail and only jumped up when I heard the small, tentative voice leaving a message. I pushed the speakerphone button so that Lucy could hear.

"Mrs. Warren?"

"Oh, you are there. I thought it was a machine."

"It was a machine, ma'am. I just got to the phone late. How are you?"

"I'm well. Thank you for asking, dear. I thought you might like to know Jeff has regained consciousness. He's expected to make a full recovery."

I didn't know what she was talking about, but I played along. "I'm so glad to hear it, I was worried."

"He did lose his position with that trucking company, but his uncle Lou may be able to get him his old job at the post office. I expect he'll call you himself once he gets those tubes taken out and is on his feet again." Only a hard pinch on the forearm stopped Lucy from making faces that were guaranteed to crack me up while I was talking to the old woman.

"Will he have any lasting health issues?" I asked. I had to keep her on the line until I could ask her some questions without appearing insensitive to her son's condition.

"Well, I guess you don't drive a truck into an overpass without shaking up your noggin a bit. He was unconscious for a few days, but they told me not to worry because it was induced — I think they called it — until the brain swelling went down." Jeff Warren really did have the worst luck. Next she'd be telling me that one of his ex-wives was back in the picture, looking for a big insurance payoff.

"Mrs. Warren, do you remember, we were talking about the Donnelley family. Do you by any chance, know what happened to Eddie Donnelley?"

"Of course, dear, everyone knows that."

And she would have told me the last time we spoke except I was too impatient and cut her off — that's what I got for interrupting a sweet old lady.

I had thought it unlikely Eddie Donnelley would have changed much after twenty years in prison, but he did have a jailhouse conversion. Of a sort.

"Folks in town thought it was all that time in prison," Mrs. Warren said, "but maybe not. People's natures are their natures. That's what I saw on CNN or HBO — one of those new stations."

I thought of Ellis Damon. Maybe Lucy had been right after all. "Did he get religion?" I asked.

"Oh, no, dear, Donnelleys always had that. His mother used to have the priests over for lunch once a week. No, that wasn't it."

Conversion, indeed. Or perhaps *transformation* was a more appropriate word. Eddie Donnelley was now Edwina Donnelley.

According to Helen Warren, rumor had it Eddie planned to use the drug money he'd stashed away for his sex change operation once he got out, but the money was never recovered, so he was making do with hormone therapy and drugstore cosmetics. Some assumed Monica had stolen the money. Others thought Kate Gustafson took it, until her suspicious death. Still others suspected a fourth partner who'd never been arrested. Mrs. Warren was in the latter camp.

"Any idea who that might have been?" I asked.

"Oh, it was so long ago. Coach Hopper got a lot of flack. People said he should have known what was going on. But how can you blame him — our team had a good record that year. Still, folks did blame him. The school never renewed his contract, and he moved away. Ohio, I think. He tried to stay in sports but had a hard time getting another coaching job because of the drug scandal. Last I heard he was a sales representative for an athletic supporter company, in Ohio, I think. Did I say that already?"

I didn't expect Helen Warren and I to have the same taste in men, but I had to ask. "Mrs. Warren, would you say Coach Hopper was an attractive man?"

"Well, now there's somebody for everybody, dear. Hop was pleasant looking, but he did have one unfortunate facial feature. I wonder he never had something done about it. I guess he didn't care and it didn't seem to keep the ladies away."

Her own son had a cleft lip and that didn't hurt his chances with the opposite sex.

"Was it a broken nose?" I held my breath until she answered.

"Well, I don't really remember his nose, dear. It was something else entirely. I hate to point out anyone's physical flaws. After all, we're all God's creatures — but Hop really did have a nasty set of choppers."

FORTY-THREE

The next morning, Lucy hated to leave, but she'd already been out of the office two days researching her fugitive story, which she'd been doing on spec. "Text me the minute you hear anything," she said, clutching the bag with the wig.

After I dropped her off at the train station, I drove to the Springfield police department. The same desk sergeant I'd met when Grant Sturgis and I were brought in was on duty. I made it sound like a personal matter.

"Sergeant Stamos. Is Mike O'Malley here? I'd like to speak with him."

"He's on patrol. I can get a message to him to call you. That okay?"

(I had to remember this new strategy the next time I was in the police station.) It had to be. I gave the desk sergeant my cell number and turned the phone on; then I headed for the Paradise.

Babe welcomed me with a big grin. "You've had a busy couple of days, haven't you?"

"Why do you say that?"

Mike O'Malley and Kevin Brookfield had already been and gone — though not together. "Brookfield thinks you're cute but crazy," Babe said. "I told him he was right."

"He's got a nice smile, don't you think?" I said. Babe confirmed that Kevin Brookfield had beautiful teeth. This was good news for the single women in town, and, what the heck, I was one of them, wasn't I?

"You are a little crazy, aren't you?"

The night before, in her quiet, methodical way Mama Warren had given me Coach Hopper's dental history. The poor man had had teeth like a broken comb. At some point he'd gotten cut-rate implants and they all got infected and had to be pulled. The last time she saw him, he just had nubs. "Like candy corn," she'd said, "that had been sitting out in the rain."

"Oh, you know who called," Babe said. "She tried you on your cell, then called here. The bulletin board is one thing, but if you expect me to take messages, too, I'm going to have to start charging you."

Babe slipped me a piece of paper. It was a number in Massachusetts where Caroline said she could be reached until 10:00 that morning. I looked at the clock — 9:45.

Babe tossed me the key to her office so that I could talk to Caroline in private. Again it stuck, but I finally got in, then dialed the number she'd had given me.

"Blue Willow Bakery."

For a moment I wasn't sure who I should ask for — Caroline or Monica.

"Is Caroline there?"

"Anyone here named Caroline?"

I heard some shuffling and then Caroline's voice. "Let me call you back on your number. There's cell service near the general store."

A minute later, my phone rang. Eddie Donnelley had gotten in touch with her — through her brother. He demanded the money he said she'd stolen or he'd testify, once again, that she had orchestrated the whole drug and gambling operation. If he did, Caroline could be sent back to prison for eighteen years.

"I didn't steal the money, I swear. Maybe . . . maybe Kate did. Where else would she have gotten all the cash she sent to my brother years ago? Paula, Donnelley knows where my children are."

"What? How?"

"My mother-in-law must be an idiot.

Grant talked to her to see how they were all doing. She said some woman called, saying she was a friend of mine, and told her to send the kids home. Eddie must have gotten a woman to call for him."

"Well, that's a bit of a story, Caroline."

"Stupid woman, she sent Molly and Jason home on the red-eye last night. Their flight landed ninety minutes ago. We're on our way, but it will take us five hours to get there if we catch a break and don't get jammed up on that damn bridge. I left a message for O'Malley, but he hasn't called back. I'm worried about the kids. Paula, if anything happens to them because of me, I'll kill myself."

O'Malley had said she should call if anything else happened, and it had. But O'Malley was on patrol. And if his antennae were up, they were up for a man, not a woman. I left another message for him and kept my cell on.

"You look pale," Babe said when I reentered the diner.

"Sometimes I wish you had a liquor license." I hoisted myself on the counter stool, wishing it were a bar stool.

"It's 10 A.M."

"I'm going to Caroline's. I've left two

messages for O'Malley, but if you see him, tell him to meet me there ASAP. Better yet, call Channel 8 News anonymously and tell them you saw Caroline Sturgis arrive home this morning. She's there now."

"Is she back?"

"No, but Eddie Donnelley is."

The kids would have used their parents' black car account to get from the airport in New York to Connecticut, but Caroline hadn't mentioned which airport they'd flown into. It would take anywhere from two to two and a half hours for them to get home, if they'd flown into a New York City airport and didn't hit traffic. Less time if they flew to Westchester. I didn't have the key to Caroline's, but if I was able to get into her garage, I thought I'd be able to enter the house. Hopefully reinforcements would get there not long after I did. I'd need more than just the element of surprise if something really came down and I was on my own.

Just as I was pulling out of Babe's, Kevin Brookfield pulled in. I jammed on the brakes and our cars were side by side.

"Smile!"

"What?"

"Nice teeth."

Brookfield must have really thought I was

crazy by now, but he did it. "Does this mean you're buying me?"

"Follow me. I need your help."

He turned his rental car around and stayed close all the way to Caroline's. Once again, I drove on the back roads, taking the water company's private road to the rear of Caroline's house. When we got there, I pushed the middle button on the roof of my Jeep and their garage door opened. I still didn't know how that worked, but I was glad it did. I slid in and Brookfield pulled in alongside me. I closed the door behind us.

Chances are Grant had left the door inside the garage open — many suburbanites did — but even if he hadn't, Caroline had once told me there was an extra set of keys in the garage. We just had to find them.

"I hope there's no one here," I whispered as I got out of my car.

He sidled up next to me. "Are we breaking in?"

"Not exactly."

Just then we heard a car door slam. Caroline and Grant weren't due for hours. I hoped it was O'Malley or the reporters that I'd asked Babe to summon. I pressed my face as close to the narrow garage windows as possible, but I was an inch too short to get the right angle. All I saw were the fringes of a sticker with a company logo and a taxi-and-limousine issue plate. Then I heard kids' voices and a woman's. Damn, they weren't alone.

I hoisted myself onto a narrow counter, flattening myself and holding on to a cabinet handle. I craned my neck just in time to see a tall slim woman shepherding the Sturgis kids into the house.

"Don't worry, Edwina will look after them."

I turned around slowly, struggling to keep my balance, and saw a very handsome but toothless man pointing a gun at me. In his other hand were two hunks of plastic and porcelain.

"Still want to buy the horse? Bridges. They have excellent dentists in Chicago when you have enough money. Once Caroline gives me my money, I'm getting implants. Good ones. Get down!" he ordered.

I did as he said, but hung back as far as I could, clinging to the edge of the counter.

He slipped the dentures back into his mouth and all I could think of was how I'd like to knock them down his throat. What would the Main Street Moms think about their new friend when they found out he was really a thief, a drug dealer, and quite possibly a homicidal cheerleading coach?

Kevin Brookfield banged on the door that led to the house and yelled for Eddie/Edwina to open up. He grabbed my arm and shoved me toward the door in case Eddie got nervous and shot first before looking to see who it was. "Eddie, let me in. It's me, Hop."

Nothing I had at my disposal could match a gun, except maybe my brain. At least that's what I was hoping. I clutched the car keys in my pocket. I could stab him with them but only if I could get close enough. Not likely. And Caroline's garage was so much neater than mine. There were no tools strewn about that I could use as weapons. Just a color-coordinated assortment of metal boxes that I knew held her neglected craft supplies, but I couldn't tell if any of them was heavy enough to deliver a knockout punch. What was her last unfinished project — origami, shell art? Dammit, why was she so neat? I tried to think like Caroline. The pastel boxes probably held light stuff — felt, rickrack, calligraphy brushes. Then I remembered something Caroline had made for me. She'd painted the word *PEACE* once on a nice flat river stone. I guessed the gray box, three feet away from my right hand.

"Don't do this," I said. "There's nothing

in this house except a couple of kids. They don't know anything. And Caroline didn't steal your money. Kate probably did. She probably hid it somewhere before she died and it's never been found. C'mon, you used to be a coach — you must love kids."

"I hate kids. I only took that job so I could ogle young girls in short skirts. Then one of them fell off the human pyramid and broke my nose. Kicked out my last few good teeth, too. Dumb broad."

Oh, brother — that was a tactical error. Overhead we heard footsteps and scuffling. Hopper called out again, but this time I did, too. And louder.

"Springfield police! Open up, Springfield police!" I wasn't even sure we were still in Springfield, but it had terrified Grant and me when we were in the nursery, so it was worth a try.

"Shut up, bitch!" He screamed at me and slammed me against the counter and his dentures slipped. He yelled again. "Eddie, it's me!" but it was so garbled, I wasn't surprised Donnelley didn't understand and respond.

"Eddie Donnelley, Springfield police! Come out with your hands up! We know you're in there!" I hit the panic button on my car keys and the car alarm went off, giving a passing imitation of a police siren. Hopper pushed me away from the door to bang on it again with his right elbow. For a few seconds the barrel of the gun was pointed up. I picked up the gray metal box and slammed it in his face. Rocks spilled out of the box. Hopper's nose was spouting blood, broken again, and he was choking on bits of his smashed dentures. The gun fell out of his hands and I was able to kick it away underneath one of the cars. I climbed into my Jeep, locked the door, and pressed the button to raise the garage door. As I did I saw a crew from Channel Eight news and an oh-so-beautiful Springfield police car.

FORTY-FOUR

The Sturgis kids were unharmed and Jason was declared a hero for pushing his sister out of the way when he cracked Edwina on the head with his spare hockey stick.

When the dust finally settled, Edwina Donnelley blamed Coach Kevin Hopper — also known as Kevin Brookfield — for everything. Donnelley had kept quiet for years, thinking Hopper was reinvesting his ill-gotten gains. Hopper didn't have a clue where the money was, but wisely kept his mouth shut so Eddie would do the same and not incriminate him. Once Eddie got out, they looked for the money together and the chance encounter between Caroline and Jeff Warren at the Paradise Diner led them to Springfield. They after paid Chase McGinley, a stock clerk Hopper had met in Ohio while hawking compression shorts and athletic supporters, to do a little reconnaissance. Always an underachiever, McGinley had heard Caroline had been seen at the diner and assumed the woman he'd been sent to find was Babe. That's how Kevin Hopper wound up camping out at the Paradise until the Main Street Moms obligingly mentioned their friend Caroline, who was considering buying a nursery.

Donnelley was charged with kidnapping the Sturgis kids and assaulting me in the Dunkin' Donuts parking lot. The panty hose were the same ones he was wearing when he went to see Nina Mazzo and hired her to deliver Caroline's pendant.

Kevin Hopper was charged with attempted murder and was also being questioned in the deaths of Kate Gustafson and Chase McGinley. When the body of Kate Gustafson was exhumed, it was learned that the deceased was actually a part-time waitress named Rosanne Lewis. Gustafson's body was never found.

Lucy Cavanaugh's freelance article "I Was a Fugitive" got bumped to the back of the newspaper when a baby whale got stuck in the Long Island Sound. To Babe's surprise, but not mine, she was consoled by Mike O'Malley. They had their first date last week, but Lucy hasn't shared details. Yet.

Under the tutelage of Hank Mossdale I have decided to take horseback riding lessons. He is working on my seat. Impressed with my skills as an investigator, Nina Mazzo has offered to sponsor me for my private investigator's license. I am considering it from a hammock on a beautiful beach in Jost Van Dyke.

And Caroline Sturgis, née Monica Weithorn, was cleared of all charges, past and present. On the day she was exonerated, she got a congratulatory text message simply signed with the letter "K."

ABOUT THE AUTHOR

Rosemary Harris has worked in marketing for Crown Publishers and American Express Travel Related Services and as a producer for Disney/ABC and WNET. She lives in New York City and Connecticut.

We hope you have enjoyed this Large Print book. Other Thorndike, Wheeler, Kennebec, and Chivers Press Large Print books are available at your library or directly from the publishers.

For information about current and upcoming titles, please call or write, without obligation, to:

Publisher
Thorndike Press
295 Kennedy Memorial Drive
Waterville, ME 04901
Tel. (800) 223-1244

or visit our Web site at:

http://gale.cengage.com/thorndike

OR

Chivers Large Print
published by AudioGO Ltd
St James House, The Square
Lower Bristol Road
Bath BA2 3BH
England
Tel. +44(0) 800 136919
email: info@audiogo.co.uk
www.audiogo.co.uk

All our Large Print titles are designed for easy reading, and all our books are made to last.